THE ULTIMATE BOOK OF

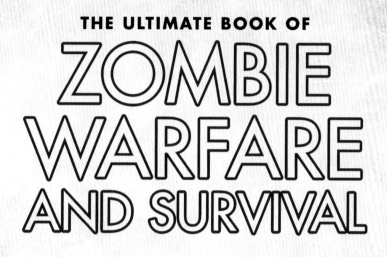

ZOMBIE WARFARE AND SURVIVAL

THE ULTIMATE BOOK OF

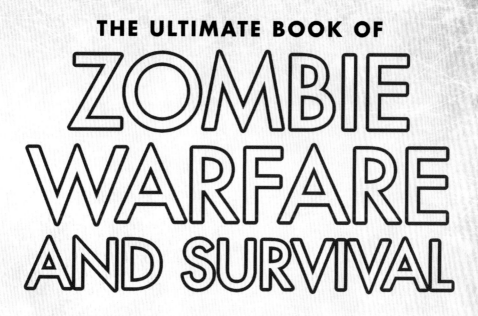

ZOMBIE WARFARE AND SURVIVAL

A Combat Guide to the Walking Dead

SCOTT KENEMORE

Skyhorse Publishing

Skyhorse Publishing books may be purchased in bulk at special discounts for sales promotion, corporate gifts, fund-raising, or educational purposes. Special editions can also be created to specifications. For details, contact the Special Sales Department, Skyhorse Publishing, 307 West 36th Street, 11th Floor, New York, NY 10018 or info@skyhorsepublishing.com.

Skyhorse® and Skyhorse Publishing® are registered trademarks of Skyhorse Publishing, Inc.®, a Delaware corporation.

Visit our website at www.skyhorsepublishing.com.

10 9 8 7 6 5 4 3 2 1

Library of Congress Cataloging-in-Publication Data is available on file.

Cover design by Danielle Ceccolini
Cover illustration by Adam Wallenta

Print ISBN: 978-1-62914-483-2
Ebook ISBN: 978-1-63220-163-8

Printed in China

CONTENTS

Foreword from the Author

Since the publication of the first book in this collection, great strides have been made in the advancement of the zombie. The undead are present in our lives as never before. From video games to books to films to television programs, they saturate our collective consciousness and shamble into our dreams. This is, of course, just as it should be.

At the time of this writing, Hollywood is filming its first $130 million zombie movie. The #1-rated new show on cable television is a zombie saga (based, itself, on a #1 graphic novel zombie saga). And the grandmaster himself, George Romero, has announced that he is back at work on another zombie film.

Yet for all this success and saturation, some still retain a profoundly shortsighted view of the undead.

Too many books, films, and games seek to portray zombies only as the enemy. The opponent. The *other*. These works meditate exclusively on the shortcomings and flaws of the walking dead. They hold zombies up as ready-made, obvious enemies, waiting to be killed (or at least avoided). In this fashion, zombies become oversimplified, throwaway villains. They get placed into video games and action movies as targets with little to do. No sooner are they presented to audiences, than they find themselves slaughtered or decapitated. They are cast off as pawns, not worth taking seriously. They end before they can begin, never examined or appreciated.

This is, of course, remarkably shortsighted.

The point of zombies is not to mow them down in waves. The point of zombies is not merely that they present an opportunity to try out your new Desert Eagle or laser-scoped M-16. Neither are they an invitation to revert to a primate state of violence, xenophobia, and hoarding canned goods on a remote mountaintop retreat.

They are so, so much more.

Zombies present a powerful new model for how we ourselves ought to be, and what we can accomplish if only we put our minds to it. Zombies have been sent here as messengers of enlightenment. They offer humans a chance to undergo a new and profound philosophical shift. They are beckoning, ready to take us to the next level of existence.

Zombies offer us all of this…and ask so very little in return.

Of course, most humans will prove too shortsighted to appreciate what has been placed before them. Only the especially astute and perceptive will grasp the lessons of the zombie. Only the most ambitious and driven will take the necessary steps to implement these lessons into their lives. This collection is designed for such people.

The benefits of pursing an existence modeled after the walking dead are difficult to overstate. The unflappable, brave, ever-stalwart zombie demonstrates a heroism that inspires us all. His lessons in "life" find applications across the spectrum. From family harmony to career advancement, from military dominance to existential enlightenment, the desiccated undead can reliably be your guide.

The zombie—who never doubts, never worries, and never feels insecure—is a sea of tranquility in a world filled with shaken souls who have lost faith in their own abilities. The zombie can show them how to restore that faith. The confused and lonely soul wonders what the purpose of his or her life can be. A zombie illustrates that a purpose can always be found, whatever the situation. Many people feel impotent and weak, unable to create real positive change in their lives. A zombie shows how to find an inner strength and make meaningful progress. The first book in this collection makes clear that the answers to your existential queries have an answer in the zombie.

The boardroom represents another great challenge in most of our lives. How does one get a job, keep a job, and make enough money to get by? Moreover, how does one crawl one's way to the top of the corporate heap, and rule it? Zombies—innately expert in conquering and crawling to the top of heaps—have much to teach the aspiring CEO. The second book in this volume contains valuable undead insight for future corporate leaders.

A zombie's might and majesty on the battlefield is likewise an inspiration to modern-day tactical commanders. Zombies raze country sides and penetrate impenetrable fortresses with alacrity and skill. No military force wants to face a zombie army, but any general who finds zombies in his command always counts himself lucky. The third book in this volume illustrates how zombie warfare can prove a valuable resource to soldiers and battlefield commanders alike.

Zombies are inextricably tied to the Caribbean. Any student of zombies seeking a tactile example of how zombies can show a path to success need look no further than zombies who ruled in piracy's golden age. From the feared privateers who took down royal navies to the pirate kings and queens who enjoyed an autonomy and power that landlubbers could only envy, successful buccaneers harnessed the lessons of the zombie—as well as actual zombies—to take for themselves what the world was otherwise unwilling to give.

In the last century, zombies also played a crucial—though little known role in foiling Nazi Germany's efforts to take over the world.

As conflicts raged in Europe, the Nazi government dispatched a team of secret agents to infiltrate the Voodoo community on the island of Haiti and wrest from this religion's adherents the secrets to zombie reanimation. The captured correspondence of these Nazi agents (included in this tome) paints a vivid picture of the devastating consequences awaiting those who oppose the walking dead, or who attempt to pervert the inherent natural perfection that is the zombie.

The zombie has made a remarkable journey. When the first reanimated corpses crawled out of cemeteries on a small, impoverished island nation in the Caribbean, no one could have dreamed that they would come to saturate every aspect of our popular culture. They weren't much to look at. They staggered about like drunken men. They were mostly unable to speak or read or perform mathematical calculations. They had numerous physical problems (including but not limited to missing eyes, skin, and entire limbs). Put these guys up against living humans—or, heck, even a group of smart monkeys—and they wouldn't look like the horse you ought to be betting on.

But zombies *are* the smart bet. If anything's clear, it's that. Zombies are power. Zombies are effective. Zombies win. When a zombie outbreak occurs, the strongest countries are powerless to stop them. Militaries find that their massive stockpiles of laser-guided smart bombs and predator drones (designed, as they are, for enemies that will "die and stay dead") fail time and again to make a dent in the hordes of approaching corpses. Governments—from egalitarian democracies to third-world banana republics—quickly slip into to anarchy as the zombies approach the capitol. Families and friendships are tested. Previously unthinkable actions become imminently thinkable (if not "Holy Jesus, the thing we have to do *right fucking now*!!! DO IT DO IT DO IT, before the zombies break through!!! DO IT NOW!!!"). Things as rock solid as marriages, religious convictions, and political orientations crumble to dust in the face of the oncoming hordes.

Zombies mean change. Zombies mean a new order. Zombies are catalysts.

They command attention wherever they go. When the living dead start to walk the earth, there is no other thing that people are talking about. Zombies, collectively, are the ultimate celebrity. They are the cast of the best reality show going, and their "antics" put peacocking weightlifters and dance contest winners to shame. When the dead crawl out of their graves and start eating people's brains, they are the only thing that photojournalists want to take pictures of. Hollywood publicists wish they could get their clients the press that zombies get without even trying.

Do *you* want to be game-changing and famous? (**Hint:** All psychological and sociological research ever conducted says that you do.) Emulating a winner is the best way to become a winner, and you're not going to find a bigger winner than zombies.

Do you seek autonomy? Independence? Freedom from a lousy boss or a family that never listens? Zombies are the key to your freedom. Nobody tells a zombie what to do. But more importantly, everybody *knows* it's pointless to tell a zombie what to do. You might as well yell at a mountain, or craft a carefully-worded missive to a typhoon. Zombies are going to do what they're going to do. Period. Would *you* like that kind of autonomy? Would you like to be your own boss (and never listen to anyone, ever, about anything)? Follow the example of a zombie, and your reputation as un-bossable will proceed you wherever you go.

Are you worried about money? I mean, let's be real here. We're living in the worst financial crisis since the Great Depression. (If you're not worried about money, I'm worried about you. Seriously.) But it doesn't have to be that way. Zombies don't worry about money. Or credit scores. Or if the landlord will stop by and notice that all the copper wire has been stripped from the house. Zombies already have everything they need. They operate in a world outside of currency. With the exception of brains—for which, the hunger can never (and *should* never) be sated—zombies depend on nothing outside of themselves for status, success, or the ability to make things happen. If financial issues have been keeping you up at night, use the books in this collection to disperse your money fears like humans dispersing before hordes of the walking dead.

Is self-esteem an issue for you? Do you not look like the people you see on TV (except maybe the weight loss competitions or makeover programs)? Do you dream of a day when you'll wake up in the morning and not worry about the judgmental stares from strangers waiting to find fault with you? Perhaps nothing in the arsenal of the zombie is more powerful than its ability to utterly obliterate any doubt, worry, or fear. All feelings of insecurity vanish before the undead. Zombies—who are frequently lacking important organs and body parts altogether—never suffer from self esteem issues. Zombies have never been made to feel bad about themselves. Though they frequently have not just one or two, but an entire *host* of physical maladies, zombies maintain an incredibly high opinions of themselves. They walk with a swagger (that may or may not be voluntary). They are immune to the judgments of others. They have no doubts and require no encouragement.

To be a zombie is to walk in power—unfettered and without fear. It is to answer to no one…and to feast upon everyone. These days, that's rare.

Have no doubt about it, our world is in turmoil. There are unpredictable international forces acting on all of us—endangering our jobs, our communities, and our very lives. Military conflicts rage across the world. A global financial depression holds us in its merciless grip. People are not constantly talking about how awesome zombies are.

Clearly, the lessons of the walking dead have never before been more necessary.

In these times of difficulty, strife, and insecurity, the world craves self-assurance. It craves consistency. It craves confident people who know who they are and what they want.

In conclusion, zombies do not dominate our culture because humans need another villain to kill with machetes and machine guns. (There are ample enemies and threats to go around right now.) Rather, zombies are popular because humans know a good thing when they see it. Zombies are, in their way, perfectly suited to navigate difficult times. They are imperturbable as Zen masters. They are, verily, the last and best hope—for themselves, and maybe for us too.

Zombies are ready to give you their power. They stand before you—a somewhat motley crew, yes—but their offer is rock solid. They are prepared to welcome you into the fellowship. They are offering you strength, clarity, and effectiveness. They want to know if you are ready. Ready to lead. Ready to win, Ready to send your problems packing.

The zombie closest to you extends his moldy, rotting hand.

Will you take it?

Introduction

This book is about the imponderable (though nonetheless real) drive within you to slough off the charnel earth of the grave and stalk through ebon forests of the night under a gibbous moon to prey upon living flesh, even though no heart beats within your own chest. It is about the quest of the zombie—the netherworld's most elegantly simple creation—and its unceasing hunger for the flesh of man.

Life's gonna throw you some curveballs, and nobody knows this better than a zombie.

You may have to move far away from home to go to the college or university of your choice. Your company might downsize you around the holidays when you least expect it. Your desiccating

> **Zombie Tip—In some languages, the word for "crisis" is also the word for "opportunity:"** In the language of a zombie, however, the word for "crisis" is also the word for "a decided lack of yummy humans to eat." (The zombie word for "opportunity" is likewise synonymous with "a school bus full of defenseless children," "a group of overconfident, naïve explorers," and "a crowded country house with the road washed out and the phone lines disconnected from a storm." . . . but you probably could've guessed that.)

corpse might be reanimated by an evil warlock's spell, a secret government nerve agent, or radiation from a UFO.

Life's going to throw stuff like this your way now and then. Need some advice on how to get through it? Look no further than our friend the zombie.

Zombies don't ask "Why did this happen to me?" They don't meditate on the *meaning* of their reanimation. Nope. It's up out of the grave and right on the hunt for brains.

Zombies have a way of making the best of a situation.

Throw a zombie in the middle of the ocean, and hey, it'll get back to land eventually. But in the meantime, it's going to fuck up some sharks, probably an octopus or two, and, damn-straight, any unlucky fisherman it gets its rotting hands on. Sure, one day its inherent drive to locate and consume thinking human brains will drive the zombie back to land—and yeah, it might be down to bone and rags by then, but that thought's not stopping it for a second.

Freeze a zombie in an arctic ice floe. Sure, it's trapped for the short term. The moment global warming reaches it, though— boing!—it springs up good as new, ready to mess you up.

Burn a zombie. Throw acid on a zombie. All I can say is that you better finish the job, because those sons of bitches will just keep on coming.

Cut off a zombie's limbs (one by one, if you like) and it will continue to drag itself after you.

See, the zombie doesn't draw the inference polite society might expect it to draw. It doesn't think: "Gee, I'm on fire. I should really stop to put this out before continuing on my way." It doesn't think: "I have no arms and legs left, and inching myself along with my neck is really taking a while. Maybe I should just give up and let the other zombies have all the fun." No! You're not going to convince a zombie it's time to give up and start pouting. It's just not done. (Or not something done by zombies, anyway.) A zombie stops only when its own brain is destroyed or disconnected from the spinal cord. Only under similar circumstances should you consider giving up on yourself as an acceptable option.

Remember to think of the adaptable zombie when life throws **you** something you weren't expecting. It doesn't have to be a villager planting a flaming pitchfork in your chest, or a machine-gun assault by a top-secret federal anti-zombie agency. It can be an irritating foot fracture, being passed over for a promotion at work, or having your car repossessed. Sure, zombies don't (usually) drive, but it isn't difficult to guess what a zombie would do in that situation.

He'd shuffle right to the bus stop, and go to work all the same. And once at work, he would eat the head of his boss (despite an irritating foot fracture).

Leadership Lessons: Learn from the Enemy

A lot of people think zombies approach their tasks lazily or without deep personal investment simply because they move slowly. In fact, zombies *could not be* more invested in their work. If a zombie moves slowly, it is because its muscles and tendons are rotted away, and attempts at quick locomotion would cause the zombie to come apart entirely. The smallest actions often require supreme effort for a zombie. A zombie lurching awkwardly toward its target may be tantamount to a person with a severe disability walking in spite of it. If a zombie is legless, it crawls. If its eyes have been gouged out, it feels its way forward (arms outstretched and flailing). If it's nothing but a skull and some spinal cord . . . fuck it! It's still crawling forward like some nightmarish inchworm.

A zombie does not stagger or crawl because it's some kind of slacker who isn't invested in what he's doing. On the contrary, a zombie is *so* invested that it staggers or crawls *despite* hardly being able to move. The focus and dedication necessary for this feat are remarkable.

For a zombie, each task it performs (opening a barricaded door, finding a way to circumvent a barbed-wire fence, herding a group of humans into a corner) is really just a subset of a larger task (eating brains). A zombie is a successful leader because it never loses sight of this ultimate goal, and it never compro-

mises (like by eating just *part* of a brain, or a monkey's brain if no humans are handy).

Don't believe what you may have seen in the movies. Effective leaders do **not** need to be physically present in order to help their soldiers win the day. Some of the best general-ing has been conducted from comfy armchairs next to warm, toasty fireplaces. Whether you're commanding an army of actual zombies, or just an army of human troops who fight like zombies, you're going to want to do one thing above all when it comes time for actual combat: **stay the fuck out of their way.**

Sending an army of zombies into battle is like unleashing a chemical or biological weapon. It's like setting off dynamite. It's like pushing the red button and choosing the nuclear option. The best thing to do is to unleash them, duck and cover, and hope that the wind is blowing the right way (because zombies are smelly). Your zombies will know what to do, and they will do it until they or your enemy are completely defeated (and possibly eaten).

Getting out in front of a bunch of zombies and attempting to "lead" them (in your little kepi and dress jacket) is just a stupid idea. You're not going to inspire them to fight any better, and you'll probably just make things worse. If you're commanding an army of actual zombies, then the zombies will likely try to eat you. Maybe you could run away from them (toward the enemy or something), but still, if they somehow catch you, you're just fucked, and then what was the point? If you're a warlock or voodoo priest and you've got some kind of spell on the zombies so they don't attack you, then that's one thing—but you're still just going to be getting in the way. Your presence won't suddenly make zombies want to eat brains any more than they already do.

1. Never Outshine the Master—When a "master" warlock or mad scientist creates a zombie, the zombie doesn't try to become a warlock

or mad scientist himself. Nope. He's off the table (or out of the grave) and on the hunt for brains. Scientists and warlocks already have their thing. As a zombie, you've got to go out and find your own.

2. Distrust Friends; Be Prepared to Use Enemies—Gee, would this be another way of saying treat everyone equally, friend or not? Because that sounds an awful lot like what a zombie already does.

3. Conceal Your Intentions—The first time you see a zombie lumbering toward you across some misty, blasted heath, you have no way of knowing it wants to eat you. By the time you've learned your lesson, it is, of course, too late. . . .

4. Always Say Less Than Necessary—Zombies tend to say only what is necessary. Necessary to them. Which is your brain. Period.

5. So Much Depends on Reputation—Zombies are "reputed" to be relentless bloodthirsty killers who will hunt you unceasingly without rest or hesitation until you are physically dead and digesting in their stomachs. Kind of makes Donald Trump look like a great big pussy, doesn't it?

6. Court Attention—Zombies get attention instantly, wherever they go. (No one, anywhere, has ever said: "Oh, that? It's *just* a zombie.") Granted, the attention they get is usually negative, but it's still attention. That's the important thing.

7. Get Others to Do the Work While You Take the Credit—Zombies aren't known to court credit. However, since the work zombies do is more or less interchangeable (eating people) it's really hard to say which zombie ate which villager, and so forth.

8. Make Other People Come to You—Higher-functioning zombies have often posed as ambulance drivers, small-town sheriffs, and

Zombie Tip—Be Respected and Feared: A misconception dating back to medieval times is that a leader must choose either to cultivate an aura of respect or fear, but that both are not possible concurrently. This is patently false, as evinced by zombies. True, most humans are afraid of zombies, and in their presence will run screaming towards the nearest subterranean military base, cold war bunker, or abandoned mine shaft. However, these same humans, when (from a safe distance) observing a zombie who has just crawled across a bed of hot lava, dodged sniper-fire, or survived a catapult attack, are apt to remark: "I know they're zombies and all, but damn, I gotta respect that."

members of the media in order to lure more victims to where zombies already are. Also, zombies tend to naturally hang out in cool places (graveyards, swamps, malls) where people already want to go.

9. Win through Actions, Not Arguments—A zombie has never won an argument. It has never had to.

10. Infection: Avoid the Unhappy and Unlucky—The notion of infection (as well as the pure unmitigated evil of this sentiment) is, of course, right up a zombie's alley. Zombies know that not everyone deserves to be turned into a zombie. Some losers deserve to be eaten entirely.

11. Keep People Dependent on You—You can "depend" on zombies to do certain things better than anybody. Say you need all human inhabitants removed from a tropical island before dawn, or you require that every corpse in a graveyard should be unearthed in a single night. Or even that a cannibalistic infection should spread from person to person until governments crumble and anarchy replaces the rule of law. Where are you gonna go for that, the Wolf-Man? Hell, no. There are some things that only zombies can be depended upon to do correctly, and everybody knows it.

12. Disarm Your Victim—Especially if he has a samurai sword or a nailgun. Those things hurt.

13. When Asking for Help, Appeal to People's Self-Interest, Not Their Mercy—Again, this despicably wonderful sentiment could only have come from one inspired by zombies. No zombie has ever appealed to someone's sense of mercy. No zombie has ever *shown* mercy, for that matter.

14. Pose as a Friend, Work as a Spy—Higher-functioning zombies are quick to impersonate living humans, especially when it will allow them to learn where more delicious humans might be. (They will also "spy" on unsuspecting victims before striking.)

15. Crush Your Enemy Totally—Zombies don't do anything halfway. No zombie ever ate "part" of someone's brain and called it a day. If you want your enemy literally decimated (and digested), there's no better agent for it than a zombie.

16. Use Your Absence to Increase Respect and Honor—Wise words. When zombies split the scene, all anybody ever seems to be able to think about is where they went and when they'll be back. The absence of zombies is never ground for presuming that no additional zombies are on their way. Also, there's no higher form of respect than building barricades and nailing windows shut.

17. Keep Others in Suspended Terror by Being Unpredictable—Check. Zombies personify the perfect marriage of terror and unpredictability. Because, hey, when you're cowering with a shotgun inside a boarded-up farmhouse, you don't know what the zombies are going to try next. They might crawl up through the sewers. They might climb down the chimney, or make a group assault on the front door. The only thing you're sure of, bub, is that they're comin'.

18. Do Not Build Fortresses to Protect Yourself—A zombie never built a fort (or anything else) to protect itself. Zombies, you see, are too busy ransacking the forts of others to think about paying architects or contractors. The zombie is the antifort.

19. Know Who You're Dealing With—Zombies are excellent judges of character. Like whether a human is the type to run away screaming, pick up a garden hoe and put up a fight, or just faint dead away as you lumber closer and closer. Eat enough humans, and you get good at picking out these sorts of details.

20. Do Not Commit to Anything—Zombies are not bound by anything, and they certainly don't make commitments. Not to say that zombies are unreliable. When a zombie is out to do something (eat you), it's getting done. It's just a question of when. Could be today. Could be tomorrow. Zombies are mysterious and have their own agenda.

21. Play a Sucker/Seem Dumber Than You Are—Zombies *obviously* inspired this rule. As a bunch of slack-jawed, shuffling grunters (who move slow and think slower), zombies appear confused or even dim-witted. There is very little about them to tell an onlooker that they are, in fact, dynamic and powerful killing machines. It's easy to underestimate a zombie, and those who do so are usually the first ones to get eaten.

Zombie Tip—Get an Early Start: The executive who makes it into the office while it's still dark out has a chance to answer emails, read industry periodicals, and catch up on work without the constant distraction of coworkers. The zombie who attacks in the pre-dawn hours has a chance to surprise people in bed while they're still groggy and much less likely to have a sawed-off shotgun at the ready. So, either way, it's good.

22. Transform Weakness into Power—The author of the "forty-eight laws" notes that humans can take power from situations that are not to their advantage by refusing to act in accordance with the wishes of their opponents. Zombies don't act the way their opponents "want" them to . . . ever. Even when zombies are facing utter ruin at the hands of humans armed with laser-guided RPGs and machine guns, zombies just keep coming. Sure, the humans would appreciate it if the zombies would come to their "senses" and just surrender. But hey, that's not how zombies work.

23. Concentrate Your Forces—Yes, do. Especially in shopping malls, abandoned military complexes, and graveyards.

24. Play the Perfect Courtier—You might not think of zombies as going in for a lot of froufrou courtly-manners-type stuff. And you'd be right. But being a perfect courtier doesn't just mean stylishly supplicating yourself in front of a king or queen. "Courting," broadly defined, just means to go after something. To pursue what you want. What zombies want is brains, and they go after it as directly, effortlessly, and yes, perfectly, as is practicable. (Sure, if your goal is to be appointed special envoy to Genoa, then by all

means don a periwig and lead-based face powder while tittering at the king's pedestrian attempts at humor even as you flatter the plain, long-toothed queen. That's your business. But if your goal is to achieve something important, like the chairmanship of a corporation, then just go right after it like a zombie.)

25. Re-create Yourself—A zombie is a master of re-creation. One minute it's a desiccated corpse resting comfortably in a historic New England graveyard, and moments later it's a supernaturally (or sometimes, scientifically) reanimated monster on the hunt for human flesh. This, really, is the ultimate "makeover." And zombies never stop remaking themselves. They lose clothing or body parts, often in hilarious or inconvenient ways, but they always adjust and keep going. They can go from "relatively human-looking" to a "mass of bone and guts sliming its way forward on its own entrails" in the instant it takes a land mine to detonate. This re-creation is just a fact of "life" for a zombie. The zombie accepts it and keeps moving.

26. Keep Your Hands Clean—While some have interpreted this law to mean that it's wise to avoid involving oneself in seedy or inappropriate activities, zombies take a much more literal interpretation. "Your hands" obviously refers to the hands that a zombie has collected from its victims. And you want to keep them clean because they taste so much better that way.

27. Create a Cultlike Following—As the many zombie cults around the world evince, zombies are masters of starting and maintaining cults. From the wilds of Haiti to the eldritch hills of Arkham, zombies put Scientologists to shame. A zombie is as effective at starting cults as L. Ron Hubbard was, but with the added benefit of not also writing terrible, terrible science fiction.

28. Enter Actions with Boldness—Verily, zombies are bold in thought and in deed. Zombies will attempt to ford raging rivers,

make frontal assaults on reinforced military positions, and walk gibbering directly into large crowds. Zombies make bold entrances and exits and attempt bolder things in pursuit of their goals. For every turn-of-the-century hot-air balloonist who thinks he's safe from the living dead, a zombie is patiently figuring a way to get up there and eat his brain. Bold? Yes. But that's a zombie for you.

29. Plan All the Way to the End—What with recently geopolitical military actions not turning out so well, this maxim is more important than ever, and no one illustrates it like a zombie. Zombies see things through to the end—which is to say, the end of whomever they're devouring. If you're going to invade a country and fuck it up all to hell, then make sure you finish the damn job. Like a zombie.

30. Make Your Accomplishments Seem Effortless—The only way a really cool action can be improved upon is to make it seem like you weren't even trying when you did it. Zombies make everything they do seem effortless. From easily sauntering along the bottom of the sea to shimmying through the tightest drainpipes, zombies do it all with the swagger of champions. And who knows? *Maybe* it is *actually difficult* for a zombie to walk miles underwater, or to contort itself to fit into tight spaces. If so, zombies aren't letting on. Neither should you.

31. Control the Options—Controlling the options of other people is something at which zombies excel. Zombies do this a *priori* in most cases. You're not going to negotiate with a zombie, or appeal to its greed, or its mercy, or even its sense of self-preservation. Those things were off the table a long time ago. With zombies, the options are get eaten or get out. The humans know it. The zombies know it. It's a system that keeps things simple and efficient.

32. Play to People's Fantasies—Especially the one about friendly zombies that aren't going to eat them. That way, you can just walk right up.

33. Discover Each Man's Thumbscrew—Thumbscrews were medieval torture devices that did exactly what it sounds like they did. However, in a larger sense, they represent the one thing that unnerves or undoes someone. Sure, you could discover them if you want to—devote time and energy to rooting out what makes this or that person flinch. Zombies, however, are everyone's thumbscrew. No one finds them anything less than unnerving, chilling, and terrifying. Which is to say, if you're looking to find your adversary's weak spot, look no further than a zombie.

34. Act Like a King to Be Treated as One—Okay, so you don't see zombies walking around in robes and crowns. (Now and then, yes, a king's corpse will be reanimated into a zombie, but these are rare cases, and they almost never get buried with the good jewels on.) Yet zombies are known to be the "kings" of the netherworld. They rule over all that they survey, and no one is safe from their wrath. Wherever they go, zombies amble forward with the confident, unhurried gait of the regal. And for centuries, they have tormented peasants (not with taxes and wars as much as by eating them). Many how-to-succeed-in-business guides advise dressing and behaving like a supervisor in order to give your bosses the "feeling" that you would be appropriate for promotion. But nobody promotes you to the **top** position. That one, you just have to seize. Like a zombie.

35. Master the Art of Timing—Knowing when to strike is key to being powerful and getting ahead, both in business and in life. Zombies provide copious examples of exactly when and where to strike. You can sneak up and eat the brain of the dedicated cop anytime during his beat, but if it's on the night he just proposed to his girlfriend and found out he got into law school, then trust me, his brain is going to taste even sweeter.

36. Disdain Things You Cannot Have—Complete sentences. Sexual intercourse. Wind sprints. There are lots of things that, while fine for other people, just don't work for a zombie. Do you see zombies pining after these things? Or complaining about how they wish they could deliver lengthy soliloquies, be porn stars, and win the hundred-meter dash? No way. Zombies go after what is still accessible to them (your brain), and completely eschew everything else.

37. Create Compelling Spectacles—If methodically stalking and eating a bunch of people—brain first, no less—isn't compelling, then dude, you really are getting jaded.

38. Think as You Like, but Behave within Group Norms—This spineless bit of advice is perfectly suited to zombies (who sometimes do physically lack spines). When a horde of the walking dead approaches you, one or two of its members might be having some doubts about the whole "eating-your-brains thing," but if they do, they damn well keep it to themselves. Group norms ensure humans end up as the entrée every time.

39. Stir up Waters to Catch Fish—If by "waters" you mean "humans," and by "catch fish" you mean "eat their brains," then, yes, this is very sound advice.

40. Despise the Free Lunch—Did you ever hear of a zombie eating a brain that wasn't inside somebody's head? No? That's what I thought. There's a reason that zombies aren't breaking into anatomy labs or turning on corpses that aren't zombies. A free lunch is at best suspicious. Be like a zombie and hunt your own lunch.

41. Avoid Stepping into a Great Man's Shoes—Eating him instead is really where you want to go with this.

42. Strike the Shepherd, and the Sheep Will Scatter—Zombies have a way of knowing exactly whom to attack. When an isolated military outpost is under siege from the undead, there's always one zombie who manages to slink away from the horde, crawl through a heating duct, and pop up inside the base just in time to eat the main-commanding-officer-guy's brain. This creates a power vacuum that allows the zombies on the outside to attack more efficiently and effectively. The same thing goes for chaperones on field trips, guards on prisoner transport convoys, and supervisors at military warehouses. Zombies have a way of sniffing out the ones who keep order, and chowing down on them first. It makes everything that comes after so much easier.

43. Work on the Hearts and Minds of Others—Especially the minds. Those succulent . . . delicious . . . minds.

44. Disarm and Infuriate—Most conventional weapons don't work effectively against zombies. Usually, removing (or completely destroying) a zombie's head is the only way to stop it. And what's more infuriating to a human who is trying to fight a zombie than learning the zombie has effectively "disarmed" you by virtue of being impervious to your rifle? (The circular saw out in the machine shed, however, is another matter. . . .)

45. Espouse "Change," but Never Actually Do Anything—The extent to which zombies can espouse opinions or hold positions on topical issues may sometimes be called into question. It shouldn't be. Zombies create a call to political (and often military) action that few politicians have ever been able to muster. By virtue of their very being-in-the-world, zombies always signal "a call for all citizens" to "stop their sectarian bickering" and instead "unite against a common enemy sent from the bowels of hell." (Or something like that.) Yet for all the strength of this "call," it is soon clear that all efforts to follow it will be quite bootless. (Zombies are going to win every time, and you know it. But hey, A-for-effort, right?)

46. Never Appear Too Perfect—No one knows about this temptation more than zombies. After all, for something so completely awesome and entirely kick-ass as a zombie, it can be a challenge to stay grounded and relate to the common man. So if a zombie plays up the staggering a little bit, or loses digits or limbs just for effect, know that it's doing it so you feel better about yourself in comparison.

47. In Victory, Learn When to Stop—Like when all the brains are eaten. That seems like a pretty good time.

48. Assume Formlessness—While some might like to wax romantic and imagine that this law alludes to becoming a powerful force that mysteriously works behind the scenes, zombies know that these words are completely literal. All zombies eventually wear down, shedding skin, organs, and bones. At the end of a long and successful career of hunting humans, a zombie may be little more than a toothless skull and a few wriggling tendons connected by a naked spinal cord. Before long, the zombie may be worn down into literal nothingness. Which is still cool. It had a good run. The point is not to fear the formless nothingness, but to anticipate it as your inevitable reward.

In conclusion, if you want to remember forty-eight laws because it makes you feel like a big man, then sure, go nuts. Whatever. But if you want to actually *be* powerful, just remember to act like a zombie. It's a whole lot less work.

Zombies never worry that they don't "measure up" as a member of the walking dead. They don't doubt themselves. They don't envy other zombies that are taller, stronger, or have more limbs than they do. Nope. Zombies only focus on getting ahead (or "getting a head"). They don't waste time doubting their own abilities or qualifications. This makes all of them "born" leaders, whom humans could stand to emulate.

You see, getting ahead in the business world can be a matter of self-selection. Every year, some employees elect to enroll in management training courses, while others put it off. When new openings a few rungs up the corporate ladder are posted on the HR message board, some employees apply for all of them, some never for a one. What separates these employees from one another—the ambitious, upwardly mobile ones from the workers doomed to spend eternity in the same desk, at the same pay rate, in the same department? The answer is: *the employees themselves.*

Thus, the real questions become "What are the factors that keep employees from reaching for more?" and "What makes a worker content with less?" Too frequently, it has nothing to do with the capacity of the employee to become an effective manager or leader. Instead, workers are likely to cite personal failings, such as shortcomings in physical appearance or charisma, as reasons why they should wait to seek a higher position within the organization.

Zombie Tip—It makes no sense to negotiate with zombies. This is obvious to everybody.

These poor souls defeat themselves before any opponent has the chance to.

The trick to overcoming personal doubts that might make you flinch from reaching (aggressively and directly) for the top of the corporate ladder is to remember our friend the zombie.

At first glance, zombies don't look much like leaders. They rarely wear designer suits or power ties. (Many male corpses are buried wearing ties, but they tend to be on the conservative side, frequently selected by relatives or morticians.) Their personal hygiene and posture are terrible. They are poor at public speaking, and sometimes lack the eyes necessary to make eye contact with subjects whom they are addressing.

When it comes to "inspiring others," the most you're likely to get out of a zombie is a moan or a shuffle in the direction of food.

Everywhere a zombie looks, it sees other people who are more attractive, more articulate, and generally more capable than it is. But does that stop a zombie from pursuing its goals? Does a zombie decide to wait until it acculturates and assimilates into the accepted mold of a "leader"? Does it ever think: "I'm too **fat** to eat that brain," or "I'm too **old,**" or "I'm too **inexperienced**?"

No way.

Zombies get what they want (when they want it) because they never convince themselves that they are somehow "unsuited" or "unworthy" to be leaders. To the contrary, zombies are filled with confidence. (Okay, confidence and maggots, if you want to get all technical about it.)

Zombies don't only win military engagements through force of numbers and combat awesomeness. Zombies win because their enemies have been reduced to quivering masses of terrified fruit preserves. No one is immune from the terror inspired by zombies.

Properly trained and attuned, a zombie army can instill a creeping dread in even the most stalwart of foes.

Fear is important. **Fear helps you win.** Great generals have always understood the role that fear plays on the battlefield.

As is well documented, the great Genghis Khan liked to send Tibetan throat-singers into battle alongside his troops. Though they provided no additional killing power, the eerie noise they made struck fear into Khan's opponents who often decided that they were demons. Something as seemingly innocuous as singers helped Khan drive his opponents from the battlefield all the more quickly.

Sometimes military commanders do everything right but still come up short. They play each card correctly, yet (one must say it) fail to achieve their ultimate objectives. History records them as having been middling or ineffective leaders, when, in truth, they could not have possibly done anything more to ensure victory.

It is into this category that one must place American Civil War General Ambrose Burnside. He was a soldier, a leader, a facial-hair pioneer . . . and quite possibly the only Zombie Commander in the Grand Army of the Republic.

Burnside understood the value of attacking the enemy like a horde of zombies and exhibited this in battle after battle. A student of military history will find no finer example of his battlefield acumen on display than Burnside's operation to take the bridge over Antietam Creek—the so-called Burnside's Bridge—at the Battle of Antietam.

On September 17, 1862, Burnside, under General George B. McClellan, engaged Confederate troops at Sharpsburg, Maryland. Antietam Creek ran through tactically important portions of the battlefield, and Burnside was ordered to secure it. To do this, he knew he needed to cross it and secure both sides. Like any good Zombie Commander, Burnside thought to himself: *How can I do*

this in a way that involves my troops just charging straight at the enemy all goddamn day?

Military historians are quick to criticize Burnside for neglecting to deduce that Antietam Creek was only fifty feet across at the widest point and only waist-deep. Further, they note, the Confederate forces did not monitor many sections of the creek. (The inference put forward seems to be that Burnside should have had his soldiers wade across and flank the enemy, or something boring and stupid like that.) These so-called historians fail to notice, however, Burnside's having been a zombie (which casts any positive estimation of their skill as historians into serious doubt).

No, when looking to take Antietam Creek, Burnside resolved to do it like a zombie. His keen zombie eyes surveyed the battlefield and lit upon the one piece of geography that would make this possible: the single, well-defended, narrow bridge that forded the creek. Here, Burnside understood, was an opportunity to use the terrain to make his soldiers fight like members of the walking dead.

All day, Burnside sent wave after wave of troops over the bridge in conspicuous, zombielike fashion. Yet, as the battle drew on (with what appeared—to the untrained, nonzombie eye—to be a lack of progress on Burnside's part) General McClellan began sending dispatches to Burnside. (e.g., "Why haven't you taken the creek?" "Why are you just marching men, three-abreast, across the bridge

War is too important to be left to the generals: Seriously. Things always go better when they're handled by a bunch of rotting reanimated corpses who are out to eat some brains. It's like: Okay Mr. General-guy, you've had your say at the press conference. Now let the experts take it from here.

again and again, effectively negating your advantage of superior numbers?" "What's this rumor I hear about you directing our troops to eat the Confederates' brains?") Eventually, McClellan lost patience and ordered other brigades to "help" Burnside take the creek by "not just attacking over one tiny goddamn bridge."

Today, we can only imagine the resounding zombie victory Burnside would have won had his efforts not been curtailed by senior commanders who insisted in meddling with his obviously awesome battle tactics.

While, on the face of it, this support appears to have allowed Burnside to be successful in completing his assigned military objective, it also failed to end the engagement in a decisive, undead fashion. To wit: Though defeated, the Confederates defending the bridge lived to fight another day (as opposed to all being eaten).

The opposing army left the engagement with a lesson running something like: "If the Union troops are being mowed down in wave after wave, they will eventually try something else (as opposed to "The Union troops will just keep coming and coming and coming until we run out of ammo and have to use our bayonets, and even then they will keep coming." [It's like: "I don't know about you, Zeke, but I'm starting to think we should just let these guys free those slaves. They seem to really want it."])

Burnside was censured and accused of attacking like a complete jackass (as opposed to being given a medal for zombie awesomeness).

If McClellan and others had simply given Burnside's approach the **time it needed to work**, then the enemy would have eventually been overtaken by Burnside's shambling, hoary army of zombielike fighters. The Confederates would have soon exhausted their ammunition, succumbed to physical exhaustion, and been completely demoralized by the knowledge that they faced a foe that would continue to attack in the lockstep manner of the undead.

Inside the (Empty) Skull: How They Think

Fortune favors the bold, and nobody is bolder than a zombie. **Period.** A zombie never has to be prompted or cajoled to do what it ought to be doing. A zombie never needed a "motivational speech" or "incentive structure" to get off its duff and try to eat somebody's brain. A zombie takes it upon itself, without prompting from others, to always be "on." Zombies are completely self-motivated.

Zombie Tip—There are No Small Roles, Only Small Actors: Some people would rather not be involved in a project unless they get to play a central role in it. This contemptible egotism is no way to get ahead (or, in the case of zombies, to get a head). Zombies know that all the zombies in a horde are playing an important role. Sure, the ones at the front of the pack who are breaking windows, tearing the bar-lights off the tops of cop cars, and ripping people's brains out might get more "attention" at first. But c'mon. The zombies waiting in reserve were important too. No task is "beneath" a zombie, and neither should it be beneath a Z.E.O.

Giving a zombie a pep talk about how it should go out and eat people is like telling water it should be wet, or telling the sun it should be bright and hot. Zombies aren't things that *sometimes* eat your brains, *when they feel like it* or when "market conditions make it appropriate." Zombies are constantly driven to eat people. They go after what they want without regard for how their coworkers feel about it, for "family time," or even for their own physical safety.

When considering a course of action (crossing a minefield, burrowing under a wall, charging a nest of howitzers), a zombie never considers that his action might be perceived as "too bold" or "inappropriately brash." A zombie flatly *does not care* about such things. A zombie's only question is "Does this course of action take me closer to my goal (brains) as directly as possible?" If the answer is yes, the zombie proceeds.

If you want to take your business career to its zenith and become a Z.E.O., you will need to cultivate a zombielike boldness. This doesn't mean that you need to charge into every board meeting, merger arbitration, or salary negotiation like a gibbering, teeth-gnashing zombie (though it couldn't hurt). But it does mean that you need to learn to take initiative, be self-motivated, and *interact with other people.*

Nothing happens in a vacuum. Not life. Not movement. Definitely not business success. No matter what you've got going for you, you will *not* succeed if you only keep to yourself.

Don't worry if you're an introvert, or you've never been good at making conversation at cocktail parties, or if professional "networking" functions make you want to stab someone in the eye with your fountain pen (this is, in fact, the healthiest reaction possible to networking events). Zombies aren't gregarious, either. Zombies aren't good at telling funny stories or making those around them feel at ease. Zombies have trouble with business casual (or dressing themselves at all, for that matter), and don't exactly "fit in" at most corporate events.

> **Zombie Tip—Stay on the lookout:** Think enlightenment will just smack you upside the head one day when you least expect it? Not likely. That's how you get hit by a truck. Whatever you're looking for (spiritual zen, true romantic love, a brain to eat) you've got to be looking for it if you expect to find it. Otherwise . . . bam! A truck. I'm not even kidding.

So if you're a little shy around the edges, or you're awkward and poorly spoken compared to those around you, **don't worry.** Zombies are, too. But if you're going to be a Z.E.O., you've got to learn from a zombie and let your temerity override your impulse to be shy.

A zombie finds a new way to take initiative and do something bold several times a day.

Most of us know a few poor souls who, for whatever reason, have difficulty dealing with reality. Their "solution" for this, nine times out of ten, is to construct a world of their own that they find more palatable than the real, actual one. This kind of self-delusion could not be farther from the earnest, reality-loving temperament of a zombie.

Don't think zombies aren't tempted to delude themselves from time to time. Believe me, there are plenty of aspects to a zombie's reality that aren't the easiest to cope with. He's an animated corpse with poor motor control and little to no speech driven onward by a desire that is never satisfied. Those who encounter him either flee or attack with all their might. He is "discriminated" against in virtually every way possible.

What's worse, when a zombie's hungry, he can't just go to the grocery store or corner market like you and me. It would be nice

Zombie Tip—Believe in yourself: Well, maybe not your living, complete and total self . . . but you know that "self" that's left when the soul has exited the body and then that leftover corpse has been stashed to rot for a few years before being supernaturally or scientifically reanimated to walk the earth and eat people's brains? That self. Believe in that.

for him if he could, but it's just not the case. A zombie has to track down living humans and eat their brains.

Despite all of these middling-to-large inconveniences, no zombie has ever chosen to "escape" from his reality into, say, a world of pills or drugs or booze. No zombies have joined religions that promise a better "next life" in the hereafter. You never see zombies joining the SCA or playing role-playing games in which they pretend to be someone else. It might be momentarily tempting, but zombies realize that they have to be where they are. They have to live in the now, regardless of how difficult it might be.

A zombie realizes that the only thing worse than having to grow up and live in the real world is what happens to you if you "decide" not to. You'll have to face reality someday. We **all** have to. Running from who you are and where you are will only make it worse when the time comes.

Some humans have living situations that are more or less tolerable, but are haunted by things and occurrences from their pasts. These people may look fine and dandy from all outward appearances, but are tortured inside by things that they did (or things that were done to them). They let these things from the past bring them down and make their lives miserable. This behavior is also unacceptable to a zombie. Zombies have difficult pasts too, but it doesn't stop them from getting on with "life."

Think about it. One moment you're lying there a corpse, minding your own business and enjoying the sweet lethe oblivion of the grave, and the next you've been reanimated by some chemicals you've never even heard of, and your life takes a turn you totally didn't expect. You're walking the earth once again under a pretty daunting set of conditions when you'd much rather be napping away in the dirt. Zombies don't waste their time pining over what might have been, however. They accept their situation and move forward (literally), always making the best of things. Always looking ahead—never backwards. Always searching for the next brain to eat. Always slouching toward the future.

No matter how adverse your current or previous situation, remember these three immutable zombie truths:

You are here.

It is now.

Eating a human brain is the most perfect pleasure imaginable.

Most of all, **do what makes you happy.**

That could be the best thing about zombies. They know what they want and they go out and get it. They go in a straight line, right to what they want. Whether it's the path of least resistance or the path of being firebombed by government troops, a zombie takes that path if it leads to tasty brains. A zombie's going to get what it wants, and fuck you if you think you're going to stop it.

A zombie doesn't hesitate, and it certainly doesn't doubt itself. No zombie ever says: "I'd really like to give the whole eating-your-brains thing a try, at least for a while. So right now the plan is to move to New York City after graduation and give it a go, but if I don't eat at least one brain by the time I'm, like, thirty, I am *so* totally moving back home and applying to law schools."

A zombie doesn't hedge its bets or give itself timelines. Once it makes a decision, it sticks to it.

It's down for (after)life.

It will pursue its goal to the very ends of the earth.

The rest of us could aspire to such dedication.

There is no general agreement, even among the most astute students of the walking dead, as to whether or not zombies have the capacity to "fail" at something, especially in the sense that you or I might understand the term.

Zombies try to do things (open doors, tunnel upward from subterranean burial mounds, bite through pith helmets) all the time. Sometimes they succeed, and sometimes they do not. Yet a zombie's ultimate goal is always to eat the brain of its enemy. If an action—even one that seems to be a misstep—brings a zombie closer to that goal, one is hard-pressed to call it a "failure."

Zombies are naturally curious creatures. In many cases, their reanimated brains contain little to no trace of the collected knowledge their bodies had in life. Thus, for a zombie, each action and interaction with something (an automobile, a power line, a flotilla of battleships) presents a new opportunity to learn about the world. I should not give the impression, however, that zombies are interested in "pure science." Zombies are interested in "eating your

Zombie Tip—Make time for yourself: With today's hectic, modern schedules, it's important for us to find ways to make times for the activities we really value. Whether it's more time with the kids, "private lessons" with your tennis instructor Hans, or eating a bunch of people, you've got to make "me" time. Nobody else is going to do it for you.

Remember: Zombies don't let emotions bring them down. Or up. Zombies stay in control.

brains out of your head." They may be fairly called curious in that they are curious about what actions may bring about this desired result. Though certain actions may fail to result in edible humans, there are frequently unexpected and (to a zombie) delightful results.

For example, zombies struggle to understand mechanisms like automatic doors, turnstiles, and elevators. Their interactions with these devices are often frustrating exercises that do not result in the appearance of edible humans. Sometimes though, the unexpected occurs. A zombie that has "failed" to locate delicious humans may accidentally touch a circular plastic button next to a bifurcated metal wall, and find that—moments later—this wall magically opens to reveal a box full of terrified humans with no place to flee (and who seem intent on mashing their own set of buttons to no avail as they scream for help that never comes). A curious zombie may search fruitlessly for humans in a series of shipping crates on a wharf; yet when the zombie is sealed inside one of those crates, transported for several weeks as part of a ship's cargo, then deposited on the docks of a coastal population center, it will find that it has succeeded in locating the presence of humans after all, as soon as that shipping crate is opened by an unlucky merchant. Consider, too, the zombie who explores the basement of a morgue or mortuary—there it will find only dead, embalmed brains (not worth eating). But if the zombie conducts a thorough search of the premises that lasts until

Zombie Tip—Meditate about it: The ancient practice of clearing one's mind by sitting quietly focusing on one's breathing was tailor-made for zombies. Zombies already sit quietly most of the time, and focus on brains only because they do not breathe. This lived-state of near constant meditation indicates a zombie's close proximity to nirvana.

dawn, the zombie may yet encounter the mortician arriving to get an early start on his day's work. (The zombie will, likewise, get an early start on eating the mortician's brains.)

The point here is that serendipitous things happen to zombies all the time as a function of their natural curiosity.

Wherever they are, whomever they're with, and whatever the situation, zombies have a way of making the best of things.

No, wait, that's actually selling it short a bit.

Zombies don't just make the best of things. At least not in the way regular people do.

When they get knocked down, they spring right back to life.

When their situation looks bad, they don't pause for an instant—**not for one instant**—to be depressed about it, before continuing on their way.

When forces that promise almost certain doom to a zombie array themselves before it, a zombie doesn't flinch (though some higher-functioning zombies **have** been known to smile).

A zombie doesn't just "make the best of it." Rather, a zombie is like a resilience-machine, designed to stay on course no matter what. Words like *ennui, hesitation, doubt,* and *depression* aren't even in its vocabulary.

There is every indication that, at every moment it exists, a zombie is doing what it loves, and loving what it does. The quest for brains is not something that a zombie's going to let come second for any reason. Keenly aware that becoming flustered, or depressed, or in any way emotionally distracted does not further its purposes, a zombie simply chooses not to lose its cool.

Have you ever heard anybody talk about a zombie that had lost its cool? You'll also never hear someone talk about a zombie "flying off the handle and trying to eat someone's brain." This is because zombies are already after your brain, which is as "off the handle" as it gets, really.

Have you ever heard of an angry zombie? (True, zombies can *appear* angry when compared to humans, but think in terms of "compared to other zombies.")

How about a sad zombie? (A zombie standing by itself out in the rain might seem, for a second, like a pitiful sight. But trust me, that thing is feeling no pain. Zombies aren't humans, as should be painfully clear by this point.)

A zombie doesn't wince at what most of us would call a "desperately dire situation" and "a tragically grave misfortune." The average human is not so lucky.

By focusing on perfection, humans make their lives imperfect.

By never worrying about doing things

perfectly, zombies experience perfect happiness.

As remarked, many self-help authors have opined that an obsession with perfection does not lead to happiness. Zombies have discovered that the opposite is also true. By never worrying about whether or not you've gotten something perfect, you tend to experience a rollicking happiness that is, well, pretty darn perfect.

 Zombie Tip—Remember that YOU have the power to change the world: Not in any real, meaningful, geopolitical way, of course. But if you're willing to scale things back just a bit, you'll see that real change is possible when you work on a one-to-one (brain-to-brain) level.

For instance, when a zombie's making his way through a day care center during a power outage, he doesn't worry about whether or not he's going to eat the brain of **every** child inside. When a zombie is locked in a to-the-death (or "death") combat with a human, he doesn't stop to worry about things going perfectly. If he's got to smash his victim's head on a rock, precious and delicious brains could be lost. If he decapitates the human in a wet or muddy battlefield, the brains could get all gooey and gross. (And who wants to eat a muddy brain? Totally gross, am I right?) Numerous things can "go wrong" in the course of combat. Does this stop the zombie? Not for a second. Win or lose, partial-muddy-brain or delicious-entire-brain, the zombie is just going for it like he always does. Nine times out of ten, the zombie finds that things go great when he just goes for it like that.

When disaster does strike, just follow these handy zombie crisis steps:

1. Relax—Zombies are always relaxed, having no anxiety, blood pressure, or heart rate to speak of. You can't think or help others if you're not relaxed and thinking clearly. Depending on the nature of the crisis you're facing (airborne tranquilizer attack, sleeping potion, invasion by dissidents with a very boring political agenda), you may already be relaxed. If so, just try not to fall asleep or anything.

2. Assess your personal situation—Are you trapped under rubble? Suffocating under waves of oily smoke? Being carried through the sky by some kind of tornado? Zombies have suffered through these terrifying situations and come out just fine. If you can remember this fact, then so will you. Taking care to secure your own person first in a crisis may seem like a selfish step, but it's important to get yourself to a safe place before you can help others or impress your bosses.

3. Assess the situation at large—What the fuck just happened? Even the smartest zombies have to stop and ask themselves this question from time to time. So once you've established that you're okay, it's time to take a deep breath and figure this shit out. Are robbers in hockey masks pointing guns at the tellers? Did an earth-quake just level a good three-fifths of corporate HQ? Is Godzilla (or possibly Mechagodzilla) crushing a warehouse full of pallets? However unexpected or far-fetched the crisis, when it's happening, it's happening, and you better wise up to that fact. Once you understand what's going on, you can take the next crucial step.

4. Just blindly charge in and go for it—Zombies didn't get where they are today (the pinnacle of awesomeness) by sitting back and carefully formulating action plans. Zombies just rush in (or slowly shamble in) and go for it, with no regard to their personal safety. At no time is this approach more called for than during a crisis.

Giving things power over it is not something a zombie does.

Of all entities everywhere (be they natural, supernatural, celestial, or something else), zombies may be the most free. With an

Zombie Tip—Love you long time: When you find something rewarding in your life that you truly love doing (mentoring inner-city youth, building houses for the homeless, consuming the still-sentient flesh of the living) make time for it, because man, you gotta have priorities.

Note: While it cannot be said that zombies make a concerted effort to consume either sex before the other, plenty of zombies *do* end up picking up girls late at night in secluded places. Especially girls with big, you know . . . brains.

existentialist flourish to make Jean-Paul Sartre blush, zombies realize they are truly able to do **whatever** they want, **whenever** they want. Zombies have noticed that no one can tell them what to do, and that the only limit on their actions is usually self-imposed.

A human thinks: "Even if I want to, I can't kill my enemy. If I do that I'll be shot at or jailed."

A zombie thinks: "If I want to, I can eat that guy's brain **and** get shot at or jailed."

The impending consequence in this example is much the same for the zombie and the human. The important difference is that the human is so acculturated and constrained that he automatically opts out of what he really wants to do. The radically free zombie keeps everything on the table.

When a human says: "Can I do that?" He usually means something like: "Is this legal? Will I get in trouble? Is it permitted?"

A zombie who wonders if something is possible is concerned only with the physical logistics. A zombie might wonder: "Can I break down this military barrier? Can that fat kid outrun me? Can I get through that doorway with this spear sticking through my chest?"

But **never**: "Will I get in trouble if I break down this door? Will eating that fat kid be in bad taste? Is it a social faux pas to go indoors with a spear?"

Did you ever hear of a zombie being nervous, or having high blood pressure (or blood pressure at all)? No. Zombies take it easy. If one human runs away, it's not like there won't be others. Slow and steady wins the race, and this is inherently apparent to a zombie.

When we talk about "being feared" or "inspiring fear in others," there are several similar activities from which we must distinguish ourselves. Activities and projects that, as zombies, we are most certainly *not* engaging in. These include bullying, gangstering, and threatening. Allow me to explain.

Bullies, unlike zombies, are fundamentally insecure. They want to be powerful and esteemed, but their insecurity requires them to create situations where they can forcibly affirm these things constantly. A bully on the playground steals milk money, not because he really needs the extra 70 cents, but to remind every-body (most of all, himself) that he can take it. That he is bigger and stronger, etc. The bully at work forces his entire staff to work late just to prove that he is powerful enough to do it, not because there is any pressing deadline to be met. This behavior is very unlike a zombie. A zombie never distended a victim's jaw while chiding "Why're you eating yourself? Why're you eating yourself?" Zombies don't do things because they need a burst of confidence, or because they want their superiority affirmed. They just want your brain, and you're right to fear them only because they're actually coming to get it.

Like zombies, gangsters also inspire fear, but zombies aren't gangsters. Whether it's the Al Capones of a bygone era or the Tupac Chopras of today, gangsters are all about building a rep and using it to build an empire, usually a criminal one. It's all about money. People fear gangsters because gangsters will kill to get what they want, and will seriously mess with you if you somehow inter-fere with their bootlegging/drug dealing/energy drink-endorsing enterprises. Stay out of a gangster's way, however, and he may be nice to you, or even help you out. Zombies, on the other hand, have no secondary interests needing protection. A gangster says "You'd better not mess with me 'cause I'll fucking kill you . . . though under the right circumstances I could be your friend." A zombie says "You'd better not mess with me 'cause I'll eat your brain if you do. Then again, I'm going to eat your brain anyway, so whatever." Gangsters are violent because they have interests to protect. Zombies are just being themselves.

Finally, some humans (many, in fact) use fear to threaten people. There is an if/then-style proposition to it all. **If** you don't let me ride your bike, **then** I'll break your arm. **If** you don't take me fly fishing, **then** I'll cry the whole way home. **If** you don't give me that promotion, **then** I'll sleep with you. There is no "if/then" in the brain of a zombie. Zombies will kill you and eat you no matter what you do. If you let me ride your bike, then I'll eat your brain. Going fishing? Getting eaten. Not going fishing? Still getting eaten. Are we seeing a pattern here? The thing to take away is that zombies don't leverage the threat of eating someone's brain against something else. What they want is the only thing they want.

Contrary to these other types, the fear inspired by a zombie is not the fear of a bully, a gangster, or somebody making a threat. The fear inspired by zombies is, in contrast, the purest kind of fear. It's like the fear of a bolt of lightning or of a hungry tiger. It is the fear of things that cannot (or will not) be reasoned with. The fear of something with no ulterior motive. It's something with no ego to flatter or hidden agenda to uphold. No amount of digging into its past will unearth a secret about a bolt of lightning that you can use to keep yourself safe from it.

Okay, so let's hold up our lists and notice once more that one is strikingly more substantial than the other. Now, for a moment, imagine this scenario, however radical it may seem at first: What if everything on your **THINGS I'M AFRAID OF**

list were magically transported to your **THINGS THAT FEAR ME** list?

Suspend disbelief for a second and drink that feeling in.

Feels good, doesn't it? That's how a zombie feels every day.

If you consider it, zombies "think positive" all the time. Though they are rotting reanimated corpses facing physical restrictions that would daunt and overwhelm the most positive among us, zombies never pause to meditate on what they **can't** do. Rather, they remain focused on what is still possible for them. A one-armed zombie doesn't think: "Damn. One arm. Shit." Instead, he thinks: "I'm gonna find a way to strangle you one-handed, bitch! It might take longer, but hey, I've got all day." A zombie whose torso and legs have rotted into a putrid gelatinous mass doesn't cry over spilled brains about the hundred-yard dashes he will never run. It slithers after humans through sewers and drains, using its natural sliminess to its advantage.

If there's one historical figure for whom the slogan "Just do it" came too late, it is the mysteriously zombie-like general Sima Yi, who commanded troops in China's Three Kingdoms era around the year 200. The period in Chinese history when it seemed like everybody was attacking everybody—and military leaders trying to make names for themselves were a yuan a dozen—Sima Yi was able to establish himself as one of the most feared badasses on the block by attacking his opponents in unexpected, innovative, and highly effective ways. In almost everything he did, Sima Yi employed a zombie's determination and fortitude.

Though probably not **technically** an actual zombie (as far as we know . . . records from 200 aren't the clearest), Sima Yi fought in ways that gave his troops many of the advantages enjoyed by actual zombie armies today.

Consider the following:

He was "unpredictable."

Sima Yi was known not only as a fierce fighter but also as a foe whose next move could not be easily guessed. This lack of predictability was a vexation for his enemies, who had a difficult time anticipating where he would strike next. He sometimes sent his enemies notes suggesting he would do one thing, then made a point of doing the other. Sima Yi became known in ancient China as an expert strategist precisely because his next move could so infrequently be determined in advance. But (here's the funny thing) when you look at what he actually did, it was just "attack, attack, attack." In almost every situation, Sima Yi's enemies would have best served themselves by anticipating an offensive.

Sima Yi almost just always attacked but allowed his foes to think he was likely to do otherwise. **Very like a zombie.**

He did things you "can't" do.

There are rules by which all combatants on the battlefield are bound. Ironclad rules. Rules steeped in tradition and history. Rules that cannot be broken . . . until someone wises up and just says, "Oh, wait. *Yes they fucking can!*" Sima Yi seems to have invented this.

In one of his first campaigns—at the Battle of Xincheng in 227—Sima Yi's enemies believed that he "couldn't" attack them prior to obtaining permission from the royal court, which they knew he did not have. However, Sima Yi (brilliant tactician that he was) noticed that this injunction against beginning the offensive without permission was really just **an abstract idea**, whereas his soldiers and war equipment were, quite to the contrary, **real and tactile** and perfectly arranged to attack the enemy, like, right now, without any waiting. Thus, before his opponents had time to say: "Wait a minute, you can't do tha—" Sima Yi had done it and won the battle with a swift offensive against an enemy that thought itself unable to be engaged by virtue of court doctrine.

Zombies, like Sima Yi, have won countless battles by doing things you "can't" do. They're old chestnuts by now, but how many times have we heard the following:

You can't survive multiple .38 shots to the heart.

You can't function as a military unit in environments without oxygen or sunlight.

You can't capture a fortified position if the defenders outnumber you.

You can't subsist on a diet entirely comprised of living human brain tissue. (You probably need, like, vegetables and stuff. . . .)

Except zombies **can.** And they **do.**

Zombies abide by no military conventions. (Hell, the bacteria saturating their own bodies is usually enough to qualify as "using biological weapons.") They respect no borders or boundaries or treaties. And they **certainly** don't wait for permission from a royal court before engaging an enemy. Zombies do what they do, and fuck your rules.

The longer it takes you to wake up and realize this, the longer zombies (and commanders like Sima Yi) are going to have an advantage over you.

He resisted provocation.

At the Battle of Wuzhang Plains in 234, Sima Yi faced a fierce opposing general named Zhuge Liang. Considered by many to be Sima Yi's nemesis, Zhuge Liang was also a brilliant battlefield tactician. However, as history shows, Zhuge Liang also wasn't above a bit of schoolyard name-calling. As the two opposing armies stared one another down, Zhuge Liang grew anxious and had a suit of women's clothes sent to Sima Yi, effectively calling him a girl for failing to attack fast enough. There may be no modern-day equivalent to the depth of this insult. Accounts tell us that Sima Yi's

lieutenants were incensed and called for an immediate attack to punish Zhuge Liang for this intolerable gesture.

Instead, Sima Yi made the greatest tactical move of all. He did not quicken his pace at all.

Just like a zombie.

Zombies don't respond to insults or taunts. You can't bait a zombie with words (though human brains are another matter entirely). You can't hurt their feelings by pointing out short-comings. For all of their rotting, limbless decrepitude, zombies couldn't care less about the way they appear. There are no aspects of their appearance about which zombies are sensitive. In fact, there is **nothing** that can be said (or otherwise conveyed) to hasten a zombie's murderous, ravenous ire.

When a zombie is ready to attack you, you'll know, **because you'll be getting attacked.** (Until then, you're just going to have to sit tight.) This tendency allows zombies to triumph in many battlefield situations where those with hotter blood (or blood at all) would see a commander provoked into missteps, lured across minefields or into ambushes, or prompted to engage an enemy before he was 100 percent prepared. Zombies are never lured into traps. They are never incited to attack when the situation doesn't warrant an offensive. They never overstep their operation's objectives by fighting for things like "honor" or "pride" or "something other than brains."

By remaining unmoved by what was—in his day, at least—the biggest insult anybody had ever seen, Sima Yi displayed a zombie's fortitude and restraint, and never allowed his enemy to prompt him into joining battle before he was good and ready.

He used physical oddities to his advantage.

As is well documented, Sima Yi could turn his head around a full 180 degrees without moving the rest of his body. (Think about that for a second. Freaky, huh?) Now, we have no way of knowing how Sima Yi *felt* about this quality that made him different from other men. Perhaps he was tempted to conceal his difference from the rest of the world.

But if he *was* tempted, he didn't give in. Instead, he said, "Fuck that; I'm going to be the best turning-my-head-180-degrees general there is!" And he **was**—using his neck-turning ability on the battlefield in full view of friend and foe alike.

There is some evidence that Sima Yi's allies even derived a morale boost from this feature. (Upon seeing this physical oddity, the general Cao Cao is said to have remarked, "This guy can totally see from all directions, which will probably help out on the battle-field or something. And also: Holy shit!")

Now, everyone knows that zombies tend to have physical "differences" that—at least on the surface—separate them from normal soldiers and/or military commanders. Zombies are frequently missing limbs or eyeballs. Zombies' bodies have usually been horribly contorted and warped from years spent rotting in charnel earth or moldering at the bottom of a well. Zombies' skins have usually turned an unhealthy shade of white (which makes for really lousy camouflage unless you're in the arctic), or a disgusting greenish brown (which is sorta good for camouflage, actually).

Everyone also knows that zombies never let their physical differences stop them. They never try to hide the things that iden-tify them as being unlike most people. They don't don makeup

Zombie Tip—Courage is being scared but doing it anyway: Idiocy is not being scared of zombies and/or attacking zombies. (It's like, dude, what are you even thinking?)

and wigs in an attempt to "pass" as humans. They don't attempt to "stand up straight" when their rotted spine compels them to lean forward awkwardly.

Yet this refusal to bend to the expectations of others is more than an acceptance of themselves as just the way God (or a voodoo priest or an evil wizard or secret government supersoldier project gone horribly, horribly wrong) made them. Zombies have realized that in many cases, their "differences" translate to "advantages" on the battlefield.

Zombies that lack body parts (or parts of body parts) can frequently squeeze through battlefield impediments that would stop a normal-sized soldier. Zombies can use their inability to respirate to ford deep rivers and withstand poison gas attacks. Zombies with gaping holes in their torsos can sometimes have projectile attacks pass completely through their bodies. And, yes, some zombies with especially loose spinal cords and vertebrae can swivel their heads around 180 (or even 360) degrees.

Zombies are dynamic, inventive warriors. Whenever they find a way that they are different from their opponents, they ask (or groan): "How can I use this to my advantage on the battlefield?"

The only thing he feared was the living dead.

For all the tales of derring-do and famous aphorisms attributed to Sima Yi, the utterance for which he is best remembered might be: "I can do battle with the living, but not the dead." He made this famous statement in one of the only situations where he is recorded to have run from a battlefield in cowardly terror.

But he had a good reason. (The best, really.)

The story runs that after Sima Yi's nemesis Zhuge Liang died (of natural causes [wuss]), Sima Yi brought his army to bear on Yang Yi, Zhuge Liang's successor. However, as the two generals engaged their forces, Sima Yi caught word that Zhuge Liang was not actually dead. Or that he had been dead, but now no longer was. Or that he was dead *but somehow had still been seen walking around.*

Though historians of the time do not record him using the Z-word, Sima Yi wisely decided that if these reports even had a *chance* of being true, he did not want to risk engaging an undead enemy. Instead of taking the risk that he would have to fight an actual zombie, Sima Yi wisely disengaged his army. When asked about this uncharacteristic retreat, he uttered the aforementioned quote by way of explanation.

Fearing zombies didn't really make Sima Yi *like* a zombie (or Zombie Commander). It just shows that he was smart and knew what was up. Even though the rumors about Zhuge Liang turned out to be false (he was still dead), Sima Yi gets credit for not even risking that shit and erring on the side of caution, which is always the best thing to do when it comes to zombies.

In conclusion, if you make Sima Yi your model, you'll be well on your way to becoming a Zombie Commander. Like you, Sima Yi was merely human, but he elevated himself to greatness by fighting his enemies (and winning) with the tactics of the living dead. And hey, that's all I ask.

Dead Lips Sink Ships: How They Communicate

Let's face it; it doesn't take much to fuck up a mission. The slightest change in weather can postpone the launch of a multimillion-dollar rocket. Choppy seas can delay (or destroy) a nautical offensive. Rioting indigenous people can totally muck up your army's plans to occupy their land and take their shit. As a zombie soldier, you always want to eliminate as many of these external factors as possible to ensure smooth sailing for whatever nefarious military offensive you are planning. And the *last thing* you ever need is for invasion plans or attack stratagems to be compromised because people heard you talking about them.

One of the advantages a zombie soldier must possess is a knack for complete silence regarding matters pertaining to the battle-field. This is even true **while on the battlefield itself.**

Zombies are known for being quiet, but are not all completely silent. The walking dead are known moaners and groaners, and probably more than half of them can articulate at least one word ("brains"). Some higher-functioning zombies can even string together complete sentences or intentionally impersonate humans. The fact remains, however, that zombies **never talk more than is necessary.** There is no zombie chitchat. There is no banter around the campfire (or the mausoleum or whatever). Zombies have no need to "talk about the weather" (literally or figuratively) with their compatriots. This silence may be due to factors such as a lack of lips and functional vocal cords, but even zombies rendered silent by uncooperative physiology **still do not attempt to communicate**

with their colleagues through other means. This, then, suggests that a zombie's lack of impulse to communicate stems from something deeper. I wish to posit here that they don't need to chat with one another, **because zombies (and zombie armies) already have a really excellent esprit de corps(e).** Most people chat idly in order to establish a rapport with people they are still getting to know and trust. But zombies have such complete camaraderie that this is never necessary. A zombie's natural silence is more than a nice thing to have on covert missions. It is one of the most important keys to the success of the zombie warrior.

Because they don't go around discussing things like attack plans and "next steps" on the battlefield, zombies never betray anything that might give an opposing army an advantage. There is no point to spying or eavesdropping on zombies. No one has ever sent a secret agent, dressed as a member of the walking dead, to infiltrate a zombie camp to see what could be learned from the zombie soldiers. (And no Mata Hari femmes fatales have ever initiated liaisons with a zombie commander to see what could be learned.)

A zombie's silence is not limited to preparations; zombies are mostly silent on the battlefield, too. However, this doesn't mean that they can't communicate when it's absolutely necessary. Zombies **do** communicate on the battlefield through a series of subtle, nonverbal cues. The most dominant of these may be called: "Just following the zombie in front of you." There is an elegant simplicity here. As a zombie's reasoning goes: *If a zombie is moving, it is because it sees an enemy (or food) and is moving closer to it. Therefore, if the zombie in front of me is moving, it must see an enemy/food ahead, and if I follow that zombie, then I, too, will move closer to an enemy/food.* No part of this process involves the need for spoken language.

Zombies can also moan in surprise or alarm when a new enemy is sighted. This typically indicates to surrounding zombies the appearance of the new enemy. (In many respects, a zombie's moan can be compared to the bark of a dog; it indicates the desire for something, and that others like it should know its presence.)

Finally, zombies have been known to moan out of frustration. For example, when humans have secreted themselves behind an iron door, zombies have been known to gather in front of it and emit low moans and groans. A zombie's moans of frustration are more than just a sacrilegious or pornographic exclamation of regret and anger. They are also a message to other zombies: "There is frustration and failure here. We must resolve the matter some other way." And the thing is, **they do.** If zombies have trapped a group of humans in a machine shed and find themselves groaning in front of the bolted door, some other zombie is always going to realize that that way is blocked and start looking for another way to get inside. It may tunnel under the side of the shed or it may find a weakness in the rear paneling and bust its way through it. The point is, when one zombie moans in frustration, another zombie takes it as a call to action and does something about the situation.

If you want to fight like a zombie, then work on cultivating a reputation as the quietest guy in your unit. You do not need to be completely mute—again, most zombies do talk *a bit*—but limit your speech to things unrelated to military engagements. Teach those around you to communicate nonverbally as many battlefield actions as possible. And if the guy in front of you looks like he sees something good, you can probably just follow him.

Seriously, no one likes a gossip or a motormouth. People who can't stop prattling on and on about endless trivialities will never get far in life. Zombies, by contrast, get very far precisely *because* they place extreme limits on verbal communication. (That is, if they don't eliminate it altogether.)

While a few zombies are completely silent, most can manage at least a moan. Some know a word or two (like "brains"), and high

> **Zombie Tip—Grunt softly, and carry your own arms should they become detached:** Not that zombies care about being called litterbugs, but you never know when arms might come in handy, you know?

functioning zombies have been known to utter entire sentences. The important thing is, nobody ever heard of a zombie talking more than was absolutely necessary.

What **is** "necessary" for a zombie?

A fair question. The answer? Brains. As many as possible. And while the average zombie's guttural moan of "…braaaaaaaaains…" may be little more than an involuntary declaration of love for what it prizes most in (after)life, the zombie who *can* manage articulate intentional speech uses it only to further his or her ends. A zombie may:

Impersonate an ambulance dispatcher to order more paramedics when all available ones have been eaten.

Use a small amount of speech with one human to negotiate his way into a situation where there will be additional humans (gaining entrance to a building, etc.).

> **Zombie Tip—Trust Your Instincts:** In business as in the nocturnal hunt for the flesh of the living, your first impulse is usually the right one. If something seems a little off about a candidate you're interviewing, or if you suddenly get the feeling that a swath of swampland might be mined against zombie attacks, then dude, it probably is.

Use a word or two to operate voice-activated doors or machines, provided this will lead them closer to actual humans.

Utter just enough speech to appear human when appearing to be a zombie would be a disadvantage (i.e., hiding; this is rare behavior, and only the highest-functioning zombies ever do it).

Moan to indicate its presence to an unsuspecting human. (This is usually done to corral quick-moving humans into more manageable locations.)

The important thing to note here is that the speech is a means to an end. There's no: "What's up, dude? How was your day? Eaten anybody good recently?" Forget that noise. A zombie talks *for a reason*, and so should you.

There is, after all, a certain gravitas to the speech of a zombie. Not that it's eloquent or pleasant to the ear. In fact, it is neither of these (and, come to think of it, probably a good example of the opposite).

Zombies are almost uniformly successful because they choose to partner up **with other zombies**. Zombies cooperate. They do this because they have the same shared goal in mind (eating your brain) and because they're already headed in the same direction (toward you). Yet as this "cooperation" begins to mount, two zombies become three and then four, and before long you have a "gang" of zombies. After a few gangs meet and merge, you have a "horde." Hordes combine and form an "army." **And then you're fucking talking!**

A lone zombie is not by any means disadvantaged. He's just not as powerful as he *could* be when flanked by a number of his brethren. An army of zombies is one of the most powerful things known to man. The only things you can really compare it to are natural disasters. A horde of zombies hits with the city-leveling power of an earthquake. It disrupts communities like a tidal wave. It exterminates (or at least moves) populations like a famine.

But when zombies do talk, people listen.

If a zombie opens its mouth, some important stuff is about to go down, that, probably, you should know about.

If you want people to take you seriously when you talk, then make like a zombie and keep your trap shut 99.9 percent of the time. Then, when you **do** talk, they'll listen as if their lives depend on it.

Okay, first of all, there's a difference between "being prepared" and "undergoing preparation."

Zombies are prepared (all of the time, at every moment of the day or night) to kick your ass and eat your brain. They don't require any prep time to be ready for a battle or engagement. Their fighting effectiveness is not bolstered by a review of the terrain or conditions they will encounter. In this connection, military briefings and mission reports are almost entirely lost on them. They may even attempt to eat the person delivering the briefing.

In this way, zombies exist in stark contrast to the rather ponderous machinations of the modern political and military establishments. Formal conflicts between nations tend to have several stages, each of which allows conventional generals to prepare their troops for combat. These stages can include:

Sun Tzu's most famous aphorism might be that "all war is based upon deception." At face value, he's talking about soldiers pretending to be strong when they are weak, pretending to be weak when they are strong, and pretending to be disorganized when they are a model of order. But what about soldiers who "pretend" to be alive, when they are technically dead, and look dead but move and fight as though they are clearly alive? What about a soldier who staggers and looks weak, but who is strong enough to kick your ass and eat your brain? What about a soldier who might appear to be "falling apart," yet nonetheless can withstand gunshots, electrocution, and having entire limbs blown away? Zombies are the "living" embodiment of Sun Tzu's ideal soldier.

A further examination of Sun Tzu's specific suggestions makes clear that the author clearly had the tactics of zombies in mind (if he was not an actual zombie himself). For example:

"Feign disorder, then crush your enemy."

Nobody seems more "disordered" than a zombie. Even in a great horde, they have trouble sticking together. Half of them can't walk in a straight line. They give away their position by moaning. They're confused and startled by shiny things and fireworks. (Hell, I might underestimate them myself if I didn't know better.) But zombies only *look* disordered, and there is an eerie coordination to their efforts. Like a zombie, it's best to let the enemy assume you are no threat. Then walk right through the entrenchments and barbed wire and eat his brain. In business, you may *appear* to be disorganized. Your desk may be a mess, and your calendar a tangle of conflicting appointments. But woe betide the coworker who assumes this means you are no threat to him. Once he has counted you out as competition, it will be all the easier to steal the corner office from under his nose.

"Attack him where he is unprepared—appear where you are not expected."

Like, say, I don't know, in shopping malls and abandoned military bases? Do you think those might be good places?

It's not hard to see how this maxim might be applied to the boardroom, but if you really want to do it well, you've got to do it like a zombie. Zombies are masters of popping up where people don't expect them and (more importantly) aren't equipped to deal with them. Zombies climb through holes in masonry and shuffle into houses where defenseless humans are waiting. They walk underwater (occasionally fighting sharks), and decimate weaponless tourists on tropical islands. Zombies take "business" to people, even if people aren't expecting it.

So "ambush" your boss the next time he takes that solo visit to the topless bar, and use the opportunity to ask about your upcoming promotion in a friendly, my-cell-phone-takes-pictures-that-I-can-e-mail-to-your-wife kind of way. It's not your fault he wasn't prepared for your question, and you deserve an answer. Then and there.

"If your opponent is of choleric temper, seek to irritate him."

Lots of things are irritating, but almost nothing is more irritating than a zombie. Zombies make your house smell bad when you just cleaned it. They moan and grunt when you're trying to get some sleep. They eat your brain when you're busy using it for thinking and living and stuff.

Zombies are experts at irritating people. And, as Sun Tzu points out, irritated people make bad, bad decisions.

An "irritating" zombie may be pursuing a small group of humans through the countryside on a dark and stormy night. What do the humans do? Split up in different directions, ensuring that at least most of them will get away? Find some kind of vehicle (like a car or a helicopter) that can take them away from the zombie? You'd think so, but no. Instead, the humans barricade themselves inside the nearest barn, giving the zombie all evening to figure out a way to get inside . . . and time for his friends to show up.

If you have a coworker you need to beat out for a promotion, employ irritation to rile him or her. Steal his employee parking sticker. Order a dozen pizzas to her office. Send him page after page of solid black faxes. If a coworker can't think clearly, a coworker can't be a formidable opponent.

"If [your opponent] is taking his ease, give him no rest."

Zombies don't rest. They wait. They stalk. They bide their time, true. But they don't rest.

Even when a zombie is frozen in ice or imprisoned in a steel drum by the Army Corps of Engineers, it is always plotting its next move.

In addition to not resting itself, a zombie actively prevents others from resting. Having a dogged, undead zombie after you tends to makes the idea of stopping for a nap seem like a bad plan. If the thing pursuing you is not going to be stopping, you'd better not either.

If you're in a business situation in which you must best a foe, use dogged persistence to unnerve and destroy him. Work while he is sleeping. Put in twice the hours he does. Make it clear to him that you are an indefatigable opponent. Even the strongest adversary will begin to buckle when he realizes going up against you means forfeiting all future prospect of rest or recovery.

"Bring your own war material, but forage on the enemy for food."

Good thinking there, Sun Tzu. "Forage on the enemy for food…" Maybe specifically on their brains?

"Use the conquered foe to augment your own strength."

Seriously, do you *still* not believe that Sun Tzu was a zombie?

Nobody knows more about using the conquered to augment their own strength than zombies. True, armies might look for defectors from the other side, or see if any of the captured POWs want to try switching teams—but you never know if you can trust those guys. Maybe they're looking to be double agents, or triple agents, or some shit.

When zombies bite and infect humans, there's no question as to the "loyalty" of their converts. The bitten humans are going to become zombies (if they don't realize what's happening and shoot themselves in the head first) and, once zombies, they're never going back.

"In the practical art of war, the best thing of all is to take the enemy's country whole and intact."

This final lesson of Sun Tzu's is perhaps the most compelling case for why the style of the zombie is most effective for one seeking military or corporate victory. It's a simple idea, but vitally important.

If you're a conquering army, then you're conquering a foreign land for a reason. If history is any indicator, you are after natural resources, infrastructure, and access to assets. If, to take your enemy's country captive, you have to firebomb it out of existence, it sort of defeats the purpose of taking it. If the cities are destroyed, the crops ruined, and the wells poisoned, then it's going to be something of a hollow victory. What's left for you to take? The spoils of war are, um, spoiled.

So in business, a hostile takeover must be executed so as to preserve the entity being taken. If your aggressive acquisition style causes the best and brightest to leave the target company, causes vendors to refuse to do business with it, and severs all its ties to the local and national politicians who helped it skirt all those pollution laws, then you've got to ask yourself if it's really worth having.

Zombies are experts at taking a countryside whole, without pillaging crops, destroying property, or wrecking historical and cultural treasures (except by accident). Any invading force (be it an army or a corporation) should look to zombies as the best example of conquering-while-leaving-intact.

To sum up, it is clear that Sun Tzu (like any bright military tactician) recognized the superior battlefield skills of zombies. The impulse to apply Sun Tzu's writings to the business world is, therefore, not entirely incorrect. Yet sources should always be credited, and in this case, the source is clearly zombies.

All's Fair in Death and War: How to Fight

Everything you know is wrong.

There, I said it.

When it comes to the art of warfare, your every conception could not be more off base.

Enemy surveillance, carefully coordinated attack plans involving feints and deception, long-range weapons . . . these are not the tools of a true warrior. These are lies. These are the tools of weaklings. Of failures.

The modern military-industrial complex seeks only to fatten itself by promulgating the untruth that expensive military equipment and years of strategy training at West Point are the most reliable tools for achieving victory on the battlefield.

I, on the other hand, am someone you can trust. I have no vested interest in deceiving you. I am here only to provide access

Zombie Tip—Know guts, know glory: Zombie warriors understand that the shortest path to achieving victory is the one that goes straight through the enemy soldiers. One by one. With their teeth.

to the laws that have allowed **zombies** to become the most effective fighting force in the world today.

You might shoot your enemies with M-16s, destroy them with fragmentation grenades, or send them through a skinless shrieking hell with a combination of napalm and white phosphorus. And that's, you know, fine . . . but notice also that you're not winning every battle you fight. You're not eliminating your enemy's entire army each time you engage it. You're not conquering the countryside with the swiftness and fatality of an implacable virus.

In short: **You are not fighting like a zombie, so there is room for improvement.**

Throughout history, the most brilliant military minds have sought to defeat armies of zombie soldiers. **All have failed.** No advance in their high-tech weaponry or cutting-edge training has ever allowed these leaders to match the tactics and fighting skills inherent in a bunch of stinking, rotted, walking corpses.

In the history of combat, there has been no foe as implacable and persistent as the zombie. Zombies have penetrated supposedly impregnable fortresses. They have forded uncrossable streams, traversed moats filled with flaming oil, and chewed through drawbridges on even the most impenetrable castles. They have risen from watery depths to overtake ships and sailing vessels—from ancient Roman barks to modern aircraft carriers—with ease and facility. They have clogged the treads of tanks with their bones. They've attached themselves to helicopter skids (then hoisted themselves up to feast on the pilots inside). They've overtaken the most well-defended modern military outposts.

Zombies get close to their enemies and tear them limb from limb. Zombies bite off noses and ears. Zombies eat brains.

While zombies are often belittled, denigrated, and (most crucially) underestimated by their opponents, they always manage to somehow have the last laugh (or last brain). **It is this "somehow"**

that this section proposes to examine, quantify, and make available to the reader in practical, easy-to-understand steps.

You need to ask yourself right now: "When it comes to zombies, do I want to beat them (clearly, an impossible task) **or do I want to join them?**"

Many soldiers wish that they could face their opponents with unflinching resolution, instead of doubt and anxiety. Many soldiers wish they were part of expeditionary forces that would operate autonomously and act with resolve, instead of requiring constant micromanagement. This section will make clear that these and other traits **can be adopted** by today's soldiers **if they copy the ways of zombies.**

Do you already have military training? Don't worry. It's nothing that can't be overcome. It's time to slough off the things you learned at West Point and replace them with things learned at Monroeville. Are you already a battle-hardened veteran? Prepare to learn more in three hours in an abandoned shopping mall than you did in three tours in the Middle East.

Let's be clear: **This is serious business.** The world needs effective soldiering, now more than ever. Today's geopolitical clusterfuck contains (but is by no means limited to):

- Traditionally warring ethnic factions
- Newly warring ethnic factions
- Tyrants and dictators who have ceased to be useful to the major world superpowers
- Insane religious leaders who encourage poor people to commit acts of violence
- Countries that are bored enough to fight over useless islands or horrible deserts in the middle of nowhere
- Third world paramilitary leaders who feel they'd do a much better job of running things than an elected president

Zombie Tip—A brain in the hand is worth two behind the hastily impro-vised zombie barricades: Count your blessings, man. When something good comes your way, go ahead and enjoy it. Don't forsake it in favor of what might be behind the next door. Cause it could be some kind of anti-zombie nerve gas the government has been working on, and then you're just fucked.

All of whom will probably, at some point, need to have their shit set straight via a military engagement. These problems aren't going away, and it's important that a capable military is around to address them. **That "capable military" is going to be you.**

The soldiers of tomorrow are going to have a lot on their plate, and their ability to do what they do—effectively and efficiently—is going to be more important than ever before. Fighting like a zombie will allow you to achieve victory, destroy foes, and settle geopolitical conflicts with the quick decisiveness of a zombie's bite.

The world needs help from zombie soldiers, and if you're reading this book, then it looks like it's going to fall to you. Ask yourself if you're tough enough to get down like a member of the walking dead. If you are, then welcome to basic training.

Everybody has different strengths and weaknesses.

If there's a lesson to be taken from this fact, it's "use what you got." It's a lesson nobody's learned better than a zombie.

The luckiest zombies are those with the good fortune to be reanimated directly after mortal life has departed from the body. These zombies, usually still wearing the clothes they were buried in (which, in the case of female zombies, almost always includes pearls and a hat), have the fortune to be mistaken for living humans. Occasionally, these lucky zombies are even mistaken for the *particular* living people they were before they died. The advantages of this are diverse and considerable. A zombie who appears to be simply a drunken or similarly incapacitated human being of sallow complexion has a much greater chance of gaining access to the places where living humans (and their correspondingly delicious brains) are to be found. Some of these highest-functioning zombies are even lucky enough to remember a word or two of human speech. (Usually these will be simple words and phrases like "hello," "yes," "no," and "I am, in fact, a neurosurgeon. Now please let me closer to that succulent frontal lobe.") These zombies are the millionaires, the professional athletes, the rock stars of the zombie world. But as long as they remain appropriately humble, we have little reason to begrudge them their success. (Zombies are not covetous of one another's good fortune. This is yet another trait we could stand to adopt from them.)

Other zombies (perhaps the majority fall into this category) are lucky enough to have all of their limbs and features, but cannot pass for living human beings. These zombies have deathly pale skin. Their grave-clothes are often generations old. Their fingernails and teeth are long and ragged. Their hair is unkempt and encrusted with soil. Still, these zombies are able to be mistaken for living humans at great distances or in the dark, and often use this fact to their advantage. These zombies can sometimes blend into crowds of inebriated people (such as at sporting events or rock concerts), and can pass unnoticed through inhabited areas on dark, rainy nights.

Other zombies still are less lucky, yet manage as best they can. Zombies in this category are often missing arms or legs. Eyes, noses, and teeth are questionable. Baldness is common. Decomposition, to some degree, has already set in. These zombies are often called the most hideous because they still possess some visible

similarity to a living human, but with the most jarring variations thereupon. These zombies induce fainting, vomiting, and the invocation of deities on sight. Tragically, they must exist in a world not designed for them—a world of staircases made for people with two legs, ladders for those with two arms, and voice-recognition software that is hard enough for a living human to use and damn-near impossible for a zombie's rotted vocal cords to operate. These zombies can't pass for human, and don't try to. They win by paralyzing victims with fear. By being a glorious abattoir-on-parade. If someone faints at the sight of them, so much the easier. If a zombie's wounds or half-decayed state is knee splittingly hilarious, then hey, keep laughing while the zombie gets that much closer, funny guy. Maybe these zombies don't look much like people anymore, but the point is, you're still getting eaten.

Some zombies appear to be normal humans, especially from a distance. They wear clothing, have all their hair and teeth, and their tendons and muscles have yet to rot, making normal locomotion more or less possible. These zombies—usually bitten while they were still alive (or reanimated **directly** after death)—may look and act like living humans in more ways than not, but each of them will have a "tell" that betrays them. You just have to look for it.

That guy shambling down the block might look like the same mailman you see every day, but look closer. Do his eyes lack their usual focus? Instead of whistling show tunes, is he drooling and moaning? Do the neighborhood dogs, who usually bark at him, now flee in cowardly terror?

How about the nice lady who works behind the deli counter at your local grocery store? Does her skin look a little more—how does one put it?—"corpselike" than normal? Are the red spatters on her apron a little *fresher* than usual? Does she give off a reek of raw meat that has nothing to do with the ham slices in the glass case in front of her?

What about the babysitter . . . ? She's a little early to watch the kids tonight, but so what, right? Maybe she's just getting a head start on things. But now that you take a second glance, her clothes appear to be a few days old, and her hair (usually so carefully brushed) is more than a little tangled. Her Keds also seem much muddier than you remember. What kind of muck she been walking through, anyway? And instead of waiting for you to leave so she can call her boyfriend, she's totally trying to eat you. What's up with **that?**

Importantly, in most of these cases, you have to get really close to these "people" before you can tell for sure that they're zombies. In each instance, the zombies will use this fact to their respective advantages. This law of deception by proximity is something that **you** must now employ in your business dealings with other companies.

Any questions?

A final category of zombie may fairly be called the Most Decomposed Zombie. Some researchers have even wondered if these creations ought to count as "zombies" at all. Here you find the walking skeleton, no more than rags, tendons, and bright white bone glistening in the moonlight. Here you find the gelatinous humanoid mass, muddily rising from a grave in the bottom of a swamp and lurching toward land caked in leaves and vines. Here the brain,

spinal cord, and gibbering skull, squirming along like a fish out of water. These zombies are not just un-human, but un-zombie-like as well. But fuck it, right? They're still coming for you, and that's the important thing. In fact, maybe that's their advantage. These zombies aren't trying to look like humans. They're mud creatures, or fish, or skeletons, or fish skeletons. They're not going to let you tell them they're not zombies. You don't "get" to tell

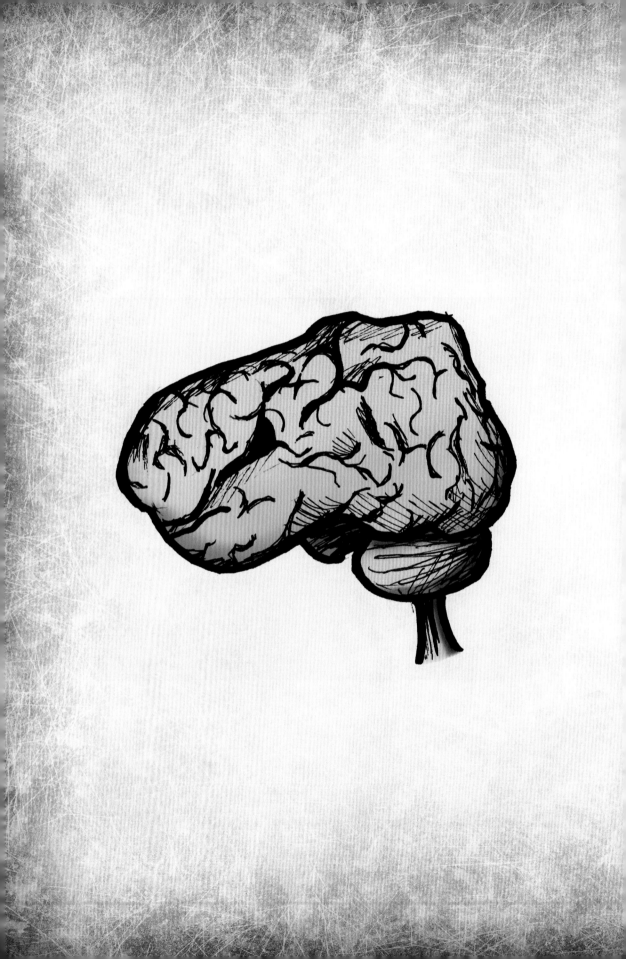

them what they can or can't be. They're going to crawl or slither or drag themselves after you, and eat your quick-to-categorize brain before it can exclude them from anything else.

In short, the zombies (in all of their various forms) remind us that to be good at what you do, you don't need to be "normal" by anyone's standards but your own. No matter what hand God, or nature, or various artificial reanimating nerve agents have dealt you, you already have everything you need to effectively achieve your goals and follow your dreams.

"No man left behind."

It's a motto that has long served some of the most impressive and storied fighting forces on the planet. It also doesn't apply to zombies at all.

Zombies, as everyone knows, are constantly left behind on the battlefield. One reason for this is that they tend to move slowly and often just get outpaced. But another reason is that zombies don't stop to bury their dead. Nor do they pause to tend to their wounded. Since time immemorial, soldiers facing zombies have known that it is bootless to wound one zombie in hope that others will stop to "help" it.

Thus, to become a true zombie warrior, you must expunge from your brain all fealty to the credo "No man left behind." Don't believe for one moment that zombies don't stop to attend to the fallen because they are insensitive or heartless (though, yes, some zombies are technically missing hearts). Rather, a zombie soldier understands that **the best way to help a fallen colleague is to eat the brain of the one who felled it.**

One thing that makes zombie soldiers superior to conventional soldiers is their ability to attack without prompting. (Conventional soldiers tend to waste valuable attacking time waiting around for "a battle plan" and similar things.) Consider the following comparisons.

If cut off from communications with HQ:

Conventional soldiers *will hold position and attempt to reestablish lines of communication.*

Zombie soldiers *will hunt and kill the enemy.*

If caused to encounter unforeseen obstacles, natural disasters, or confusing signs from the enemy:

Conventional soldiers *will wait for word from senior command on how they ought to proceed in light of this new development.*

Zombie soldiers *will hunt and kill the enemy.*

If faced with an overwhelming foe they cannot possibly hope to defeat themselves:

Conventional soldiers *will call for reinforcements, request an air strike, or just run away.*

Zombie soldiers *will hunt and kill the enemy.*

See a pattern here?

Zombies also use their slow speed as a tactical advantage in many situations. Zombies walk but don't run, so fleeing humans usually understand themselves to have a little time to run away. However, in doing so, these humans reliably make very bad decisions, of which zombies will happily take advantage. For example:

Ack, zombies! We just have time to barricade ourselves inside of an abandoned house and nail all of the doors shut, effectively sealing us in until the zombies catch up.

Ack, zombies! We just have time to run deeper into this abandoned mine (or system of caves), which we can only assume must go on forever.

Zombie Tip—Never put off until tomorrow what you can do today: Especially when it involves violent, lawless mayhem and cannibalism. Those brains aren't going to eat themselves. Hop to it, dude.

Ack, zombies! We just have time to run to the other side of this tiny island (instead of, say, fixing our boat), where I'm sure there won't be *more* zombies waiting for us.

In each of these cases, it is the impression zombies give that they can be at least temporarily outrun that leads their victims to make these bad decisions. Time after time, the zombie's victims ironically place themselves in situations where the zombies' lack of quickness will no longer be a factor.

We've covered the advantages of Always Just Marching Straight Ahead in the direction of your enemy. One contingency to be prepared for is the result of this tactic when employed against an enemy whose troops are fewer in number and/or more tightly packed than your own. Namely, your troops will encircle your enemy.

Note that this is more than just a "side effect" of marching a bunch of soldiers (who don't want to patiently stand in line behind one another) toward a smaller encampment of enemies. It is a tactic that has been used by zombies since the beginning of time and should be adopted by you whenever possible.

In dialogues pertaining to combat, generals speak of wanting to flank and rout one another's armies but rarely of "encircling" them. This is because most generals have in mind the goal of compelling the opposing army to either run away or to surrender. Very few military leaders have the goal of "eating every last one of the enemy's brains, no matter how much time or how much effort we must expend to make that happen."

If you have access to powers that can **actually** raise the dead, it will certainly help things out a lot. People in this category might include:

- Voodoo priests (or at least researchers who've synthesized the zombie-creating powder used by voodoo priests)

- Magic Users level 34 or higher who have mastered all Raise Dead spells and are of lawful evil alignment
- Funeral directors who've been lucky enough to save some of the mysterious glowing goo they found in the asteroid that landed on their property that one time
- Scientists who've been shunned by the mainstream establishment for conducting experiments into the reanimation of necrotic tissue
- Industrialists overseeing large toxic-chemical facilities who have seen fit to circumvent EPA standards by stashing hazardous waste in graveyards (I mean, who's gonna ever know, right? And plus, who's it hurting? The dead people? Ha! [Takes long, fitful draw on Davidoff])
- Socially isolated teenagers who found a copy of the *Necronomicon* in that occult bookstore over on Milwaukee Avenue

(**Note:** Those with the power to create actual zombies will be able to skip ahead to the end of this chapter.) But what if you're **not** a voodoo priest, magic user, or smug factory owner richly deserving of comeuppance? What if you're just some guy or gal who bought this book?

Fighting like they're dead is something zombies do because they **actually are dead.** (The word "like" hardly needs to be applied, really.) Being dead brings with it several advantages, however, that often give zombies the edge they need in combat situations. Chief among these is an almost total and complete lack of fear.

Most soldiers on the battlefield have—if we're honest about it—two priorities:

- Accomplish mission (e.g., kill enemies, blow up supply bunker, assassinate Saddam/Hitler/Osama)
- Not die

And they aren't necessarily prioritized in that order. Usually, for one to happen, the other has to happen, too. But when it comes right down to it and a soldier has to choose one, what are the things that would make him or her choose to accomplish the mission **even if doing so would mean his death?**

The answer is: the notion that death is a certainty.

If you're going to be KIA no matter what, you might as well try to get the job done, whatever it is. I mean, what else are you gonna do? Just sit there and wait around to get killed? Hell no. If you're going down, at the very least you want to take a few of the bad guys with you.

The trick is gaining the sense that death is inevitable. To make the point clear, let's start with a less extreme example. Like jogging.

Let's say you've let yourself go for a few years, but now you want to get back in shape, so you decide to start jogging again. But with your flabby gut and man-boobs, you feel a little self-conscious about getting back out there. It'll be embarrassing. You'll be "the fat guy" in the park or on the treadmill at the health club. So, consequently, you start to put it off more and more. You find excuses not to go. You procrastinate. **Maybe you fail to go jogging at all.**

Why? Because you're afraid you'll be embarrassed as "the fat guy."

> **Zombie Tip—I regret that I have but many, many zombie "lives" to give to my country:** How many times can you reanimate a blasted-apart zombie and get it back into fighting shape? I dunno, but let's find out!

What's the solution? (No, not "work out at home" or "jog at night.") Don't **take the risk** that you **might** be embarrassed. Instead, **ensure that you'll be embarrassed.**

Make yourself a Day-Glo T-shirt with lettering that reads: "Get a load of my ginormous man-boobs!" Compose a route for your jog that takes you past the homes of all your ex-lovers and former business partners who are now more successful and thinner than you. Wear jogging shorts that are far too tight and expose parts of your backside that should never, ever be seen. You've got to make it more than a daily jog. You've got to make it a daily-jog-and-exercise-in-total-humiliation. You can be like: "Honey, I'm going out for my daily-jog-and-exercise-in-total-humiliation. Time to get my heart rate up while bawling like a little girl at my own shame! Be back soon!"

When the fact that something **might** occur is dissuading you from taking an action you need to take, you need to **ensure** that it occurs and, in doing so, give your fears no place to go.

Anyhow, let's leave the fat jogger and go back to the battle-field. Obviously, you don't want to ensure that you die—like shoot yourself or something—but you need to be ready for that possibility. (This is war, after all.) Just as our self-conscious jogger has to stop thinking, "I could be embarrassed if I do that," a soldier who truly wants to fight like a zombie must never allow the phrase "I could get killed if I do that" to prevent him from acting.

Zombies can of course be "killed" (or "killed again" or "rendered still") by disconnecting their heads from the rest of their bodies, or by penetrating or destroying their brains. Zombies do not walk with a swagger because they are invulnerable. Rather, they take the battlefield with the confidence of one well prepared for the eventu-ality of death. (Also, they've died once already and probably have the sense that it's not all that bad.)

WORKING TOGETHER!
...FOR BRAINS!

To be clear, zombies never **try** to kill themselves. They don't leap into lava pits, position themselves in front of artillery cannons, or turn melee weapons on themselves. (There is no record, anywhere, of a zombie suicide.) Zombies are merely open to the **possibility** of another death. They accept it as part of the general condition of being a zombie, and do not allow it to deter them from their efforts to eat the brains of as many humans as possible.

Now, it is true (believe it or not) that zombies can't accomplish everything. Some chasms are too deep to cross, some government missile silos are too tightly guarded to infiltrate. But no zombie ever looked at itself and the task before it and decided not to try. Zombies are so successful because they try *everything possible* to

Zombie Tip—History has shown that those who presume to know what zombies want almost always meet an untimely end—usually because they forget that zombies, more than anything, just want to eat them.

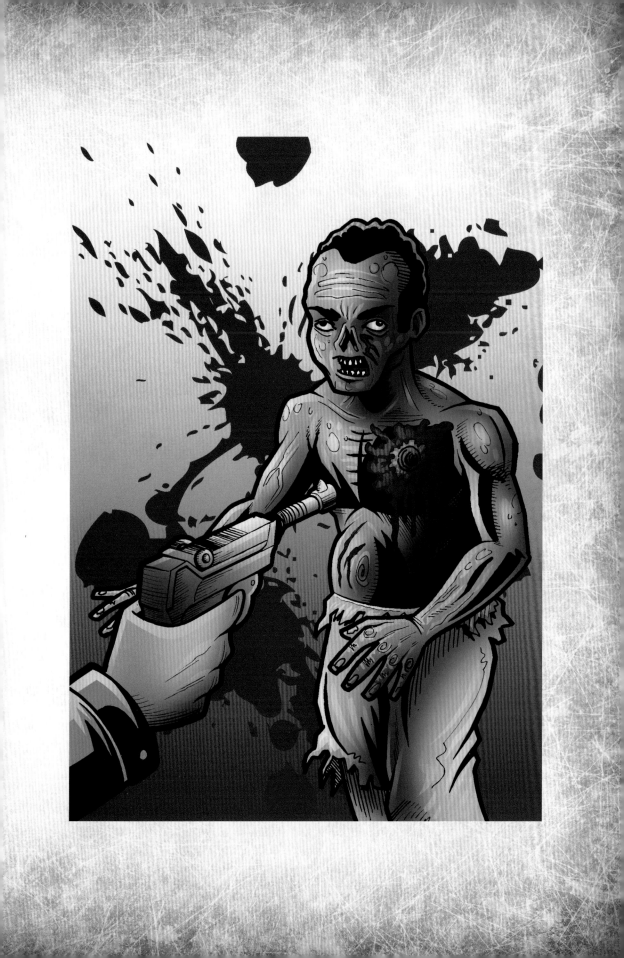

get what they want, regardless of any physical setbacks. In some cases, they are even able to turn their physical "inadequacies" into advantages.

A zombie with no arms or legs can inch along on its haunches, or slither like a snake. Sometimes these inching-slithering types can find their way through grates or fissures in castle walls that a regular zombie would never be able to negotiate. They can wiggle through and stoop under barricades that might hold a regular zombie at bay.

Plus-size zombies (originally fat people, now obscenely bloated by the process of natural decomposition) can use their inhuman girth to block doorways and corral humans into corners. They are dynamic, walking barriers of death. (No one is *ever* too fat to be a zombie.)

Ugly zombies—those missing jawbones or other significant maxillofacial components—can use their ugliness to their advantage. Most humans are horrified upon seeing a zombie, but still possess the sense to run away. Yet if a zombie is *especially terrifying* to look at, a human may be completely paralyzed with fear. Then, all the ugly zombie has to do is saunter up and start munching.

Severely decomposed zombies can use their physical decline to their advantage by passing for offal or meat-rendering by-product. In the case of a zombie like this, most people won't know *what* it is . . . until a mouth appears somewhere in that gelatinous, fleshy mass and takes a bite out of them.

 Zombie Tip—Remember: Instead of "No man left behind," a zombie's creed is "No. Man left behind."

Kicking ass like a zombie is as much about what you *don't* do as it is about what you do. And one important thing that zombies don't do—ever—is obey conventions, treaties, or rules of any kind governing their behavior on the battlefield. No zombie has ever agreed not to eat the brains of women and children, or not to eat the brains of prisoners of war, or to refrain from using certain tactics on the battlefield. Zombies do not allow themselves to be bound by documents or contracts, and so find themselves unfettered killing machines with infinite options when it comes to *kicking your ass*.

Sometimes people assume that battlefield techniques lacking in complexity must be outdated and ineffective. People are attuned to watch for the new, the surprising, the cutting edge (or leading edge, or bleeding edge, or the edge of a zombie's teeth as it eats you). People are ready to credit a complicated tactic with being able to accomplish wonderful things but are suspicious of an approach known for its "elegant simplicity."

Sometimes the best ways of doing things **are** the oldest and simplest. **There are some models upon which no improvements can be made.** And one such a model is the attack pattern of the

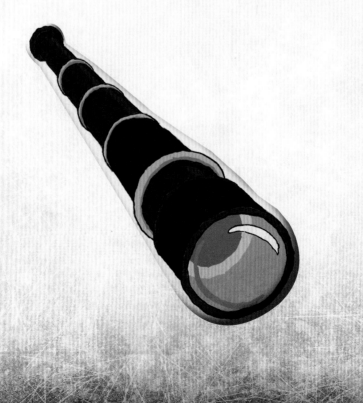

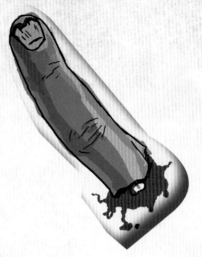

zombie (a.k.a.: the first thing you must learn if you are to become a Zombie Commander).

A zombie army is always moving. (Not at the quick step, certainly, but they're always making forward progress.) Moving brings you closer to the enemy. Moving makes things happen. Moving keeps things interesting.

Zombie soldiers neither bivouac nor "hold their position." If a zombie army isn't moving, it's because humans are nearby and the zombies are trying to figure out how to get at them. Yet the main function of this tactic is not merely to locate the enemy and have a nice change of scenery. Always Just Marching Straight Ahead will endow your soldiers with numerous **advantages on the battlefield** once combat begins.

The first opportunity for this strategy to help you will be the moment your army first comes into contact with the enemy forces. Throughout history, large armies have tended to "make camp" once sighting their enemies—pausing to consider a plan of attack, determining how the terrain might best be used, and sizing up the enemy's strengths and weaknesses. (Sometimes, based on an unfavorable analysis of the latter, the armies elect not to engage

one another at all!) Weapons are prepared. Battle plans are drawn. On some occasions, representatives from the two sides actually meet face-to-face to see if the conflict can be avoided (and, if it's unavoidable, then they discuss the "rules" and parameters of the upcoming engagement).

When you locate an enemy army to engage, you will do **none of these things. You** are not a typical commander, and **you are not commanding a typical army.** That is why you will win the day and crush your enemy utterly.

When a horde of zombies comes on some tasty humans, the horde doesn't draw up a plan of attack. It doesn't wait till dawn because doing so is poetic or traditional. It just attacks. Then and there. It could be dawn's first light or two in the morning. It could be sunny, stormy, foggy, raining locusts, or earthquaking. Zombies don't care. They will still attack.

Moving slowly. Preying upon things. Sound like anybody you know? Of course it does. It sounds like zombies.

Zombies are natural pirates because they are already attuned to a "life" of roaming and attacking. They take what they need (brains), and leave what they don't need (everything else). Zombies also understand—or *seem* to understand—that remaining stationary means destruction.

Zombies, like pirates, aren't hard to kill on a one-on-one basis. They die with a simple decapitation or musket ball to the head. They tend to move slowly. (Pirates may have peg legs, but zombies have crushing rigor mortis and tendons that have often

Zombie Tip—You must become expert at waiting patiently if you wish to fight with the effectiveness of the walking dead.

rotted away entirely. While pirates are often drunk and/or delu-sional, zombies comport themselves with the kind of massive loss of function that only comes with years spent moldering in a graveyard.) If you want to catch up with a single roaming zombie, it's not going to be hard to put him down provided you have even the most basic of weapons. A *stationary* zombie is completely a lost cause. (A stationary zombie is also not going to get to eat anybody's brain.) That's why every zombie—no matter how desiccated and bony, no matter how many limbs or appendages it may be missing—always drags itself along and is always in a group. Movement and comradeship mean survival and the possi-bility of delicious brains. Inactivity and isolation mean destruc-tion and no brains.

While a single roaming zombie may seem like a threat to very few—and may, in fact, seem quite comical and amusing—a horde of zombies (or a pirate ship bursting at the seams with them) is a terri-fying sight to behold. Zombies and pirates move slowly, but as long as they move (and as long as there are a lot of them) they are still a threat.

When a stuffy British navy lookout cries "Pirates off the star-board bow!" it may still be a full hour from this first sighting until these piratical aggressors have moved close enough to put their cannons in range.

Yet, the fact that it will, you know, **be awhile** before the pirates get here does nothing to diminish the alarm and anxiety that the British sailors suddenly feel. Same thing with a zombie outbreak. When the first few walking corpses shamble into the fledgling settlement that will one day become Port-au-Prince, the villagers can easily evade and avoid these slow-moving visitors.

However, the abject terror they feel will come not from these two or three brain-seeking interlopers, but from their knowledge that the main burying ground just outside town holds *hundreds* of corpses—who at this very moment may be clawing their way out of the earth and heading toward the smell of living humans.

In both cases, slow is scary. In both cases, the fact that any real physical danger is like an hour away does **nothing** to quell the concerns of those who will be preyed upon.

As a zombie pirate captain, you're going to be doubly slow. Your boat is slow and your pirates are slow. The good news is that you're also going to be doubly terrifying to your enemies (and just doubly awesome, generally). When a trading ship laden with spoils from the New World sights your rotting zombie bark off the starboard bow, the captain will understand that your ship is a massive pirate barge (slow) and—when he looks more closely—that your crew is composed entirely of lumbering, loping zombies (slower). Your lack of speed, however, will cease to occupy the unlucky merchant's mind to the same degree as your lack of compunction about eating him and everyone else aboard. He will also, as he thinks about it, become creepingly aware of the terrifying advantages that **zombie** pirates will bring to bear against him.

Though their ship might move slowly through the water, the zombies steering it will never tire or rest. They will never need to sleep. They will never run out of provisions. While a merchant's crew is prey to every human weakness and failing, your **inhuman** zombie pirate crew can work around the clock to chase the merchant to some craggy shoal where he will have to choose between fleeing overboard or putting up a (bootless) armed resistance. As much as he may hate you, he will not have time to scuttle his craft.

As you internalize the Code of Zombie Piracy, embrace your inner slowness. Understand that it works for you, and not against you. Zombie pirate crews—much like hordes of terrestrial zombies on foot—always get their man.

Eventually.

The Zombie Army: What power-hungry despot *hasn't* considered making some sort of deal with the devil in order to command a host of the undead? And sure, a zombie army might look attractive at first. The advantages of zombie soldiers are plentiful. They don't need to be fed, paid, or billeted between battles. They can march all night without stopping. They don't complain about being sent to their almost certain destruction, and they can keep fighting after sustaining injuries that would leave a normal soldier prone and shouting for a medic.

That said, there are important ways in which the zombie army fails to perform essential functions of human armies. Prisoners, for example, are usually eaten by zombie troops before they can reveal to you any useful information about enemy encampments. Tactical withdrawals and disengagements are not usually in the zombie soldier's vocabulary. (Once a zombie smells brains, it's on!) Further, your enemy can usually disengage your zombie army whenever he wants (provided his troops can manage a slow jog), whereas your force will have considerable difficulty in pursuit. Most troubling of all, zombie armies tend not to disband when the military campaign is concluded. Instead, they'll turn on the residents of whatever country or kingdom you've used them to capture, turning the very prize you fought for into a desolate wasteland that only a zombie could love. Then, when there is nobody else left, the zombie army will turn on you. But hey, what did you expect? When you dance with the devil, he always gets to lead. And in this case, he'll lead you right into the middle of a zombie army with nothing else to do.

The important lesson to take here is that a zombie works only for himself (or herself). Sure, a zombie's self-interest may momentarily coincide with your own, but at the end of the day, a zombie looks out for number one. So should you.

Don't get me started on "regular" pirates.

Oh sure, *being* a pirate is one thing. It's all "Yo, ho, ho, and a bottle of rum, and when do we get to go on the next murderin', plunderin', womanizin'-spree?"

Being a pirate is fine and dandy.

But *leading* a group of pirates? That's a pain in the ass right there.

Did you ever wonder why pirate captains like Long John Silver and Blackbeard and Captain Kidd have reputations for being such dicks? Trust me, they didn't start out that way. Blackbeard and others of his ilk got to be complete and total bastards for one reason and one reason only. They were called upon to do the impossible: **manage pirates.**

Think about the worst employee you ever saw at the worst job you ever had. Think about their self-centeredness, their inability to be a "team player," their proclivity for physically attacking coworkers whenever they felt like it. Now multiply those traits about a thousand times, and you've got **some** sense of the workplace behavior you find in somebody who wants to be a pirate.

Wait! You're not fucking done yet. Now take that worst-coworker-times-1,000 and multiply him or her by **an entire crew of pirates**. And now imagine **you're** the one who has to get these ADHD, violence-prone, self-centered drunkards to somehow focus and work together. Even a veteran behavioral psychologist would grant that these people are not going to respond to "positive reinforcement" and "disciplinary timeouts." (Also, Ritalin is still like three hundred years away.)

So what's left? Well, as any pirate captain—no matter how initially beneficent—always learns, pirates tend only to respond to the most base, primal motivators. They want gold and plunder, and they want not to die (probably in that order, but hey, it's not hard and fast with these guys). To get regular pirates to do anything, you have to **threaten to kill them** or **reward them with treasure**. Anything less, and it's just one more step toward an ineffective crew that is going to start thinking about how good a mutiny sounds. For a pirate captain seeking to motivate his crew, the "carrot" has to be brimming with gold and jewels, and the "stick" should be the tip of a cutlass or the end of a plank.

The captain of a ship of **zombie pirates** can remain a **totally awesome dude** (or **seriously cool chick**) while still managing a crew effectively and efficiently. Why? Because you don't have to be a violent jerk to get zombies to do what you want them to do.

Zombies are easy to lead, at least compared to pirates. Zombies don't want money. They don't seek fame or fortune. They don't lust for sexual intercourse. Most important for you, zombies don't aspire to be pirate captains themselves, so nobody's gunning for your job. In fact, they don't care **at all** about rank or promotion. (You won't have lickspittles falling all over themselves wanting to be first mate.) Zombies have no egos or career aspirations. They have only an uncontrollable thirst to feast on the flesh of the living. (This is something that, as a pirate captain, you ought to be able to provide them if you're worth your weight in sea salt.) Pull your bark alongside a British merchant vessel or Portuguese caravel, point them in the right direction, and the rest is a cakewalk.

Further—in sharp contrast to conventional, living pirates—zombies are infinitely replaceable. While a pirate captain commanding human pirates might flinch at the cost (both in human life and capital investment) of sending a boarding party to their almost-certain doom against a better-armed foe, the captain of a zombie crew need have no such compunction. When you know the right voodoo shaman or enchanted burying ground, zombies can be replaced with relative ease and at a reasonable price. Also, you can send wave after wave of zombie pirates to be destroyed without any deleterious effect on the morale of the zombie pirates who must follow after them. They will still be willing to fight for the death for you in any situation. This brings me to my next point . . .

Zombies have **complete faith in your judgment**. So what if your last ten voyages ended in ruinous defeat? So what if you've been defeated by European navies so many times that your nickname is "The Bitch of the Seas"? Zombies will not lose **one single ounce** of confidence in your leadership ability, no matter how much of an incompetent starveling you might appear to be (or might actually be). Zombie pirates will always follow you to the ends of the earth (or at least to where there are brains).

Zombies are also stalwart fighters compared to human pirates. As the cannonballs and grapeshot start to fly, you'll be glad to have them on your side. When you employ zombies for piracy, you get a crew that will fight to the "death" every time. Both zombie pirates and regular pirates are fundamentally selfish entities, **but**, for zombies, the selfish motivations are quite simple. Zombies want to kill humans and eat brains. That's it. Regular pirates want a slew of things (plunder, women, fame, blah blah blah), but they also want to not die or be destroyed in the course of getting stuff. Zombies do not have this keep-living-and-not-die "hang-up" appended to their collective psychology. Zombies just go for the gusto. A crew of zombie pirates will not hesitate to attack larger vessels, it will not flee or surrender when the tide of battle (or the literal tide) goes against them, and they will never show "fear" in the traditional sense of the word.

Speaking of fear, perhaps the greatest advantage of commanding a crew of zombie pirates is the amount of fear you will strike in the hearts of your enemies. Regular pirates are, of course, already pretty frightening for merchant ships laden with goods and passengers. Pirates go into battle drunk and singing songs. They don't wear uniforms. They howl like animals and smoke hashish and set their beards on fire. Most terrifyingly of all, pirates don't play by the rules. They recognize the legitimacy of no government or treaty. The captured will live or die on the pirates' whim. Station, title, and wealth will not protect anyone in the presence of a pirate. However, at least pirates are, you know, **human**. They can be (to a point) reasoned with. Propositions like: "If you spare my life I'll lead you to where my treasure is buried" at least have the capacity to be *entertained*. Human pirates have been known to allow captured voyagers to become pirates themselves and "enlist" in the crew (which can be an attractive option when the other choice is walking the plank). Zombie pirates don't dance or cavort as they go into battle—and they certainly don't drink rum—but they have the capacity to inspire a terror even beyond that of a traditional pirate. When a merchant or enemy navy encounters zombie pirates, there are only going to be three possible outcomes— defeat the zombie pirates, outrun the zombie pirates, or get eaten by the zombie pirates. **No other thing is going to happen**. You will not reason with them. You will not bribe them into letting you live. You will not flatter them into submission. It's kill or be killed. **That's it**. And speaking of killing, zombies are also hard-to-kill, tenacious fighters, so suiting up to fight a bunch of zombie pirates is way, way more daunting than getting ready to fight conventional pirates.

Whereas the sound of drunken pirate song (and the sight of a Jolly Roger) rightly inspire fear in merchants and navies alike, it is the wafting stench of charnel earth, the eerie stillness and unflinching focus of a pirate ship **crewed by zombies**, that inspires the ultimate, cosmic terror in those who behold it.

Also, we've got to look at job performance. Zombies are the ultimate nautical warriors. Zombies are equally effective on land or on the sea. Or **in** the sea. When they're not busy fighting sharks or other awesome things, zombie pirates can walk or swim underwater with relative ease. They can also attack. Whereas human sailors who fall overboard in the course of nautical warfare tend to drop their sabers, get their powder wet, and suddenly focus less on "attacking the enemy" and more on "trying not to fucking drown," zombies who are tossed overboard and fall into the sea simply begin attacking from a new direction. In situations where human pirates will selfishly want a rescue, zombie pirates require no intervention.

One thing to take from all this is that if organizing and running a zombie pirate crew sounds like a lot of work, just stop for a second and think about how hard it would be to run an actual human pirate crew. Suddenly, guys who stumble around and moan for "braaaaains" won't be such a big issue for you.

For these and other reasons, the Code of Zombie Piracy directs that you shall be the only human pirate aboard your ship. From here on out, it's **all zombie**.

Undead on Wall Street: Winning on the Corporate Battlefield

In times of increasing economic uncertainty, the slow and steady gait of a zombie can be a supremely effective model for those seeking to improve their station in life vis a vis a rise through the corporate ladder. For what is the marketplace of unfettered capitalism if not a battlefield? What is the boardroom, if not a military HQ? And what is the office supply closet, if not a cache of the deadliest and most advanced weapons of slaughter ever known to man—and maybe also a place to make out with attractive coworkers where nobody can see?

Achieving success in a traditional corporate setting is about two things:

1. Fitting in with the culture, and
2. Making sure the job gets done.

Zombies come from varied backgrounds, but always make sure to be uniform in all the ways that count. They come fat and thin, tall and short, with all four limbs still intact and with just a few clumps of gristle (that might have once been appendages) attached to a torso. But their gait is the same. Their unseeing (all-seeing?) thousand yard stare is the same. Their desire to consume living human brains is definitely the same. Zombies are identical in all the ways that are truly meaningful. They also know how to deliver where and when it counts. Corporate leaders want to see top producers. They want employees who can deliver the goods. And when "deliver" means "eating," and "the goods" means "a school bus full of screaming, terrified children" zombies become the most effective model available for comporting oneself in a way certain to make those in the corridors of corporate power take notice. Zombies deliver. They make things work. They are always working. For them, distinction between work and play has lost all meaning. And, in this, they have found true meaning. An aspiring business executive setting his or her sights on a corner office would do well to attempt the same.

Are you instead interested in going out on your own? The tech startup entrepreneur has plenty to learn from the slavering legion of undead. Finding small holes in the landscape that have not yet been filled, and then working to fill them before any of your business school chums can, is very like a zombie. The undead are excellent at surveying landscapes and finding openings and holes to fill—especially when those holes are entrances to castles, hastily fortified farmhouses, or abandoned prisons. Zombies have an innate sense of where opening might exist, and know all about exploiting those opening for the maximum brain-eating advantage possible. Perhaps your goal is to upset and destroy a traditional business model like taxi services, restaurant reviews, or physically going to a store to buy anything at all, ever. Zombies shall serve as your example here as well. Zombies are the original agents of destruction and chaos. In their rampaging wake, entire lines of business can be decimated (or at least irreversibly altered), and exciting new "innovations" can spring up in their wake. From corpse decapitation services to lawnmower weaponizing, zombies are catalysts of innovation and capitalism. They seed new businesses wherever they tread. Where they have gone before, the landscape is indelibly altered for good. And at the end of the day, isn't this what any corporate leader really wants?

By making the zombie your model, you will enjoy the slow, steady, and reliable rise to corporate power and success that only comes with the total dedication of the undead.

Don't Remember Who You Are (or Were Before You Became a Zombie)

Conventional wisdom says that staying grounded and humble is fundamental to being an effective C.E.O. Most business books will caution against the sins of pride and hubris, and hold that even the most powerful executive must never lose sight of the humble circumstances from which he or she arose.

This advice could not be more misguided.

For a Z.E.O. (as for an actual zombie) losing track of who you used to be before you became a powerful entity is not only recommended, it is compulsory.

You see, it isn't clear exactly how much of their former lives zombies remember after reanimation, but there are indicators that some of the undead recall at least a little about who they were and what they used to do. Zombies have been known to respond to their former names, recognize faces and places that were once familiar to them, and to salute superior officers in military situations. Sometimes preferences or tastes a zombie had in life will remain after zombification. Zombies also seem to have a way of remembering who their enemies were in life, and have a knack for wreaking some form of revenge upon them.

However, no zombie ever attempted to leverage his status or previous station in the world after becoming a member of the walking dead. No zombie, seeking entrance to a fortified dormitory, ever said: "Hey, I used to be an important tax attorney and a trustee at the college. Based on this, you really ought to take the boards off the door and let me in so I can eat you." The zombie *knows* that's not going to work, and the people inside know that whatever *used* to be true about this trustee (nice guy, important businessman, local Little League coach), the fact of his *now being a zombie* pretty much overrides it.

But hey, it swings both ways. No reanimated-soldier zombie believes for a second that his old army buddies won't shoot him in the head just because he used to fight alongside them. Zombie cops and zombie judges may have once enforced the law, but that counts for nothing the moment they're zombified—they break every law they can, just like any other zombie. Zombification severs all important ties to who someone once was. Astute is the zombie who realizes this fact instantly (as is the human who would avoid being eaten by zombies). As you climb the corporate ladder and eventually assume the mantle of Z.E.O., you would do well to remember this.

True, you may still have friends and supporters toiling in the lower echelons of the organization who want to convince themselves that, since becoming Z.E.O., "You're still the same guy/ gal" and "You haven't changed." Though these beliefs are patently inaccurate, you may still use them to your advantage (just as a zombie allows foolish humans to labor under the misconception that a zombie they knew in life won't try to eat them).

The fact is, when you become a corporate leader, you have to become a different person. Just as a human's priorities (spending time with family, saving up something for retirement, not getting eaten) differ starkly from a zombie's (brains), so must your priorities change when you reach the top of the corporate ladder. No longer will you focus on the Machiavellian mechanics of a rise to power. You will now be required to turn your attention to holding on to the reins, increasing corporate profitability, and ensuring your workers labor with the methodical loyalty of zombies. If you

Zombie Tip—Preserve Your Top Performers

Maybe in brine and dill or something. That way, they'd taste like pickles.

were to "remain the same guy/gal" the results would be disastrous, both for you *and* for the organization. You owe it to your employees (and the shareholders and yourself) to change for the better when you make it to the top.

There isn't much use in getting sentimental about it, either. Wistfully recalling your early days as a records clerk as you sit behind the big oak desk isn't going to drive up the price of shares one iota. (And, honestly, the best lesson to be taken from being a records clerk is usually that it sucks to be a records clerk.) Likewise, as a Z.E.O., the benefits of identifying with any group (other than zombielike leaders) should pretty much be off the table.

Teddy Roosevelt once said: "There is no room in this country for hyphenated Americans." And while this sentiment would probably qualify as hate speech today, it comes from a genuine attempt to forge a community so great (America) that it would transcend factors of ethnic origin. Teddy liked the idea that when you became an American citizen, you could just say that you were an "American." You wouldn't have to qualify it with the continent on which your ancestors evolved.

Teddy's vision is similar to what happens when you **become a zombie.** Few people think to note a zombie's ethnicity, religion, or cultural background when identifying it. A zombie is a zombie is a zombie. (One notable divergence presents itself in the form of the 1932 Bela Lugosi film *White Zombie,* but that was a movie about the *first* Caucasian zombie *ever,* so c'mon, you gotta make an exception.) By and large, zombies don't need to be "more diverse." Being a zombie is diversity enough.

"Connect" to Others

Zombie Tip—Find the Right Fit

Just because a corporate recruiter finds you a job with more pay and a bigger title, it doesn't mean you have to take the gig. It may be a good job, but is it the job for you? Zombies are masters of waiting for the "right fit"—especially when it's a way to fit into a storm drain or through a small basement window. Approach any new opportunity with a zombie's careful discretion.

This book would not be the first to point out that it's important for a manager to establish connections with his or her employees. However, in the vast majority of cases, modern business books err by advocating a C.E.O. create false or forced connections. The idea that a leader would actually want to be, in any *real and meaningful way,* **connected** to the working stiffs that labor in his or her factories and offices is left off the table entirely. Rather, the advice typically given in business books seems to implicitly argue

for the forging of **fake, forced** connections between employee and employer. These books do a great job of advising C.E.O.s how to *appear* to be connected to employees, but not how to *actually* connect with them. These books presuppose contempt for the worker—and seem to assume that a natural, organic connection would not be appropriate or possible. Based upon this, they suggest that leaders create situations that will give employees the "feeling" of connectedness, while not actually linking you to them (or them to you).

Following such advice has been the downfall of many a C.E.O.

How many times have we seen suit-wearing corporate leaders awkwardly attempting to have a beer with the warehouse workers, pretending to care about employees' families at the company holiday party, or gently spoofing themselves and other Microsoft executives in a widely circulated company-produced video? Hurts just to think about, doesn't it? Well, it hurts the executives even more.

More than just the temporary awkwardness of interacting on false pretenses is involved.

These ill-advised corporate leaders (believing the errant and misguided business books they have read) will **falsely** assume that their efforts to achieve a connection with employees **have been effective.** And, as long as nothing rocks the corporate boat, this does not present any real peril. Nothing will contradict the executives' incorrect assessment that they are beloved. However, as soon as times get tight or a crisis arises (see earlier chapter), a C.E.O. will need to rely on a connection with his or her employees, and it will become devastatingly apparent that no such connection exists. Just when the mistaken C.E.O. starts counting on the workers to "suck it up" and "roll up their sleeves" (because you're all, you know, buds), they will instead start "doing the bare minimum" as they "look for other jobs on the Internet all day."

Zombie Tip—Have Undaunted Curiosity
Staying curious throughout your working life is a trait that great leaders and great zombies have in common. Whether you're wondering how customer satisfaction levels could be raised, or how villages could be razed (and their inhabitants eaten) cultivate your natural curiosity and it will take you to the top of your field.

The error here, really, is with neither the workers nor the C.E.O., but with the business manuals that continue to insist that a holding company sack race means your employees love you and will work unpaid overtime.

But if sack races are off the table, then what **can** provide meaningful connections between employees and an employer?

The answer: Zombies.

Zombies are masters of connection. The most important connection, for a zombie, is connecting its teeth with your brain. But that isn't the *only* connection a zombie understands. Zombies, you see, are **connected to other zombies.** This is because zombies are *like* other zombies.

No matter if a zombie is fat or thin, short or tall, was reanimated five minutes ago or has been shambling across the earth for a thousand years, zombies have deep and meaningful commonalities. Zombies are undead. Zombies want to bite and eat people. Zombies like brains. Zombies don't bite other zombies. Zombies don't make chitchat.

Elegantly simple, the common code shared by zombies runs deep and remains constant. Zombies act as a cohesive, connected unit because they **are actually connected.**

As noted above, a typical misguided C.E.O. will try to find connections with employees **where they don't exist.** This will seem forced, and it will be awkward for everybody.

A Z.E.O., in sharp contrast, will find the real commonalities **that already exist** between himself and employees, and, in pointing them out, demonstrate that they have always been connected.

In summary, if you respect your employees' intelligence, and don't feed them a bunch of bullshit about how you "care" about them as a part of your "family," they will come to esteem you as an honest, plainspoken, and fair executive—which, really, is the best you can hope for. After all, you never heard of a zombie who tried to inspire other zombies by saying they were a family that deeply loved one another.

Zombies are just a bunch of decaying guys and gals who want to eat brains.

Sometimes, that's enough.

It's safe to say if you're reading how-to-succeed-in-business books, you're not starting at the top. This is good. If you *were* already at the top, it would probably mean that you got there using (ugh) traditional business tactics. Or maybe you inherited a family business or married the right person. The point is, to become a Z.E.O.

(instead of a dime-a-dozen C.E.O.) you need to climb the corporate ladder *like a zombie*, starting with the very first rung.

As it stands, you probably answer phones at a desk, work a press at a factory, or complete ream after ream of mindless paperwork. Don't be disheartened. Zombies also start in modest or less-than-glamorous places—like shabby country graveyards or crumbling, vine-encrusted family crypts. This is no impediment to their eventual success.

They're getting out. And so are you.

The first step to transforming yourself into a Z.E.O. is beginning to *think* like a Z.E.O. From day one, this means a new focus on priorities. A zombie knows *exactly* what it wants and goes after it. A zombie ignores everything inessential to its desires and devices.

Begin, then, by identifying the essential. If you work an office job, make a list of your *essential* daily tasks. Then, make a list of the inessential things that actually take up your time. If you need to, take a whole day and write these things down as you go. Be patient and detailed. It's important that you do a thorough job. Also, note how long your tasks take. Some essential tasks can be time consuming, but others can be accomplished relatively quickly. Likewise, many inessential things can take up a deceptively large amount of your time.

At the end of the day, stop for five minutes and read over your list. If you're like most people, the results will surprise you.

You may find that you spend two hours a day (or less) actually writing memos, responding to e-mails, and taking phone calls that are "essential to business," and six hours or more on other tasks. This wasted time can include obviously nonwork activities—spacing out on the Internet or engaging in e-mail flame wars about the latest superhero movie, sure—but it can also be spent politely chatting with colleagues who drop by your cube, e-mailing or talking on the phone with coworkers about nonessential aspects of work, helping your colleagues with their nonessential projects, and working to temporarily correct or compensate for situations and inefficiencies that other people have caused.

Be brutally honest in your assessment and documentation of these nonessential things that take up your valuable time. Did a coworker stop you at the water cooler for five minutes to chat about the game last night? Put it on there. Did you stop and flirt with the new intern from Wellesley for a good half-hour? This is the place to 'fess up, old boy. I promise not to tell.

The first step on the road to becoming a Z.E.O. is to discourage these distractions from happening to you.

I word the above advice most carefully. Many so-called "motivational experts" are apt to tell you that the first step to success is to adopt an internal (as opposed to external) "locus of control." What that means, simply put, is that you must think of the world as a place in which you make things happen, instead of a place where things happen to you.

Wrong. Wrong. Wrong.

Sure, if you really wanted to have to steel yourself every damn moment of the day, you could actively try resisting all of the distractions and temptations that crop up in the workplace. And yes, it's *possible* that you might have the fortitude to succeed at such an incredible challenge. But why not take an easier (and more effective) route to the same place by discouraging these temptations to inefficiency from ever occurring to begin with?

Let's go back to zombies for a moment. Have you ever heard of a zombie being asked if he saw the big game last night, or how her kids are? Do people have the urge to walk up to a zombie and see if it can help out on a new project? Do sugar-free-gum-snapping secretaries ask zombies if they could "find the time" during their day to provide feedback on a report?

No, no, and no.

Rather than asking them for input, help, or advice, most people tend to *run away screaming* when they see a zombie. While there are advantages for everyone in avoiding unnecessary work, the first and foremost advantage for a zombie is that it remains free to do what's really important (i.e., methodically stalking humans to consume their living flesh).

Now, the question is, how do *you* enjoy these kind of zombie benefits? How can *you* comport yourself in such a manner as to make the notion of walking up to you and handing you a memorandum a laughably idiotic act?

The answer is: **Start small.** Start with your cubicle (which probably *is* very small).

Is your cube a friendly place? Are there photographs of cute, smiling children or relatives? Is there a jar of your coworkers' favorite candies? Perhaps some clever Dilbert cartoons about various absurd aspects of the corporate environment?

Zombie Tip—Avoid Office Dalliances

Having no sex drive at all gives zombies one less distraction from their all-consuming greater lust for the flesh of the living. Z.E.O.s lack this advantage, but should still try to keep things reasonable. (If the only way you can pick up a chick is because she's your secretary, then dude, you're just being a giant douche.)

. . . because, if there are, then—amusing as they may be—*these things are working against you.*

A friendly workspace, where humans are not afraid to go (and perhaps even feel *invited* to go) sends the **wrong** message. Where do zombies, the pinnacle of efficiency and focus, get their "work" done? A cursory answer might include misty midnight graveyards, shafts buried deep inside forgotten nuclear testing facilities, and rotting ghost ships of the undead. None of these places invites humans (at least not *sensible* ones).

Starting on **Day One,** go ahead and remove everything from your workspace that might make it attractive to other people. Candy jar on your desk? Get rid of it. Pictures of your family? In the trash. "Certificates of Completion" from those Quark and InDesign classes you took? Into the recycling bin. (You don't want people asking for help with "page layout" when they could instead be imploring "Please, please for the love of God, don't eat me!")

Am I advising, then, that your cubicle walls should be entirely bare? Not by any means. Fill your cubicle as you see fit . . . with things that will make people think twice before bothering you.

Your first impulse might be to put up a sign that says "Go Away!!!" or even "Fuck off." Besides being uncreative, this would probably also get you fired (which is *not* your goal). Your decorations should say "Go away" the way a zombie's appearance says "I'm about to *fucking eat you.*" A zombie doesn't carry a sign or wear a T-shirt announcing this—instead, a zombie "announces it" via the gore dripping from its incisors and the murderous, inhuman look in its eye. You've got to be subtle in advertising the fact that you are not someone to pester. Subtle like a zombie.

So don't loudly announce, "Once, I fucking killed a guy" at a staff meeting. (Even though it might be fun.) But *do* conspicuously leave court documents around your cube pertaining to a murder case in which you were the defendant . . . who was unexpectedly let off on a technicality (the witnesses' brains kept getting mysteri-

ously eaten). Souvenirs of weird-looking witch doctor stuff from Haiti? A *great* idea for workplace decoration. Medieval woodcuts of torture and shit? Super! (Say they're part of your ethnic heritage if people from HR give you a hard time.) Make your cube a reflection of you . . . a "you" who doesn't want to be bothered with unnecessary interactions.

Do keep your computer (you probably need it for, you know, work), but make sure you at least find some sort of screen-saver that's really off-putting. (Something with zombies would be good.) Keep your office chair, too, but see if you can find some way to make it "scary" when you're not sitting in it. Hanging a jacket or lab coat with a mysterious red stain over the back of it would work. And if you have a scanner, be sure to leave something disturbing in it when you're not using it. Eighteenth-century manuals of gynecological surgery have a way of sending the "right message" to a neighbor who would otherwise interrupt you to ask if you'd mind scanning a picture of his kid's soccer team.

Like a zombie, send a *clear but nonverbal* message that you should not be bothered with petty requests or pleasantries. Doing so will free up your schedule in a way that will allow you to take the first crucial steps toward business success.

It should go without saying that you can also feel free to ignore all of the indirect appeals to your time. Posters in the lunchroom for company softball teams, sexual harassment prevention trainings, and compliance classes that are "required for your recertification" can safely be ignored. If it's not about your immediate work, then it's not for you.

Then, take all of this newfound time, and use it to accomplish more than you ever before have.

"But wait," I hear you asking, "what if I can get all my 'regular work' done in two hours? If that's the case—because, like, I'm so smart and efficient—then what's wrong with me taking a little time to smoke out with the guys from shipping and receiving, or playing hours of Mario Bros. on an online NES simulator?"

The answer is, nothing . . . **unless you want to become a Z.E.O.**

"Storming the barricades"

The third quarter will be the most pivotal of all in your quest to become Z.E.O. It will also be the most dangerous and difficult. It will be the quarter in which you and your staff are tested and in which you learn whether all of your careful planning and calculation have paid off.

The third quarter is about installing yourself as Z.E.O.

Now maybe that sounds dangerous or intimidating to you. Perhaps you're thinking "Gee, I've already accomplished *so much*—I'm Employee of the Quarter and I have all these cool zombie coworkers I made—do I really *need* to storm the boardroom and attack the current C.E.O.? That sounds so violent. Can't I just stay here and be happy with what I have so far?"

Not if you want to be a Z.E.O.

Z.E.O.s *take* power. It's not something they wait to be given. There's a big difference between installing yourself and waiting for promotions to go through. Why? **Because you want to have things while you're still young enough to enjoy them.**

It is important, here, to say a few words on this idea.

Under the old twentieth-century business model, control of a corporation was handed over to an executive who had "earned it" through many years of service. This executive had "paid his dues," both inside and outside the boardroom. He and his wife attended all of the right soirees. He volunteered for company charity events and played on the company softball team. He learned to dress and talk the "right way." And for this self-effacing, personality-destroying regimen, he was rewarded with the reins for maybe five, ten years tops. He was already white-haired when he got control of the company, and at the slightest downturn in business or correction in the market, folks started whispering that maybe it was time for him to retire.

So here he is, this guy who gave his whole life to the company, and he has only a handful of years at the top. And he's the *fortunate one*. What about all the other corporate losers who groomed themselves for the corner office but never made it anywhere close? Poor bastards.

But, as I said, this was the old model.

The new model, the twenty-first-century model, is that of the Z.E.O.

Money is connected to time. Inextricably and forever. (Zombies, who can pretty much "live" forever, are experts on time.) An executive who waits until he's sixty to become the head of a major corporation has only a few years in which he can expect to be the top-salaried employee. In contrast, a Z.E.O. who installs him or herself at, say, thirty will have many, many years of earning *at the peak of the pyramid*. Forget how much you put in the 401(k) each month. Fuck your 401(k). They're all worthless now, anyway. Your number of years in the top spot is where the *real* key to financial success is going to be found.

Look at it another way. Take a guy in his late sixties. He's worked hard and saved his whole life by living simply, socking away as much as he possibly could. (In many ways, this man is the wet dream of most finance-book authors.) He's just paid off the mortgage on his house. He owns a small business worth a few hundred thou. He's bought a few stocks that are maybe doing okay. And say he also owns some land—it was in the family or something—that a developer would like to buy. Now, add up all of this guy's stuff, plus the cash in his checking account, and his net worth is probably a million dollars. Maybe even a couple million.

Now imagine someone like Paris Hilton. She is twenty-five years old and has at least a million dollars *in the form of dollars in a bank account* that she can do whatever she feels like with. She doesn't have to live simply or modestly, but can instead live lavishly—eating at fancy restaurants, wearing designer clothing, and traveling by saffron-powered hovercraft. She has millions of dollars *that she can enjoy.* See the difference?

Many authors of business and finance books would have you believe that the two people in the above examples *are the same thing.* Seriously! After all (say most business book authors) they're both millionaires, aren't they? And you said you wanted to be a millionaire, *didn't you*? (I'll say it for you: **Not like this, I didn't!**)

Obviously, Paris Hilton and a scrimping, saving septuage-narian are *not the same thing at all.* Don't agree? If you had to choose one of these existences for yourself, which one would you pick? The person facing the sunset of his life with little to show for it except a bank statement with seven figures, or a freewheeling socialite using money to have fun and be the center of attention? Aside from a few incorrigible hermits, most folks will choose the latter.

This exercise points to a question that most business books fail to ask, and that is: *Why* do you want to be rich? Is it so you can act like a millionaire (replete with top hat, cigar, mistresses, mansion, and top-shelf liquor), or is it so you can act like a "millionaire" who saves and scrimps his whole life?

Consider it another way.

If asked, "Would you like a million dollars?" Most people would instantly respond in the affirmative. But likewise, if queried: "Would you like a million dollars that you can see on a statement

Zombie Tip—Using "Temps" is Always to be Discouraged

For the Z.E.O. as for the zombie, the idea of a "temporary worker" is a risible obscenity. It's like, let me get this straight. . . . You want to come onboard for part of the time, and then just leave after a few months? What? Nobody has ever been a zombie temporarily. (Once you're a zombie, then dude, you're a zombie for good.) A Z.E.O. should only select workers with zombie-like dedication who want to work with him on a permanent basis.

and just 'know it's there,' or would you like a million dollars that you can use to buy things and have fun?" most people are going to say that they want the second kind of million dollars.

You, my friend, can have **either.**

If it's the first kind you want, then you don't need any special advice from me (or from zombies). You don't need the secrets in the rest of this book. Just start saving as much as you can, and buy appreciating assets. Even if you don't make a large salary, if all you do is save, it's really quite manageable. Don't bother trying to become a Z.E.O. Just sock away $25,000 a year for forty years, and you'll have a million dollars . . . *right before you fucking die!* Maybe you can use it to upgrade to a gold-plated respirator in the nursing home or something.

If that doesn't sound good to you, then don't wait for those few, fleeting years at the end of your professional career when you maybe have *a chance* of becoming a richly compensated executive. Instead, call on the hoary zombie army you have amassed and use it to *install yourself* as commander in chief of a company. Business is not a democracy, and an occasional military junta is called for.

If you're brave enough to take this step—and if you want to be rich while you're still young enough to enjoy it—then you are in the right place.

Day One

At this point, if you have successfully executed the directives prescribed so far, you should have a small army of zombie employees at your command. It needn't be a majority of employees in the company—or even a majority of your department—but it does need to be large enough to have an impact. *At least* 10 percent organization-wide is a good rule of thumb. If you're not there yet, don't despair. (However, you may want to weigh the benefits of setting aside another quarter for recruiting.)

With zombies, the readiness is all.

Here's a list of questions to ask yourself about the "army of the undead" you have amassed. (Be honest. These questions are designed to help you know if you're ready to storm the boardroom.):

Is my army 10 percent or more of the total office population?

Does my army think and act alike? (That is, do they all "get the idea" about this whole "acting like a zombie" thing—or are they still figuring it out?)

Is my army making an impact on the organization? (Have managers noticed the uptick in productivity from these "zombified" employees? Is quality and profitability steadily improving throughout the company? Is the company seeing drooling and moaning at record levels?)

Once employees are "bitten" by zombie business excellence, do they *stay* bitten? (You're doing something wrong if they don't.)

Are other, nonzombie employees reacting appropriately to your converts? (Are they confused, horrified . . . but eventually intrigued? Then you're spot on.)

That last item could be the most important. Many of the signals that you're on the right track will come, not from your army of zombies, but from the "normal" employees. You want a zombie army with a "zombieness" that is undeniable.

You want mid-level managers to say: "At first I thought I could just ignore these guys, but this is really getting out of hand with so many zombie employees."

You want a *presence* to be felt. Anxiety-about-zombies, for lack of a better phrase, is good. It will help the employees who will not be directly involved in the coming zombie coup (which is to say, the vast majority of them) to accept it when it occurs.

You want a feeling of tension and irritation to pervade the nonzombies. You want them to feel that the tectonic plates of the company are shifting. You want them uncomfortable and looking for some form of resolution.

For your plan to work, the average worker must have the feeling that "something *has* to happen soon" and that matters are "*coming to a head* with these zombie employees." That way, when actual escalation begins, bystanders not involved in the conflict will accept it. "It was inevitable," they will say. "I just hope it ends soon," they will say. **And it will.**

It is this tendency to want things to "be over" (with little regard to how they are actually settled) that you must use to your advantage in this affair.

So, if, on this first day of the new quarter, you have confirmed that your zombie minions do, in fact, meet the salient criteria, and that your corporate organization is ripe for the taking, then go home and sleep well. For tomorrow, great events begin!

Week One—Planning Your Attack/Mustering the Troops

Almost every major corporation has had a top executive who has been "asked to step down" at one point or another. There are too many examples to list. Usually, the reason that he or she is "deposed" is declining profits. It can also arise from declining quality, or unethical behavior. (When the Feds show up and lead him away in handcuffs? Yeah, that counts, too.)

Yet it is a rarer (though not altogether unheard-of) thing when an older executive leaves because a new executive has *installed himself.*

Typically, when an executive is simply *asked* to leave, the board of directors arranges for his or her departure well in advance. Media conferences are called. Press releases are sent. The executive in question gets a severance package and sometimes a buyout. Anxious stockholders are mollified with reassurances that an executive search will be swift and effective, and that a new leader (one who was born ready to right this foundering ship) will be located with all speed.

However, when an executive *deposes* an old C.E.O. and *installs himself* as leader, these same warm reassurances are not present. It is the new leader himself who must convince employees, board members, stockholders, and shareholders to recognize and accept as legitimate his claim to the leadership of the organization. (A mouthful to say, and a bitch to do. But no worries. You're already halfway there.)

The key in the first week of machinations is to position your opening moves so that at the conclusion of events (which is still as much as three months away) you will be poised as a legitimate heir to the throne.

Begin by checking alliances and allegiances.

Alliances are important, both internally and externally. Let's start by looking at external ones.

"Wait a minute," you might be saying. "*External* allegiances? But I want to be the Z.E.O. or whatever of *this* corporation, not any exterior company."

Hold those horses, kiddo. In *any* situation where control of power shifts, it is important that that shift be recognized externally to lend authenticity to the new claim to power.

Let's say there's a tiny Third World country that has just had its president (and his cronies) run out of the presidential palace by a group of rebels. Both groups are claiming to be the legitimate rulers of the country. The president says: "Even though I'm not in the presidential palace anymore, I'm still the president." The rebel leader says: "I'm in the presidential palace, so I must be the new president." The people are probably divided on the issue of who is really in charge, so how does it get decided? Well, in most cases, through *recognition by other countries.* If the United States or the United Nations says it recognizes the new rebel leader as the legitimate president, then the country can continue doing business with the United States and other countries. (**Hint:** *That's really fucking important.*) Likewise, if the new rebel leader is *not* recognized globally as the legitimate ruler of the nation, then he will be paralyzed. His throne in the presidential palace will be just another chair. Other nations will refuse to negotiate or trade with him, because his claim to leadership will have no legitimacy. The country will wither and die under his grip (though he is likely to be overthrown by yet other rebels before it ever gets that far).

When you take control of the company where *you* work, you want the battle to be swift and decisive, but you also want your victory to be legitimate. You want the vendors and distributors and contractors and consultants (who work with you every day and are necessary to your operations) to recognize that you, as the new leader, have the authority to take power and be the new boss.

Create a task force spearheaded by your top zombies to explore this issue. Start with the exterior elements who are most important to the continued operations of your company. For example: the truckers who take your product to market, the retail locations that sell your product, and the vendors who sell you the raw materials you need in order to manufacture your product. Try to gently find out whether they would continue doing business with you if they learned that someone else was in charge . . . someone a little more like a *zombie.* If you encounter resistance, find out what you need to do to get them amenable to the idea.

Suggested water-testing talking points include:

"We here at Company X pride ourselves on making top quality products, and are always looking for ways to improve. How would you feel if a change to zombie management resulted in improved products on your shelves?"

"Word is, some new employees with their eyes on management positions have really been 'taking heads' and 'eating brains.' Look for big things from them this quarter. If some of them were to claw their way to the top, you wouldn't object to doing business with them, would you?"

"Isn't it great to work with people who are driven, focused, and don't make idle chitchat all the time? . . . or, really, say much of anything at all? Because we're thinking of making that the new, corporation-wide policy for employee comportment."

> **Zombie Tip—**
> Sitting in the boss's chair doesn't make you the boss—other people acknowledging you as the boss makes you the boss.

Yeah, it can be tedious to have these conversations, but you'll be glad you did. You don't want to take power and then find yourself paralyzed. (Nothing is more pitiful than a paralyzed zombie. Like when a mortician or a scientist has you chained down to a table or something, and is getting all in your face with the whole "Tell me . . . *why* do you want to eat our brains?" spiel. It's like, damn, I dunno. They just taste good. Why've you got to be such a dick about it?)

Of course, it's equally as important for you to plumb the depths internally to learn what allegiances exist *within* your corporation, and what can be done to use them to your advantage.

The best possible scenario for an aspiring Z.E.O. is to be at a company with low morale, weak performance, and (most importantly) a C.E.O. who is ineffective and disliked. If this is where you find yourself, then thank your lucky stars and get ready to take the old bastard out.

But things may well be more difficult for you. Your company may be profitable and successful. The C.E.O. may be affable, competent, and well liked. The employees may be contented and pleased.

If this is where you find yourself, do not despair. Many coups have toppled prosperous regimes, and many competent leaders have been unseated by those even more competent. **Plus, you have zombies.**

Above any general sense you may have of your company's condition, you can test the allegiance of employees to the current leadership in many ways. Some suggested steps include:

Putting a life-size cutout of the current C.E.O. in the employee lounge. If, in a few days, it is covered with gum and has been used as a dartboard, you are in good shape. If it has been carefully maintained and/or decorated like a shrine, you may have problems.

Starting a rumor that the current C.E.O. is planning to leave his or her post. Is this rumor met with relief, excitement, and joy, or is it met with dread, resentment, and anger?

Starting a "Party Planning Committee" for the C.E.O.'s next birthday. Put a sign-up sheet in the cafeteria. If you get more than a few signatures by the end of the week, you may be in trouble. (Note who does sign up so they can be zombified ASAP.)

If your coworkers are already unhappy and ready for a change in leadership, great. You can skip ahead to the next section. If, however, your coworkers are pleased with the current leadership, then you need to foment dissent. This will prepare your zombie troops for "battle."

The first step is to blame people in power for things above and beyond their control. This has been the tactic of those wishing to cultivate aggression in a populace since the beginning of time. **You see, there are two great truths of life (which all zombies know):**

1. Life sucks most of the time.

2. It sucks for no reason.

Most people are willing to openly agree with the former statement (based on all the suckiness they endure daily), but many are skittish about admitting the latter. They get all: "If life sucks for no reason, then aren't we just afloat in a meaningless, godless netherworld where zombies might rise from the dead at any moment and eat our flesh?" (It's like, doye! Of course we are.) But because people *don't like* the idea that life sucks for no reason, they're always looking for an explanation of *why* it sucks. A scapegoat. A culpable party or parties. A cause for all the suckage.

That is where salespeople come in.

In ancient times (or in today's Third World and Middle Eastern countries), when a king wanted his subjects to rise up and make war against a neighbor, he made sure to emphasize that the kingdom he wanted to attack was the source of everything bad in his subjects' lives. Even if the connections were tenuous or made no sense, the king repeated them until they started sounding true.

Why is it so crowded? Because that neighboring nation stole all of our land a long time ago. That's why it has *always* sucked here. They're holding on to space that is historically ours! We need it to grow crops and move around and shit. They stole it . . . *so we should take it back.*

Why am I so sick all the time? Because immigrants from that other country are taxing our medical system so you can't get adequate care. If that other country doesn't do something about its surplus population . . . *then maybe we should do it* for *them.*

Why can't I get my shitty novel published/unwatchable film distributed/terrible play produced/poorly rendered artwork exhibited? Why? Because of our neighbors! They stole our indigenous culture and imported their own. They snuck in and installed themselves in top positions at our media companies—so when your novel/film/play/painting gets rejected or panned, it's not because you're terrible . . . it's because you're not like *them.*

It sounds crazy, I know. But this sort of thing has worked for all of recorded history. (Also, don't worry that you won't actually be able to improve people's lives when you do take power. History also shows that that never happens, but for some reason nobody ever complains.)

Your task, going forward, is sowing these seeds of dissent *in a business context.* In your case, the "oppressor" is not a neighboring regime, but a dictatorial C.E.O. who needs to be overthrown. Even if the current head of your company is talented, compassionate, and charismatic, consider using variants of the following to create an atmosphere in which you can urge the employees to help you unseat him or her:

Why don't I make more money? "I hear the current C.E.O. is keeping base salaries low as part of an incentive-based compensation plan that only benefits top-level executives. We'll *always* be screwed as long as they keep running things this way. . . ."

Why are our workspaces and facilities so shabby and dreary? "Who knows? But I hear that they just installed a solid-gold bidet in the C.E.O.'s washroom. Kinda makes you think, dunnit?"

Why can't I ever seem to get a promotion? "I'm surprised by that, too. You're clearly a handsome genius who is destined to be a part of our next generation of leaders. Maybe it has something to do with the current C.E.O.'s policy of only promoting his friends, family, and fellow university alumni."

Be creative with these talking points, and tailor them to your own work situation. Find a way to tie the problems and foibles at your own office back to the current management. It's easier than you think, once you get started.

If you do your job effectively, you won't need to (and, indeed, shouldn't explicitly) suggest that a new, more effective C.E.O. is what's required to correct the problems besetting your office. It will be all the more effective if you allow your coworkers to come to this conclusion themselves. And, even if they don't, when you "appear" (looking like a new C.E.O., astride your zombie army) it will suddenly "make sense" to them that this is what's required.

Understand this: You *must* position yourself as "the guy/gal who's here to solve the problem" in order to win the approval of your company's employees when you take power. Obviously, you're not going to appear reluctant, or as if you were drafted into becoming the next C.E.O. (Z.E.O.). However, you must also act in such a way that it appears employees' problems and grievances would be addressed if you took power. Nobody's going to say you're acting selflessly, but people may say something like: "Yeah, it looks like he is staging some kind of coup, but at least he's trying to make it *better* around here."

It is this *gradual betterment* that will be the key to your assumption of the company's top spot being acknowledged as legitimate. You don't have to have a plan or platform to solve every problem (that would look weird and suspicious). You just need to appear to be a step in the right direction.

Month One

It is in this first full month of the third quarter that you must truly set things in motion and begin your zombielike assault on the corridors of power. The time is now.

So far, you have zombified yourself, "bitten" other employees to zombify them, and taught them in turn to bite others. And in the first week of this quarter, you have ensured that your zombie coup will be recognized after it takes you into a position of power. You have also sown dissent (if workers at your company were not already dissenting on their own)—a key step in any successful move on a base of power.

Now you're ready to stage your zombie-corporate takeover. (Deep breath. Here we go. . . .)

Step one: Disobedience

Sometimes the things we do are less important than the things we *don't* do. And one thing zombies don't do well is obey. Not supervisors. Not C.E.O.s. Not soldiers with flamethrowers and machine guns. The zombie's natural inclination toward disobedience will serve you well as you get things going.

The 10 percent (or more) of the workforce that you have zombified will already have some command of disobedience. Since zombification, they will have been "disobeying" things like company dress codes and HR directives to "be pleasant" to other coworkers. Now, however, you must take your zombie minions to an entirely new and dramatic level.

We know whom zombies *disobey* (practically everyone) but whom do zombies *obey*?

The answer is: Their creator.

Whether a Haitian voodoo witch doctor or a medieval wizard dabbling in the black arts, the only dude who's even got a shot at controlling these fuckers is going to be the one who made them in the first place.

And that's you.

Starting here, in the third quarter, your "zombified" employees must be instructed to obey you—and only you—going forward.

Certainly, the zombie employees should keep working under their respective supervisors. (That is vital to the continued success of the corporation you hope to inherit.) However, they should only work at your say-so, when *you* say so, on projects that *you* deem important. The key is to demonstrate your control of the zombie employees to the rest of the company.

Stress to your zombie followers that they don't need to be confrontational with their regular, nonzombie supervisors. After all, zombies aren't *confrontational* about rules, just *disobedient*. When a frustrated police officer yells at a zombie: "Turn around and put your hands on your head," or "Don't come any closer," or "Stop eating that guy's brain," the zombie doesn't stop to argue with the officer. He doesn't even stop to acknowledge the question. He just keeps on doing what he wants to do. Instruct your own zombie followers to mimic this behavior.

When nonzombie supervisors give them tasks to complete and meetings to attend, your zombie followers should nod placidly and smile. They should not argue or verbally refuse when instructions are given. Afterward, however, they should only perform the tasks that you have approved for them, and only attend meetings that you—as their true master—have okayed for them to attend. Again, the point here is not for your zombie minions to "not do any work." Rather, it is for them to do "zombie work only."

And, of course, all their work should be done in a zombie's slow, methodical, yet superior style.

Step Two: Accountability

As your zombie workforce implements its policy of disobedience, ripples of its effects will slowly reach up the chain of command. Be patient, and let this happen gradually.

For the first few days (or even the first full week), nonzombie managers and supervisors may simply think that some of their employees are having an off week. They'll wonder if maybe morale is just low. (Did we forget someone's birthday? Did I accidentally insult one of my employees somehow? Has a local sports team lost a championship?) Human Resources may be called on to intervene with team-building exercises or employee satisfaction surveys. Supervisors may try one-on-one lunches with their staffs. Motivational speakers may be brought in to explain why the fact of their being born without legs should make office workers feel like "They can do anything!" (These efforts will, of course, be fruitless.)

As managers throughout the company begin to collectively realize that many of their employees are behaving differently, they will also notice that productivity and quality are coincidentally up. It may take them a while to correlate these two phenomena (we *are* talking about managers, here), and when they do, they will not know how to react. It is your job to step in and "help" them.

As it becomes clear, corporation-wide, that something is "up" with certain employees, you should let it drop that you might know something about it. Be subtle. Don't send out a company-wide e-mail announcing your dominion over an army of the undead.

Instead, start a rumor. Leave something on the copier about it that can be traced back to you. Interested parties will eventually come calling. When they do, your goal is to sign up as many managers as possible.

Don't look desperate—even if that's how you're feeling. Don't act like you *need* them. Instead, when a pustlegutted mid-level manager nervously lopes into your office to ask about these "zombie" workers, you just tell him how it's going to be. Make clear that things are already in motion. This new zombie way of doing things is going to be the model going forward. Pretty soon (sooner than later) it's going to "infect" the entire corporation. Tell the mid-level manager that he can be a part of it if he wants to, but nobody's going to force him. He doesn't have to make the change now. The change is, however, inevitable. There's *no question* that it's coming. The only real question at this point is: Does he want to be one of the people who joined voluntarily? (When he had the chance to be on your *good* side . . . ?)

Depending upon the effectiveness of your salesmanship, you can expect to recruit and "zombify" between 50 and 75 percent of the curious parties who come to you. Most of those who decline will go peacefully. Some will have to think over what you've said. Some will think you're a nut. Others still will see you for what you truly are—the progenitor of a dangerous virus that is spreading quickly and could be lethal to the current management structure of the company. Those in this latter category—if they are loyal to the current C.E.O.—may eventually go to the board of directors and alert them of your sedition. When this happens, it's time to make your pitch.

Step Three: Making the Pitch

You knew this day would come. In fact, **you've been looking forward to it.**

By the time the board of directors (or other elite body) at your company hears more than one report of a zombie worker infection, they're going to want to come talk to you about it. You should welcome this interaction. After all, it is a necessary step for your rise to Z.E.O. However, you must also handle it very carefully.

Likely, your visitors from the top will begin with a list of charges, of which (let's be honest) you are 100 percent guilty. The charges are likely to include:

- Subverting direct orders from supervisors.
- Failing to complete work assignments on time, and encouraging others to do likewise.
- Completing employee directives only as you see fit.
- Failing to attend mandatory meetings and performance reviews.
- Failure to complete almost all paperwork sent to your office.
- Encouraging other employees to become "followers" and adopt your idiosyncratic workplace standards.
- Something about zombies . . . or something.

When the huffing, furious chairman of the board is through delivering this litany of transgressions—vibrating with anger as he waits for your response—prepare to dispel him by using two of the most magical words in the business lexicon: "Yes, and . . ."

Stare down that overblown gasbag of a corporate chairman with confidence. Every one of his charges is accurate and true. There may even be some things that he's left out. But use the magical phrase "Yes, and . . . " and watch his mind begin to change. Sell him on all the *positive* aspects of all that you have done, and hint at all that you are prepared to do.

Say, "Yes, and . . ." :

- Employee productivity, among myself and these "selected" employees, is up more than 50 percent. Overall productivity is up 15 percent corporation-wide.
- Employee job satisfaction and morale are increased.
- Product quality has steadily risen in direct proportion to the number of "selected" employees who have adopted my "new standards" for quality work.
- While attendance at some nonessential functions (team-building exercises, all-employee meetings, corporate retreats) *is* down, attendance at meetings to vital business projects is perfect.
- The recent uptick in corporate profits *directly correlates* with employees trying out these new "workplace practices."
- And anyhow, zombies rule, you bloated old gasbag! (Optional.)

While this takes a moment to sink in, hit him with some questions that are easier for him to answer. (Also, if the rest of the board is around, invite them in to your cube/office. If you have been summoned to them, so much the better. You want as wide an audience as possible for this.)

Ask the chairman questions like:

- "You do like quality work, don't you?"
- "The goal here *is* to increase productivity and profits, right? I mean, *that's your job,* right?"
- "It is a good thing, isn't it, when employees learn valuable workplace skills with no additional investment in our already-bloated training budget?"
- "If there was something I could do that would increase bottom-line profitability, employee-satisfaction, and work quality, *at no cost,* you'd want me to do it, wouldn't you?"

Get him saying "Well . . . yes," and, "I suppose theoretically . . ." as much as you can. Give him the old razzle-dazzle. Don't let him stand back and look at the big picture. Don't let him reflect upon the unprecedented magnitude of the changes you are proposing. **No.** Keep him focused. Keep him looking at specifics. You want him saying "yes" as much as possible in front of the other chairmen.

Do this until the very moment you are excused or dismissed.

Though you might be tempted, in this first moment of confrontation, to sell the board on complete corporation-wide zombification, you need to hold back a little. Soon enough, the idea will begin to bounce around inside their heads like a pinball. They are a committee. By the very virtue of who they are, they decide nothing quickly. But the results you have shown them are undeniable.

"Gee, we *are* supposed to increase profitability . . . ," one might begin by saying.

"The shareholders want any action that increases their return," another will point out.

"It's not like this guy's doing anything that violates Sarbanes-Oxley, or is, you know, *actually unethical,*" yet another might say.

"What would it hurt to let him continue a while longer?" one will finally posit. "After all, if it starts to go poorly for any reason, we can just shut it down and fire the guy."

"Ooh, ooh," another will suddenly declaim, "and if it *does* go well, we can say it was our idea and take all the credit."

When the board is finished deliberating, all eyes will turn to the chairman. Yes, you may have called him a "gasbag." Yes, your methods are unconventional, confusing, and off-putting. But darn it, *results are results.* Eventually, his thoughts will turn to his compensation—which is largely tied to stock performance and company profitability. And, after adequate reflection in this arena, he will conclude that he wants what you've got.

That, my future Z.E.O., is when the tide turns.

Remainder of the Quarter

Sometimes in life *you ask*. Other times, **you get to tell.** This is about to be one of those times when you get to tell.

Probably, the communication from the board and its chair will arrive in the form of a phone message or e-mail. If you've carefully followed the steps and talking points prescribed above, there is little doubt that they will respond in the affirmative. They can't be seen to go on record as *officially* endorsing your project of corporate zombification, so their message will be subtle and nuanced. Be ready to read between some lines.

They may simply say that they have chosen not to act at this time . . . or that your project, while morally questionable, has yet to violate a specific corporate rule. ("Legal is still reviewing it.") They may put you on "corporate probation" or something similar. They might say that your project will have to be shut down "very soon." (Just, you know, not quite yet . . .)

You should count any such communiqué as a complete and total victory, and prepare yourself for the next step.

As the rest of the third quarter goes by, the board is going to watch and wait. They will examine you and your entire zombie operation as closely as they possibly can. They are going to look for *any reason* to shut you down. Don't give them one. Make sure that zombie discipline among your troops is tight . . . and keep on recruiting.

As corporate profits, productivity, and quality all continue to creep higher and higher, the board will have to admit you're onto something. The ball is now back in *their* court. Possibly, they will eventually return to you and let you know they appreciate your efforts—despite your unorthodox approach—and would like to move forward by facilitating some kind of "arrange-ment" regarding you and the top spot in the company. It is more likely, however, that they will not approach you. Instead, they will simply allow you to keep making more "zombies" and keep increasing profits.

If this *is* the case, then it is *you* who will have to take the final fight to *them*.

Set something up near the end of the quarter. Don't make it sound like a big deal. Say you'd like a five-minute chat with the board of directors to "knock around" some new ideas you've had. If other board members are around, they can stick their heads in, sure. But seriously, just five minutes. That's all you need.

On the appointed day, you can stride into the boardroom (dramatically, like a zombie overlord, if you like) with confidence that you now hold the upper hand.

When you begin addressing the chair, speak casually—as though a very minor point were being discussed. Ask him if he likes the improvements that workers adopting your "style" have implemented around the organization. Then ask him if he wants you to keep it up.

"Keep it up?" he'll likely stammer. "Of course, yes," he will respond. "You're doing a wonderful job!"

Then tell him, "Yeah . . . Gee . . . Here's the thing about that. . . ." Go on to explain that you have been offered the top spot with your company's largest competitor. (This is called a "lie." You may have heard of them.) Further, note that the employees who have been exhibiting such wonderful productivity over the last quarter (they may now be over 50 percent of the workforce), would want to come with you, if you left. Probably most of them would find a spot with this competitor, or would at least quit their current posi-tion out of loyalty to you. At the very least, they wouldn't be able to continue working in their enhanced capacity without you around to inspire them.

"So here's the thing," you might say, as the chair's jaw continues to drop, "I've seen in a vision that I'm going to be a C.E.O. *somewhere* by the end of the quarter. That's not in question. That's not up for debate. The only real question is: *Where?*"

A bold move? Yes. But necessary, and, again, you hold the hand with the aces.

If you like, you can add some sympathetic pronouncements that will also serve to remind the board members that you are more than just a candidate for C.E.O. You can say: "I'd just love to stay here, and so would my team. We hate to even think of leaving—and taking all of the profitability we produce with us. But, darn it, I'm going to be a C.E.O. by the end of the quarter. So if it's not gonna be here then, darn, I guess I *do* have to take that offer with our competitor . . ."

The important thing is that the chairman and his board understand the full length and breadth of their dilemma. If they lose you, they don't just lose one worker. They don't just lose all the workers who are loyal to you. They lose the mysterious, magical "work style" that has increased productivity and quality, boosted profits, and made the board members look so good to the shareholders. If you leave, you take *all of that* with you.

Before the board members agree to make you C.E.O. (and they will, eventually), they will try several feints and compromises. You must recognize and avoid them all. Some likely variants include:

- *"We need more time!"* They will point out that the end of the quarter is just days away. They'll argue that they can't be expected to make a decision of this magnitude on such short notice. But they can. And they will.
- *"What if we just give you a raise? We'll give you twice what the current C.E.O. makes!"* This is unacceptable. It's not *just*

the money that you want; it's the power that comes with being C.E.O. (and Z.E.O.). Explain to the board that, regrettably, it is necessary for you to be C.E.O. to continue to optimally implement the programs that have made the company so profitable.

- *"What if we promote you just underneath the C.E.O., or make you co-C.E.O. with the guy/gal we have now?"* Again, power. Zombies don't share with anyone, and neither do Z.E.O.s.

- *"You're asking us to make a top-level executive change, on a moment's notice, without vetting it with our shareholders, based upon a* threat *from you?!"* In a word: Yes. These board members may repeat your ultimatum back to you to make it sound absurd. Remind them, if they do this, that what's really *absurd* is losing a huge fraction of your workforce and dropping your company's performance back to its original levels—when you could have just as easily kept your workforce and increased performance *even more.*

- *"You're really being a dick, you know that?"* They've got you there. But hey, you're not there to make friends. This is not *about that.* Right at that moment, you're there to present the board with a binary—a yes-or-no proposition. They can say "no" if they want to. You're not forcing anybody to do anything.

Even under the most felicitous conditions, the chairman and his board will probably not be able to make a decision right then and there—during your five-minute meeting. If they ask you for some time to think it over, then by all means, give it to them. Simply be sure to remind them that the deadline does not change.

You need an answer by the end of the quarter.

The End of the Quarter—"Reaching Capitulation"

You don't need people to like you. You don't need people to like what you do. These are two truths that zombies know all too well.

The general populace definitely dislikes zombies, and certainly dislikes what zombies "do" (especially when it's being "done" to them). But zombies don't allow this prejudice to interfere with their goals. Instead, zombies draw strength from it. In fact, when people are complaining, running in terror, and arming themselves with scythes and dynamite, then zombies know they're doing something *right*.

As you wait for the response of the board, remember that your goal is not for the board members to "like" you. (If they do like you, you're probably doing something wrong.) You are not here to be buddies. You are here to install yourself as Z.E.O. and make your zombie management tactics the standard, company-wide. An important first step to attaining your goals may be to reexamine your own definition of positive feedback.

If you've worked a standard office job for most of your life, your conception of what qualifies as "positive feedback" may be grossly, grossly skewed. Don't fault yourself for this. Since child-hood, you've been conditioned to respond to a kind of feedback that employers manipulate to keep you in your place.

When you're a kid, following basic rules and instructions around the house will get you a cookie. When you're a student, success in your studies is rewarded with good grades. Then, when you become a member of the working world, you're rewarded for completing assignments and projects on time and under budget. But *what are* these rewards, and who's giving them to you?

Simply put, these rewards are products of the current power structure, and are designed to keep you in your place. A few extra vacation days or a cost-of-living raise only serve to make your current position a little more bearable. Promotions, when they are given out as a reward, only place you in a part of the power structure where you can make yourself useful to others. Employers have conditioned most office workers to believe that traditional "rewards" signal advancement, when in fact this is usually not the case. You may be moving up the ladder, but it's at *their* behest . . . as it is useful to *them.*

What about you?

When you make a move that propels you—and only you—toward the rewards you almost certainly deserve, expect to find that the feedback varies sharply. If this variance, at first, is jarring, remember our friend, our model, the zombie. The closer a zombie is to its goal (eating someone's brain), the *more* resistance and "bad feelings" it is likely to encounter. A zombie doesn't get to where it wants to be through a series of gradual promotions after being vetted for years and time and again proving himself reliable. He gets what he wants by taking it—taking it directly, and in the most straightforward way he possibly can. Sure, the feedback is less pleasant. No one is smiling at the zombie. No one is telling him he really earned this brain, or that it's long overdue for him. They're attacking him and calling him every name they can think of. But it's all part of the game for a zombie.

And so, for you.

When the board returns its decision (it will be in your favor) do not expect it to come, as it were, wrapped in a big red bow. These people are going to hate you. They're going to stare at you the way a villager stares at a zombie who's just eaten his best friend. They will look upon you as the source of a deadly, terminal outbreak. They'll scowl. They'll sneer. Nobody is going to smile. (Well, *you* can, if you want to.)

Remember, though, that these are good things. This sort of feedback indicates 1) that you're getting what you want, and 2) you're getting it *like a zombie.*

There is no doubt that the board of directors will agree to make you the new C.E.O. They simply have too much to lose by failing to give you the position under the conditions you request.

Your goal for what remains of this quarter is to reach capitulation, not just from the board, but from the company as a whole. Yes, you do have a loyal army of "zombified" followers, and you have just been appointed C.E.O. of the corporation, but that doesn't mean that everyone working with you will like you. For those who haven't been paying attention (or if the old C.E.O. was popular, and the company profitable), it may seem like your promotion comes entirely out of the blue. Others may vaguely associate you with the new "zombie workplace techniques" that seem to be gaining traction in the different departments, but will have no idea that you deserve the credit for their implementation and the success they have brought.

If you're young, older employees will resent your quick promotion and question your qualifications. If you're older, then younger employees will assume you're doddering and out of touch. If you're a woman, a member of an ethnic minority, or an adherent of an unpopular religion, some within the company may assume your promotion is affirmative action–based, and doubt that you have any real leadership skills.

If you've learned anything so far about zombies, it's that they don't care what other people think of them. Thus: *Your goal is not to dispel every misapprehension your new employees may have about you.* Your goal (at least at first) is only to reach a level of coexistence with them. You need to establish that, like it or not, you are the new C.E.O. That being the case, everyone will have to find a way to work together going forward.

Throughout history, many persons who strongly disliked zombies have found ways to coexist with them. Make this your model. Some humans have done this by learning which Haitian burying-grounds to avoid after nightfall. Others have found that the roof of a mall can serve as an improvised racquetball court. Others still have found that traveling through a zombie-infested necropolis is more or less tenable if one's automobile has been steel-reinforced and equipped with rotating machine guns. The point is that employees who say they "can't work with zombies" just aren't thinking hard enough. There's always a way to work out some sort of arrangement that both parties can "live" with.

Just as your goal with the board members was not to make them like you (but to make them hand you control of the company), so will it be with many of your new employees.

A good start is identifying shared beliefs and values. You might choose to work like a zombie, and they might choose to work, you know, the regular way . . . but you're *all* invested in the future of the corporation. You all want the business to be successful. You all want to make more money and retire wealthy.

And what about the things you *don't* want?

You can all agree that you don't want to waste time in endless meetings. You don't want the company to fail or stagnate because of antiquated, twentieth-century business processes. You don't want to perform meaningless assignments, or get so obsessed with perfection in every last detail that you miss the big picture.

You can also win over your new employees through consensus. Consider collecting testimonials (both from people around the company, and from outside vendors) about what it's like to work with you. Former employees who have worked under you can attest to your superior managerial style.

That said, winning over employees is all well and good, but there may come a point at which a faction simply refuses to be convinced of your worthiness. No matter how you connect with them, or how many testimonials they hear, they'll remain skeptical. Don't waste too much time dialoguing with these guys. Instead, *prove them wrong.*

Some people just want to believe ridiculous things . . . from remote, nonzero possibilities, to patently false statements like "vampires are cooler than zombies." There can be no convincing these people. One can only prove them wrong publicly. And that happens in the next quarter.

The important thing is not to let these folks unnerve you. Every great leader has had his or her critics and naysayers.

The proof is in the brains . . . er, pudding.

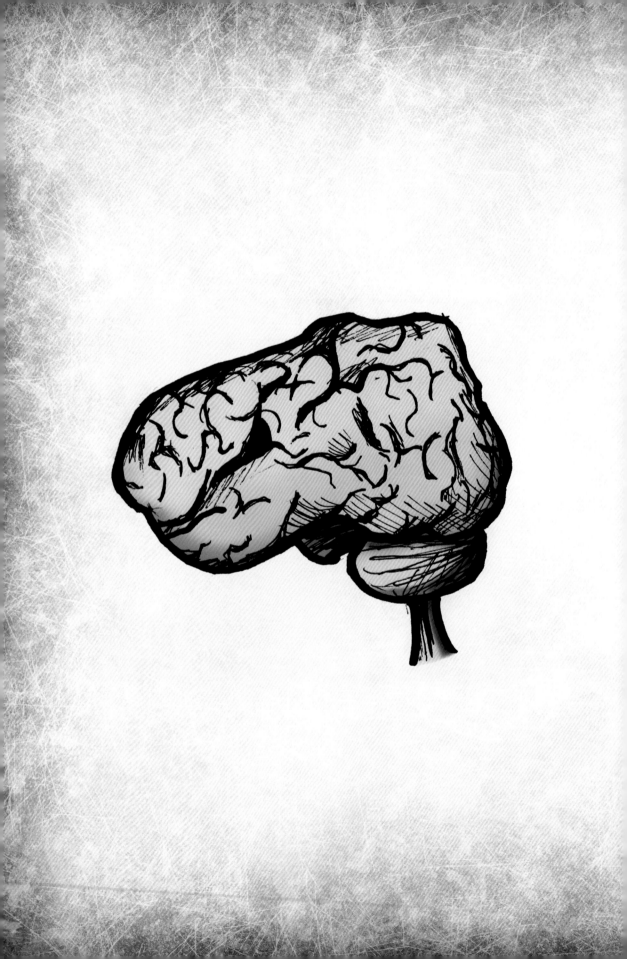

So You've Been Bitten: Making the Most of Your New (Un)Life

Becoming like a zombie is, let's face it, the most important step toward self-improvement that most people are likely to take. And why wouldn't they? You could do worse than a zombie. Much worse.

Zombies dominate in every situation. They bring self-reliance, problem solving abilities, and general resilience to any obstacle in their paths.

In an era when charismatic religion leaders routinely defrocked amid shameful accusations, television physicians are censored for proffering questionable advice, and the FDA changes its recommended daily allowances every other Tuesday, the way forward for those with an earnest interest in self-improvement is not always clear.

As this chapter maps out for you the many ways in which a zombie's ass-kicking traits may be emulated, consider that a zombie has never retired from anything under shameful circumstances (or, indeed, felt shame at all). A zombie has never represented itself as being about something, and then failed to deliver on that promise. A zombie is what it is. It is uncontaminated by pretense, artifice, or deception. (Zombies cannot deceive, except accidentally.) With zombies, you know what you're getting.

And what you're getting is pretty damn cool.

Zombies are winners and problems solvers. They know what they want, and they take it. They never doubt themselves. They never falter in their purpose. They never let anything short of a headshot keep them from obtaining their goals. An investment in becoming more like a zombie is an investment in yourself. And that will always be true.

The 24 Habits of Highly Effective Zombies

It is obvious to any close observer that zombies have benefited from a combination of carefully cultivated habits and tendencies in order to become the superior specimens they are today. By identifying and emulating these habits, humans can enjoy many of the successes that zombies do.

Zombies don't worry. Not about themselves. Not about others. Not about climate change. Nothing.

Zombies have "enough" of what they need in life (with the exception of living brains). Yet are, at the same time, "driven" with a passion and intensity that any CEO or motivational speaker would envy. Zombies don't stop. Zombies don't rest. And yet, zombies are at peace with this ceaselessness. And you can be too.

Zombies have moved beyond the pressures of society. A zombie never feels it "ought" to do something. A zombie never feels that it "should" be doing something (or avoiding something else). A zombie simply is who he or she is, and is at peace with that fact.

When you adopt the habits of a zombie, it's like a fast track to the effectiveness you seek and the self-actualization you've always yearned for. Being like a zombie cuts right through the treacle of life. Cuts right down to the heart of the matter. (Then, when that heart has stopped beating, it has the brain for supper.)

If you want to become a better person and improve your life, you need to start taking on the habits of zombies.

Rugged Individualism

What is the true spirit of an American?

Is it a man traveling alone on the open plain, fueled by nothing but his own gumption and "sticktoitiveness?" Is it self-reliance in the pursuit of your goals? Is it pulling yourself up by your own bootstraps?

Because, if it is, guess what? Boom! Zombies again.

Now sure, there are a few differences between our forefathers' version of the American dream and that of a zombie. The first American settlers wanted a place where they would be free to practice their dumb-ass religions. They wanted not to be taxed by the King of England. They wanted to exploit native peoples and take their stuff. (In some cases, they even wanted to find the "Fountain of Youth.") Later Americans dreamed of luxurious Southern plantations, railroad monopolies, and careers in moving pictures. Today, the American dream seems to involve participation in a reality TV program, saving enough money to pay for gastric-bypass surgery, and securing an adequately wide audience for one's weblog.

But if we stop to look for the vein of essential "American-ness" running through these pursuits, we come back to self-reliance and rugged individualism.

There's so much to be said for self-reliance.

It's a very important trait. Maybe the **most** important (after, of course, brains). After all, who do you expect to do everything for you?

Your parents?

Ha. They're sending you off to boarding school as soon as you're old enough.

Your so-called "friends?"

They're gonna be out of here as soon as your last credit card is maxed.

"What about Jebus?"

I hear you asking, all suddenly pious-like. Hey kid, everybody knows, Jebus helps those who help themselves!

If you want something, you've gotta go out and get it yourself. Zombies are an excellent model for this.

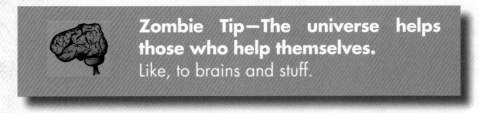

Zombie Tip—The universe helps those who help themselves.
Like, to brains and stuff.

Zombies don't sit around waiting for things to fall in their laps. They go out and get. See, zombies are "doers." And they "do" things like form hideous armies of the night that scour the countryside, eating anybody who gets in their way. They "do" enjoy corralling humans holed up inside of abandoned shopping malls and elevator shafts. They make sure to "do" the things that create environments where humans can get eaten alive.

You never heard of a zombie on the welfare dole, did you? Or some kind of government-subsidized brain-assistance program? Or a zombie who needed help at all?

No.

Think about that for a second. Zombies never ask for help. They don't have to. They help themselves. Zombies find a way.

DIY. That's a zombie, and that should be you, too.

We're Here! We're Animated Corpses Irresistibly Drawn to Feed on the Flesh of the Living! Get Used to It!

Throughout American history, different groups have had to assert their right to be part of the national fabric of this great country. It hasn't always been easy.

These groups and subgroups have had to fight for their right to exist. To stand up and be counted. To be somebody.

And yet each of these groups has, in its own way, made invaluable contributions to society, science, and the arts. Each one distinct. Each one no more or less American than the other. Yet it has not always been easy for those who at first appeared different in some way.

We love America, warts and all, but sadly zombies cannot hope to be exempt from Americans' initial lack of acceptance for cultures and practices that might appear new and different. We can, however, learn from their perseverance and be inspired by their success. Zombies are all about breaking down barricades, both the cultural and the very, very literal. If there's one thing zombies know about, it's barricades. And about being left out, and even forcibly excluded.

You don't have to be an immigrant to be the victim of prejudice. You don't have to have a different skin color or different-looking clothes to be an outsider. You may be descended from people who came over on the Mayflower. You may have attended a fancy prep school and an East Coast college. But even so, something totally beyond your control may drive total strangers to deride and exclude you.

A zombie feels your pain, gay and lesbian America! It's not cool to make fun of someone for their preferences, especially if those preferences have every indication of being innate. Even in this day and age, a lot of people still think zombies "choose" to eat brains. It's like, get a clue. If zombies had any choice in the matter, they'd be eating a steak like everybody else.

Would a gay guy "choose" to like other men, even though he knew it would mean facing a lifetime of intolerance, prejudice, and censored *Sex and the City* reruns on TBS?

A zombie wouldn't "choose" to be a murderous reanimated corpse if he knew it would mean being shot at, exploded, and beheaded whenever someone could manage it. Zombies can't help their preferences any more than you or I. And why should they have to?

Dammit, this is America! And in America, you get to be yourself. Even if it goes against the belief systems of others. Even if it contravenes accepted norms and conventions and laws of nature. And even finally, yes, if it means that you may forfeit your very brain itself.

Who knows? One day, the governor of a northeastern state may even call a press conference to subvert an impending scandal involving clandestine meetings with handsome undead men in hotel rooms, and announce "his truth" that he is a Zombie-American.

Live in the Real World

Most of us know a few poor souls who, for whatever reason, have difficulty dealing with reality. Their "solution" for this, nine times out of ten, is to construct a world of their own that they find more palatable than the real, actual one. This kind of self-delusion could not be farther from the earnest, reality-loving temperament of a zombie.

Don't think zombies aren't tempted to delude themselves from time to time. Believe me, there are plenty of aspects to a zombie's reality that aren't the easiest to cope with. He's an animated corpse with poor motor control and little to no speech driven onward by a desire that is never satisfied. Those who encounter him either flee or attack with all their might. He is "discriminated" against in virtually every way possible.

What's worse, when a zombie's hungry, he can't just go to the grocery store or corner market like you and me. It would be nice for him if he could, but it's just not the case. A zombie has to track down living humans and eat their brains.

Despite all of these middling-to-large inconveniences, no zombie has ever chosen to "escape" from his reality into, say, a world of pills or drugs or booze. No zombies have joined religions that promise a better "next life" in the hereafter. You never see zombies joining the SCA or playing role-playing games in which they pretend to be someone else. It might be momentarily tempting, but zombies realize that they have to be where

Zombie Tip—You're just as God made you.
Whether you were made to help and inspire others, to forge lasting connections, or to break connections between spinal cords and heads, it's no use trying to change it. It's your nature. (Even if what you do is very, very unnatural.)

they are. They have to live in the now, regardless of how difficult it might be.

A zombie realizes that the only thing worse than having to grow up and live in the real world is what happens to you if you "decide" not to. You'll have to face reality someday. We **all** have to. Running from who you are and where you are will only make it worse when the time comes.

Some humans have living situations that are more or less tolerable, but are haunted by things and occurrences from their pasts. These people may look fine and dandy from all outward appearances, but are tortured inside by things that they did (or things that were done to them). They let these things from the past bring them down and make their lives miserable. This behavior is also unacceptable to a zombie. Zombies have difficult pasts too, but it doesn't stop them from getting on with "life."

Think about it. One moment you're lying there a corpse, minding your own business and enjoying the sweet lethe oblivion of the grave, and the next you've been reanimated by some chemicals you've never even heard of, and your life takes a turn you totally didn't expect. You're walking the earth once again under a pretty daunting set of conditions when you'd much rather be napping away in the dirt. Zombies don't waste their time pining over what might have been, however. They accept their situation and move forward (literally), always making the best of things. Always looking ahead—never backwards. Always searching for the next brain to eat. Always slouching toward the future.

No matter how adverse your current or previous situation, remember these three immutable zombie truths:

You are here.

It is now.

Eating a human brain is the most perfect pleasure imaginable.

Remember, It's Just Stuff

Zombies don't focus on material possessions, and they certainly don't "keep up with the Joneses." Neither should you.

After all, nobody likes keeping up with the Joneses. Especially if they have a car or can run fast. As soon as they see you, they're just going to take their tasty craniums and high-tail it right for the bomb shelter. And no matter how fast you stumble after them, it's

> ### Zombie Tip—Stay on the lookout.
> Think enlightenment will just smack you upside the head one day when you least expect it? Not likely. That's how you get hit by a truck. Whatever you're looking for (spiritual zen, true romantic love, a brain to eat) you've got to be looking for it if you expect to find it. Otherwise . . . bam! A truck. I'm not even kidding.

usually a lost cause (unless one of them has a broken leg or is in a wheelchair or something). Don't worry though, because there's a lesson here. And that lesson is, forget the Joneses, and completely forget trying to keep up with them.

Plenty of self-help gurus throughout the ages have preached about the danger of growing too attached to material possessions. It's a point they drive home, and with very little subtlety. Why? Because for whatever reason, this is an idea that will simply not sink in for most people.

We all must know, deep down on some level, that the trappings of this life amount to nothing in the end. No favorite piece of clothing can give our lives the happy ending we desire. No exotic artifact, no matter how rare or imported, can come with us into the afterlife.

House. Car. Stamp collection. When you go it's just going to get picked over by relatives you never even liked that much.

We've seen it happen to other people.

We know that it's going to happen to us.

And yet . . .

Something deeply instilled in the very core of our beings makes us refuse this obvious truth, that possessions are fleeting and material things cannot last.

What is it about our possessions that cries out: "Hold on to me! Even when it makes no sense to do so. Even when the task of preserving me is time-consuming, expensive, and (at the end of the day) impossible! Hold on to me at all costs!"

Whatever the impulse, it isn't one of our better ones. How can this be known for sure? From the fact that in the most excellent zombie, one finds absolutely no trace of this characteristic whatsoever.

A zombie has no respect for possessions, period. Not for its own possessions, and certainly not for things owned by other people. A zombie keeps its goal (brains) foremost in its mind. It doesn't allow itself to get distracted by anything else. A zombie has no difficulty "letting go" of things.

When in pursuit of a victim, a zombie may lose articles of clothing on tree branches or door frames. It may leave one or both of its shoes when it chases someone through a muddy field. Eyeglasses or glass eyes. Tiaras or tube-tops.

Once they're gone, a zombie isn't stopping to pick them up.

Attachment to possessions would only hold a zombie back and would only waste time. Stopping to retrieve a lost shoelace or a treasured childhood knick knack would only distract it that much from its prize (a victim's brain).

You see, a zombie understands that time is valuable, and material possessions are expensive in more than one way.

Here's an example. More than one person has pointed out that if you worked out Bill Gates's compensation to an hourly wage, then he's making something like $50 every two seconds. So, theoretically, if he's on the job and accidentally drops any amount of money less than $50, it's not worth his time to take two seconds out of his workday to pick it up. In that two seconds, he'd make more money by staying on the job.

Think about that . . . Let's say he drops $49. That's a lot of money. You could eat a pretty nice steak dinner for $49. You could do a lot of things with it. And it's not even worth **two seconds** of Gates's time.

It's the same deal with zombies.

Nothing is more valuable to a zombie than eating somebody's brain. Thus, attachment to (and corresponding care of) material possessions doesn't make sense for a zombie (unless, somehow, it brings the zombie closer to that goal).

So when you see a zombie comically lose its top hat while passing through a low doorway, remember that there's a good reason why the zombie doesn't stop to pick it up.

Think back to Bill Gates.

When you see a shabby-looking zombie dragging itself after someone, remember: "**Here's** a guy who's got his priorities straight." Sure, his graveclothes may be missing a few buttons. His hair, fingernails, and teeth (to which he was very attached in life) may now, in the afterlife, have been left behind entirely. His pants may be trailing after him, hanging by a thread and dragging in the mud. But he's not stopping to mess with any of it. He's going right after what he wants.

Material possessions be damned!

> **Zombie Tip—Simplify, simplify, simplify!**
> Simplicity is key to the freewheeling essence of a zombie. The more things you can eliminate from your routine (like persona, hygiene, clothing, and complete sentences) the better.

It's a resolve that humans could stand to cultivate.

The Preparation

In the week leading up to the start of your zombification, you'll want to get your affairs in order. Not like some who's going to die . . . or rather, not *exactly* like someone who's going to die.

That's sort of the point.

In the week before starting this program, you'll probably want to put your most valuable possessions into storage . . . anything you wouldn't want smashed or trampled. Imagine, for a second, a zombie bouncing around like a lost pinball inside your trendy bachelor apartment or cute little single-girl condo. What would get broken, or smeared with goo, or partially eaten? Ask yourself these questions seriously, because that zombie pinball is going to be you. Also, mail forwarding? A good idea. Automatic bill-pay on your computer? Set it up, brother. That is, if you want the lights left on.

Pets that can forage (dogs, cats) will probably be okay, but if you've got a bird in a cage or something, it might be time to let Mr. Budgie spread his wings and soar off the edge of the building. You're going to have more important things to think about in the coming months than birdseed and fresh newspapers.

Zombification is challenging enough when the conditions are right and your dedication is a hundred percent. Advancing only part-way towards becoming a zombie is very dangerous. Zombie-conditioning is hard to reverse. You could find yourself presenting a PowerPoint one moment, and screaming for brains the next. If you go in with any doubts or conflicts, the chances of your finishing are small indeed. Which is a problem.

The lessons in the early weeks will get you started down the right road, but a little knowledge is a very dangerous thing. Make like a zombie in the wrong time and place, and the fallout can be catastrophic, fatal, and extremely unpleasant. (You'll notice you've never heard of a "semi-zombie" walking around, or a guy who was "a little bit zombie now and then." That's because they don't last long, those types.)

Finally, you must tell no one what you plan to do. It can take you right out of the zombie frame of mind to have nice Mrs. Perez from across the hall popping over to see "how the zombie project is going."

At the other extreme, you don't want an enemy of yours to get wind and use this as an excuse to call in the social workers and have you taken away (or, failing that, calling in a military air strike). Your condo association showing up with torches is also a bummer.

But more than any of this, you want the effect of your zombification to be that of a striking transformation. It's one thing to see someone become gradually more like a zombie over the course of weeks. It's even better when you don't see them for three months and then run into them at a social function after complete zombification. That way, there won't be any of that "Gee, you've changed a little" or "Something about you is different . . . No, wait. Don't tell me."

Instead, it'll be more like "Holy fuckface mother of shit!!! Bill, you're a **zombie** now???" And you can be all suave and play it off like "Oh, yeah, I guess you're right. I almost hadn't noticed."

Zombies don't do it for the attention, or the fame, or the free concussion grenades, or any of the other things that come their way. They do it because it's the right thing to do, and the one truth path that they inherently understand they must follow. Are you ready for this kind of dedication?

Now's the time to find out.

Love Zombie

Everyone wants to find love in life.

Platonic love. Fraternal love. Rutting-like-an-animal love, sure. But **especially** romantic love. A self-help book, even one about zombies, would not be worth its salt if it didn't include a guide to maximizing your romantic potential. After all, you deserve love. You have the right to love and feel loved. And you're probably sick of sitting and waiting around for that love to appear.

"But wait," I hear you saying, "aren't zombies sexless beings, utterly incapable of showing love? Don't they lack entirely the inclination to physical romance or emotional openness? Wasn't there a previous section of this book ("Bros before hos") about how zombies show no interest at all in the opposite sex (or the same sex)?

It is true that zombies don't show love (or feel love), but it turns out that their tactics prove expert for obtaining it. Remember, zombies go after what they want. Zombies want brains, but you might want a loving mate with whom you can raise a family and grown old. Don't worry. This impulse is not contrary to your zombification. Rather, because virtually all humans have desires to this end, it is very like a zombie to go out and get the man or woman (or even the she-male from the back page of the *Village Voice*) of your dreams.

In this week's lesson, we will learn how the tactics of a zombie prove expert in the quest for love, and we'll put those tactics into action.

We've talked before about how zombies are good at shattering misconceptions and stereotypes. Love is full of misconceptions.

- Men only want sex.
- Women only want attention and prescience and expensive presents.

There are others, sure. Too many to list here. But the biggest misconception shattered by zombies is that the chase is better than the catch.

Even though this position has been long maintained by many (verbatim, in fact, by no less a netherworld expert than Lemmy Kilmister), it is one readily shattered by the zombie.

For reasons unknown, the stereotype persists that, once obtained, love is never as good as we think it will be. Or that love necessarily fades over time. Sadly, this falsehood keeps some people from going after love at all. It is true that bad relationships (and, of course, bad sex) do sometimes happen, and that courtship, will all its razzle-dazzle and bank account-clearing expenditure, can seem more compelling than the prize at which it is all directed.

Yet true love remains a real and compelling possibility for many, and a bad past relationship is no reason to write off dating as an exercise in disappointment.

Zombies know all about the chase.

And the catch.

And no matter what your cynical sewing circle or drunken frat buddies have told you, the chase is nothing compared to the catch.

While romantic humans involved in "the chase" face humiliating rejection, painstaking preparation processes, and the prospect of blowing a whole goddamn paycheck for a kiss on the cheek on a Friday night, zombies have it even worse. A zombie on "the chase" faces everything from fortifications hastily constructed in an abandoned house, to full-fledged military arsenals directed against him. A chasing zombie (which is most zombies, most of the time) faces bullets, explosives, and voodoo spells, but that's not stopping it. Because a zombie wants what it wants. And the zombie knows that no matter how difficult things may get during the chase, the brain-eating phase will make it all worth it. Remember also, that no zombie has ever eaten a brain or two, but then decided all the fuss wasn't really worth it. No zombie has retired to a solitary life of cats, X-Box, and/or daytime TV.

In your own life, you may have loved once or twice before, and found that love not to be lasting. You may have endured all-night shouting matches, breakups that splinter groups of friends, and alimony payments that never end. I'm not saying these things don't suck. They do. They really, really do. But remember the zombie.

Even if the last brain it munched wasn't the tastiest, there's no hesitation to get right back on the horse. A zombie keeps after what it wants. It knows that true love (brains) is out there.

The first step, then, to loving like a zombie, is to banish forever all doubts that true love is out there, and worth the hassle of courtship.

If you keep mementos of failed relationships around your home, throw them out. You don't need that souvenir tote that reminds you of the time he took you to the Grand Canyon, if it's only going to lead you down the slippery slope of wondering why he also cheated on you with your best friend, and if all men are like that, and if really you should just try to be happy on your own. That, my friend, is loser-talk. And zombies only talk like winners (when they talk at all).

Photos of exes, likewise, have got to go. I don't care if there are other people in the photos. If they're saved on your computer, just use the "delete" function, or at least Photoshop out the offending person.

If you're forever carrying around *memento mori* of bad relationships, you're not going to be motivated to get on to the next one. Trust me, picking through your scrapbooks this week may be a hassle, but when *amore* comes a-knockin', you'll be glad you did.

Are the offending items erased and waiting in a plastic bag out on the curb? Very good, we'll continue.

The next romance myth that zombies shatter is the one that insists that nobody would love you for you.

From the smallest dab of makeup to cover a blemish to the most elaborate exaggeration of one's wealth, status, and penis size, the quest for love often involves prevarication and deception. Why? Because we feel (erroneously) that we are somehow not good enough. So we lie, sometimes directly and sometimes indirectly.

We know full well that, if things go well, our partner will eventually notice that we do, in fact, get pimples when we're stressed. Or that we're not really titled shipping magnates who play billiards with George Clooney and Brad Pitt on the weekends, and that we pack it downstairs. We know this will make our partners feel deceived and confused, and may very well plant the seeds for a break-up. It makes no sense to lie like this, but we do it out of a feeling that we're not "good enough" as we are, and that it's the "only way" someone would fall in love with us.

You never see zombies lying or prevaricating because they don't feel "worthy" of someone's brain. Doesn't make much sense, does it? A zombie knows he (or she) is good enough just as God (or the voodoo priest, or the nerve reagent) made him. A zombie says, "Here I am. I can only be myself. Take me as I am. Give me your brain. "

A zombie doesn't need a bank account full of money, a fancy Ivy-League degree, or a clean felony record to feel worthy of its heart's desire. A zombie presents itself openly for what it is. Sure, high-functioning zombies pass for human now and then, but there's always that moment when the elevator doors close and the zombie lets its real self shine through.

Be Open and Direct

A zombie requires neither sex nor money, but it certainly has needs. Zombies put their own needs first. In every situation. All the time.

Just as a policy of complete honesty with romantic partners can seem like a lousy idea at first (or at least a counterintuitive one), looking for love by putting your own needs first (and keeping them there) might seem to contravene the rules of dating no less deeply.

Putting your needs first is, however, directly connected to a policy of honesty and openness in the quest to love like a zombie.

When a zombie wants to eat somebody, he will make that clear. He's not stopping to consider that person's needs. Or the needs of his/her friends and family. Or even the needs of other zombies who may also be advancing towards the potential victim.

Part of a zombie's refreshing openness is its way of acting in a manner that says: "It's great and all that you're 'too young to die.' And that you 'need' to go on living. But right now, it's not about you. Right now, this is about what I want. I have a right to my feelings, and I 'feel' like I'd like to eat your brain. This is who I am. I never claimed to be anything else. I'm sorry if you thought otherwise."

See? What a gentleman.

A zombie knows inherently that it'd never get anywhere if it stopped to take into account all the feelings and desires of others that might conflict with its own.

A zombie wants to move a step closer to brains just like you want to move a step closer to true love. If that's something that somebody else can't get on board with, then it's their problem, not yours.

Be dogged, dog

Another way in which lovers can learn from zombies is in a zombie's pure doggedness and endless patience. When a zombie wants someone, it stays on the scent. It doesn't take "I already have a drink" or "my boyfriend will be right back" or "this shotgun is filled with rocksalt, you stinking zombie" as an answer.

And while **unreasonable** romantic doggedness can result in restraining orders or even jail time (and is, therefore, not suggested), there's no harm in asking someone out a second or third time. If at first you don't succeed, think of a new approach.

Zombies know that there's more than one way inside a fortified farm house. Sewers and storm drains can be opened. Gambrel roofs can be scaled, especially when you have all night. If all else fails, a zombie can go a lot longer than a human without eating. Many a zombie has starved a victim out of his or her fortification, and while waiting around is never fun, there's nothing else a zombie's got going on.

When there's someone you want to go out with, and for whatever reason the stars aren't right, remember the dogged patient zombie.

Your target may already be in a relationship. He or she may be physically removed from your part of the country. You may even have been rebuffed by him or her directly. Dear friend, all hope need not be lost.

Relationships end, and people go back on the market. People move back to their hometowns after a couple of years off "finding themselves" in the big city. People who once wouldn't return your calls may lower their standards as time goes by.

If you really want to find true love, you have to be open to the possibility that it could involve some waiting. But while you wait, wait like the zombie outside the fortified farmhouse.

The waiting zombie usually stays visible.

If the farmer screws up his courage and peeks through a crack in the door he's nailed shut, the zombie will be right outside waiting. If the object of your affection is dating someone else, let them

Zombie Tip—You never get a second chance to make a first impression. Zombies know they only have one shot to give people the correct impression. (That impression being that they're about to get eaten. Cause, you know, they are.)

know that, if they ever get bored with Mr. Whatsisname, you'll be right there, waiting to offer love, intimacy, and long, sloppy fellatio sessions.

When you can't be directly visible to the object of your affection, it's important to find other ways to let your presence be known. The zombie might not be right outside the farmhouse's front door anymore, but the creaking footsteps on the roof let the farmer know he's still the center of the zombie's world. You might not be able to stay physically near that gorgeous girl from college who said you'd never make anything of yourself, but your note to the alumni magazine about your JD from Harvard will let her know you're still out to prove her wrong.

It's important to note that only you can decide whether waiting is the right thing to do. Even zombies have to make tricky calls in this connection. Yes, a zombie will wait all week for an isolated farmer to risk venturing outside, but if there's another, un-fortified farmhouse just over the next hill, a zombie is no less of a zombie for going in search of other prey.

Go where the action is

The final lesson zombies embody for those desperately seeking someone, is to seek out a target-rich environment. It might sound a little inelegant for a chapter on finding true romance, but trust me, it is advice you need to take.

Have you ever noticed that when zombie outbreaks occur, they invariably start in cities? You've seen it before. One city falls, then another, as zombies radiate out from them. Humans who survive the zombies longest are the ones living in the flyover.

What attracts zombies to urban centers? The number of people-per-square-mile, of course. Cities are where zombies have the best chance of finding what they're looking for, and they instinctually

know it. That's not to say that there might not be some very tasty brains in rural Montana or the Mojave Desert. Probably there are. But a zombie knows its best chance of finding brains to eat will be where people are packed as tight as they can be (and paying through the nose for it, no less).

Now before you go into a diatribe about how not everyone can live in a big city and how there are many positive aspects to a rural existence, hear this loud and clear: I am not suggesting that you must live in a city to find love. At least, not necessarily . . .

What I am suggesting is that you do need to look for the kind of person you want to meet in the kind of place where that person lives. This doesn't automatically mean you need to pick up stakes, but you should consider the benefits of focusing your efforts on a target-rich-environment.

If you're idea of an ideal mate is someone who works in publishing, television, or art auctioneering, someone who likes to dress in black, and someone who enjoys live theater, then yes, you may be heading off for the Big Apple. But there are plenty of other qualities worth seeking. Your list may be very general (liberal or conservative, introverted or extroverted, outgoing or a homebody), or painstakingly specific (I want to meet an Orthodox Jewish dentist who enjoys Indian food and reads Saul Bellow). Whatever the case, you need to begin by asking yourself, honestly, where you are likely to find these types. Otherwise, you're just wasting your time. Frequently, just the smallest adjustment can yield results to make any zombie proud.

If you've always wanted to date a cop, but you spend your evenings in a bar where criminals congregate, your chances of meeting a handsome young police officer are pretty limited (at least, an off-duty one). If, on the other hand, you try the cop bar by the police station, your chances of success increase greatly.

If you want to meet a reader, go to the bookstore. (If you want to meet a broke-ass reader, try the library).

Someone athletic, hit the gym.

Many of us might like to imagine that someone who's a perfect match for us will just fall into our laps one day, or ride up on a white horse. But when you get tired of waiting, make like a zombie and go to where the targets are. You'll be glad you did.

To Recap:

Zombies know the catch is well worth the chase.

Zombies are up front about who they are, and what they need.

Zombies are dogged in their pursuit.

Zombies stick to a target-rich-environment.

To prepare for your next romantic encounter, whenever it happens, you need to prep yourself for the world of dating as a zombie.

Zombie History

Those who do not study history are doomed to repeat it, and when you're up against the undead you could be repeating it for a very long time. In this chapter you will learn not only about the great moments in zombie history, but also learn the truth about some historical figures that may not have been as alive as you think.

Construction of Stonehenge in Ancient England

While no one knows exactly who the Druids were (or what they were doin'), ancient British zombies were prescient enough to understand that building a confusing stone obelisk would be enough to bring edible humans to an otherwise empty stretch of land. (This, being before cities existed in northern England, was actually less effort than trekking down to London.) To this day, the odd tourist is lost to the zombies who still frequent the spot.

Construction of the Pyramids in Ancient Egypt

Though some historians still profess to be "baffled" at how ancient man could have had the sufficient technology, motivation, and endurance to create these monuments to the dead (clue), more open-minded anthropologists have long understood that the implementation of zombie-labor could be an important missing ingredient. (This was, of course, prior to the great Zombie–Mummy rift, when it became apparent to all that mummies were just unambitious rich kids who wanted to play in their enormous houses but never wanted to come outside and try actually **working** for a living.)

Destruction of the Knights Templar

Saracen invaders and Papal conspiracies tend to dominate modern theories as to the extinction of this ancient order, but few know that the "Knights of Malta" actually retreated to their island as a defense against zombies more than anything else. (This defense was not effective.)

Disappearance of Amelia Earhart

Stowaway zombie.

Loss of Ocean Liner "Titanic"

Stowaway zombies (navigator eaten).

Jebus

People get sensitive when you bring **Jebus** into things, especially things like zombies. The hypothesis that **Jebus** himself might have been a zombie (and the corresponding religion he founded something like a zombie-cult) is just too radical for most people even to consider. So instead of asserting anything directly, let's just look at some facts and let people make up their own minds:

Everyone agrees that the big J is known to have died, stayed dead for three days, and then to have been magically reanimated to walk the earth once again. That is to say, he rose from the dead.

He was known to raise the dead himself when it suited his purposes.

Zombie Tip—If you see the Buddha on the road, kill him: Specifically, by eating his brain.

Jebus wore rags, sandals, and had an unkempt beard. (Zombies are also known to appear in this fashion.)

Jebus was attacked on sight by the "authorities" of his day, who regarded him as "dangerous" and "a threat to society."

When he was put to death, a "regular" execution simply wouldn't do the trick. It took a "special procedure" to keep him down.

Jebus had a crew of 12 others like him, and they traveled together and worked as a team.

His people stumbled through the desert.
He taught that everyone can be, in a sense, resurrected.
His followers were frequently covered with open wounds and sores.
He could apparently traverse water without drowning.
Jebus *was never really in a hurry. He didn't run a lot. Slow and steady won the race, wherever he was going.*

The organization founded in his honor maintains blood-drinking and flesh-eating rituals to this day.

Important religious works of art in his tradition have shown God endowing humanity with the gift of . . . **brains**.

He is known to have been "fathered" or "created" under mysterious, unnatural circumstances.

*To this day, followers of **Jebus** are still known to congregate in malls.*

Finally, the religion **Jebus** founded has a way of catching on. It gets passed from person to person. "Conversions" seem to be involved, and so forth. A member "infects" non-members, making them like himself. Then it spreads exponentially. Like a virus.

The late Gerald Ford is rumored to have been a zombie for the last several years of his "life."

The famously "soft-spoken" Calvin Coolidge was actually a very talkative zombie.

Terrifying 1960s film actor Tor Johnson was, of course, a zombie—though atypical in at least one important way. (Most humans *lose* weight when zombified . . .)

Anna Nicole Smith . . . Towards the end . . . Yeah . . .

Actor and Republican political strategist Ben Stein has built his entire career aping the diction and tone of a zombie.

Al Gore has lulled many a political opponent into a false sense of calm using zombie-based speech patterns.

At least one "surviving" member of the Rolling Stones is a very high functioning zombie.

Rob Zombie is, however, not a **zombie**.

A Lost History of the Walking Dead

Several years ago, through a series of coincidences, a manuscript came into my possession which you will see excerpted in this chapter. (It has also been thoughtfully published in its entirety under the title *Zombies vs. Nazis: A Lost History of the Walking Dead.*)

While the annals of history are full of confirmed or likely instances of zombie attack, this account seems especially salient to students of the undead for several reasons.

That—at the height of their power—the Nationalsozialistische Deutsche Arbeiterpartei might have sought to harness the awesome power of the zombie as a nefarious tool of warfare is hardly surprising. However, as this newly uncovered account makes clear, the remarkable missteps and hubris of the Nazis doomed their enterprise before it had even begun.

To approach zombies with anything other than the awe, respect, and fear they are inherently due is the height of folly. The German agents in this account failed to accord zombies anything approaching the appropriate level of deference, and so failed completely.

By seeking to subjugate zombies as servants of the Third Reich, the Nazis showed a complete lack of understanding of the very things that make zombies so great in the first place. Zombies will serve nobody. They will attack everybody. But they will especially attack those who attempt to subjugate or use them.

The Nazis had no excuse for not knowing this. Within the excerpted text, we see their familiarity with the 1932 film White Zombie, an excellent example of the problems that can arise when zombies are subjugated or used to further the desires of others.

What the Nazis did not see—as villains never do—is that zombies are an unstoppable force of individualism and self-reliance. Their goals and desires are their own. When zombies act in such a way that your own goals are furthered (like, maybe they eat one of your enemies or something), it is only ever by coincidence. Zombies cannot be induced to join your side, and they can never be forced to participate in anything they wouldn't do anyway. One can hardly blame the Nazis for dreaming about controlling so powerful and awe-inspiring a force as the legion of the undead. But a dream it must remain.

This account, then, should make clear the implacable, unbending nature of the zombie. And the folly of those who—against all better judgement, and all the evidence of history—still insist upon trying to make zombies work for them.

Because, it's like, dude, that's never going to happen.

Communication 8

March 2, 1940
From: Oswaldt Gehrin
To: Reinhard Heydrich

My Obergruppenführer,

This letter contains details of our first encounter with an actual zombie. It verifies many hypotheses formulated at the outset of this mission, and disproves others. Most importantly (obviously), it verifies that zombies actually exist. Yet, as we saw that night on Bell's Hill, it also potentially amends our definition of what a zombie actually is.

Perhaps, my dear Obergruppenführer, you are familiar with the popular filmed entertainment *White Zombie*? It was released by an American movie studio in 1932 and features Mr. Béla Lugosi. I must confess that I, like many Germans, first formed my impression of zombies from viewing this film. (I enjoyed it greatly, seeing it more than a few times at the theater in Baden-Baden.) In *White Zombie*, the reanimated bodies lorded over by Mr. Lugosi's character were like robotic automatons. They stumbled forward slowly, their eyes unfocused, their senses numbed. Lugosi was able to command them, and they displayed perfect obedience to him. These zombies obeyed without question, like robots wearing the skins of dead men. (The application for such a perfectly obedient soldier in the cause of the Reich is, of course, easy to see.) These zombies would serve him, kill for him, or march themselves to certain doom at his bidding. *They were frightening because they could be commanded to kill, and they could not be reasoned with once given this command.*

I must report, however, that the actual zombie is even more troubling, alarming, and horrible to behold than those of Mr. Lugosi's film!

Just as the first sightings of mermaids by explorers in the New World were in fact only charitable descriptions of sea cows, so have descriptions of the zombie been rosily colored by the lens of the fabulist (and the lens of the Hollywood movie camera). The zombie that accosted Inspector Baedecker and myself was *very different* than the well-appointed butlers, obedient footmen, and sturdy millworkers portrayed in American films. In truth, Obergruppenführer, when described in total, the nature of the zombie we encountered may be shocking to you. Prepare yourself.

To set the scene: Inspector Baedecker and I had been waiting for some time under cover of camouflage when two shadowy figures approached our position on the hill. One was an older man of curious mien. His hair was long and braided into thick strands. He wore a dark apron around his waist, and his feet were entirely bare. His chest was bare also, save for the adornment of several rope necklaces that held strange ebon talismans that dangled together in a cluster. The heavy clack of these wooden ornaments told of his approach even before he came into view. (They seemed to weigh him down. I guessed they could not be worn for aesthetic pleasure but doubtless served some other purpose.) The old man gripped a metal chain, by which he led his partner, who stumbled like a drunkard and moaned audibly.

Its eyes! My god, how can I describe the sight? There was no life in them. They rolled madly in their sockets in a way no living human's do—and yet they saw! (My skin crawled when the zombie's idiot stare chanced upon me. My blood chilled. My stomach knotted.) The zombie's rotting cloak was worm-eaten and reeked of a lengthy internment *beneath the soil*. Odors wafted upward, and from my elevated perch I smelled the horrible fumes of rot and decay that do not accompany the living. Yet most disgusting of all was its mouth. Between hideous low moans, the thing gnashed its teeth and slavered strands of drool that glistened in the light of the gibbous moon. It was a mouth that no longer spoke coherently yet longed to express some inexpressible inner longing that made the zombie stagger on.

It was with some courage that I descended from my spot and engaged the pair. (Inspector Baedecker was closer to our visitors, but instead of revealing himself, he took to shaking quite violently as they neared. As the man and his zombie paused to examine the large oscillating bush, I was able to approach them.)

I emerged from the foliage and identified myself as a visiting lepidopterist, in search of nocturnal Monarch butterflies.

The Haitian man's first words, delivered in a thick accent, were an inquiry as to whether the vibrating bush nearby had anything to do with my research. As carefully and clearly as I could, I assured him that this was the case, and explained that the odd vibrations were related to my scientific experiments.

As we spoke, the zombie—whom he held at the end of a chain like a dog—slavered and salivated in my direction. Several times, the thing extended its arms as if to snatch my clothing (or scratch my throat), and each time had to be restrained by its handler.

Feigning ignorance, I thanked him for his concern on my behalf. Then, cautiously, I asked after the "man" on the chain, inquiring as to whether he might be insane, a criminal, or suffering from a tropical brain fever.

My ignorance seemed genuine, and it was with some amusement that our guest cautioned me that some things were better left unprobed. I quickly convinced him that, as a man of science, I took an objective and detached interest in the man who gibbered and snarled next to us. Our guest soon relented and imparted in hushed tones that the thing on the chain was indeed a zombie.

At this, the bush next to us vibrated again, and it took additional efforts on my part to convincingly attribute the motions to a nocturnal butterfly mating ritual. When this was accomplished—and the vibrations had subsided somewhat—I asked our guest why it was that a zombie should be led through Bell's Hill in the middle of the night. He smiled—even as the zombie bucked and strained in his grasp—and gave a sly reply, saying that an important religious event was to take place nearby. When I asked about the chain—wondering if the zombie was being punished (or was uncharacteristically aggressive)—the shirtless Haitian laughed and responded that if I was a man of science (as I claimed), I was not a very good one. Zombies, he explained, were known for an innate aggressiveness and propensity toward cannibalism upon the living.

"I have heard of zombies sent as agents of murder," I explained to the man, "but you are saying that a zombie will attack humans in its . . . *default* state, without being directly ordered to do so?"

My visitor replied in the affirmative.

Yet when I pressed for more detail, his good-natured demeanor soured substantially, and he refused to speak further, hurrying away into the night (his wild-eyed, groaning zombie trailing after him).

Not wishing to abandon the constrained Inspector Baedecker, I elected to remain as our guests departed. Though no further surveillance was essayed that evening, several important and useful advances in our research have been made.

While it may be the case that the zombie we encountered was somehow atypical or anomalous in its aggressiveness, it is more likely that the aggressiveness of the zombie has gone underreported. This may be due to unreliable reporting, attempts at "cultural sensitivity," or the simple fact that those who have encountered these creatures in their typically aggressive state have not survived the encounter. (Indeed, even as I prepare these very words for the encryption machine, I shudder to recall the horrible look on that zombie's face. Its rolling, soulless eyes seemed to look into horrible distances beyond mortal imagining. Its teeth gnashed like a rabid animal's. Its hands were like talons, and they gestured violently as if to rip the air. It seemed capable of anything.)

Other questions are also raised by our encounter. Why did the zombie not attack its handler? Did the zombie understand verbal commands? (If so, to what degree?) Was it like a dog, able to comprehend a few basic words, or was it more like a human? Did it follow our conversation, or did it understand nothing of what we said? Did the metal collar and chain restrain the zombie, or were they merely used so that passersby would not be alarmed?

Clearly, we have more to learn, and our investigations here must continue.

It is my cautious hypothesis that while zombies still maintain the potential to be of great use to the Reich, in light of these events, we may have to reevaluate the specific role we expect them to play.

Yours respectfully,
Oswaldt Gehrin

Communication 11

April 3, 1940
From: Oswaldt Gehrin
To: Reinhard Heydrich

My Obergruppenführer,

I am pleased to report that our team has made additional contact with Haitian zombies. The salient details of this encounter run thusly:

After the successful encounter of March the second, subsequent overnight watches on Bell's Hill resulted in no less than three sightings in a four-week period. I write "sightings" because only in the final instance did I and Inspector Baedecker—who exudes a general reluctance to act hastily—interact with the zombies in question.

In the first encounter, we spied a team of armed men transporting what appeared to be a group of prisoners. The group was shackled in the manner of a work gang, and their chains rattled as they approached our hiding places. As they drew near, I amended my guess and wondered if it could be a group of insane being transported to an asylum. (Of course, my hope was that this guess would be wrong and we would see that they were in fact zombies!) The chained men gibbered and drooled like maniacs, and the guards urged them along with the butts of rifles—correcting their loping trajectories when they wandered off their path. At the rear of the phalanx, we saw a stout woman who fit the descriptions of one steeped in Voodoo. She wore a headdress of beads and feathers, and clothes embroidered with wild patterns and bright colors. Around her neck was a rope from which a carved wooden figure dangled and danced upon her duggardly chest. Though the men around her prodded the chained figures, I saw that it was her own verbal urgings (sometimes augmented by a cane bearing the freshly decapitated head of a chicken) that truly urged the shambling parade forward. It was then that I understood for certain that these were not conscripts or schizophrenics, but fifteen or twenty *zombies* who were being transported past Bell's Hill (in, I noted, the same direction that our previous zombie had stumbled). I was intrigued, and strongly desired to interact with the group—as did Inspector Baedecker, or so I guessed from his excited vibrations— but we were outnumbered, both by zombies and armed guards. I reasoned that if the group should prove unfriendly, our Lugers might not be enough to protect us. Thus, we allowed the parade to pass unmolested. (Though there *was* a point when the Voodoo woman seemed to look directly at my position on the tree branch. Yet she did not acknowledge having seen me, and only smiled to herself . . .)

The second encounter occurred at the end of an evening's watch that had yielded no zombies (or passersby of any kind). I had removed myself from my arboreal post, Inspector Baedecker had extricated himself from his complicated foliage costume, and we were in the process of departing from Bell's Hill to return to our headquarters to sleep. Dawn was breaking around us as we walked, and this natural illumination allowed Inspector Baedecker to notice a group of five or six figures—who lumbered with the loosey-goosey gait of the zombie—silhouetted against the blue-gray dawn at the top of the hill. He alerted me to their presence with a more-than-adequate shriek. This allowed me to turn and follow his shaking finger as it reached, outstretched and trembling, toward the cavorting zombies. This group appeared at first to be unaccompanied, but upon closer inspection, we saw what has become a familiar sight: a human draped in the loud and unusual attire of the Voodoo practitioner bringing up the rear. Inspector Baedecker and I attempted to pursue this group, who soon lumbered out of sight; but by the time we reached the spot where they had been, all that remained were muddy footprints, a few scraps of torn clothing, and feathers from what must have been a very small bird. (Not a chicken.) Although it did not involve direct interaction with zombies, we felt this encounter was important because it established that the zombies can move about during daylight hours. The (presumably) mythological vampire, for example, is known to avoid sunlight on peril of destruction. Zombies are usually seen at night, but do they harbor similar nocturnal limitations? It appears that no, they do not. For as the morning sun fell on these undead subjects, they exhibited no discomfiture or alarm. Why, then, do we not see more zombies during the day? This is a question that remains to be solved. (I am confident, however, that this means a zombie army in service of the Reich would be able to attack, say, France, as effectively during daylight hours as it could after the sun has gone down.)

The final encounter was the most remarkable, and hints at deeper things, which we may be on the cusp of discovering.

It happened near midnight on the night before last. Inspector Baedecker and I were observing Bell's Hill from our customary positions when two figures came into view. The first was a hoary old man who waddled slowly and carefully. Around his neck were several of the totems of a Voodoo priest. He strode through the forest astern a single frail zombie who had sunken eyes and a great gaping mouth. On first spying them, I exchanged an excited glance with the bush that was Baedecker and readied my Luger. Here, finally, was a group we might overpower if we so wished. The older man was obviously unarmed, and the zombie looked as though it posed no threat that could not be contained by two hale Aryan men.

Unified in our purposes, Baedecker and I emerged from our covers at the same moment and confronted the figures, our weapons drawn. The waddling old shaman paused, and so did the zombie. (Near to the cadaverous thing, the horrible rot of the grave assailed my nostrils, and I wondered how the old man stood it.) Before anyone could speak, the old shaman began to remove something from his pocket. Mistaking this for a hostile gesture— for it was later revealed that he was merely reaching for a flask containing clarin, a native rum of crude distillation—Baedecker suddenly squeezed the trigger of his Luger, and the shaman fell to the ground, dead as a stone.

"Oh . . . ," declared Baedecker when the consequences of his action became clear to us. "Whoops."

Our human guest no longer with us, we turned our attention to the zombie. Its deep-set eyes were trained forward, unfocused, and it seemed not to regard us. It showed no aggression, and apparently failed even to notice that its handler had been executed.

"Well, it's not attacking us," I said, stating the obvious.

"What do we do now?" Baedecker asked, looking the zombie up and down.

"Can we take it with us?" I offered. "If we could safely transport the zombie back to our headquarters, I could take blood and tissue samples. We could then verify the claims of those who suggest the zombie is created through medical means, such as the introduction of a toxin to the living or the recently deceased. With the shaman dead, *Baedecker*, we have no way of extracting any secrets from *him*."

"Yes, but . . . ," Baedecker began, and paused.

"But what?" I asked.

"But he hasn't got chains or a rope around his neck like some of the others did. How do we get him to follow us?"

"He looks light enough to carry," I said. Baedecker blanched, and I must confess I shared his revulsion at the notion of carrying the stinking, desiccated thing for any length of time.

Then, as if magically sensing our conundrum, the zombie began to shuffle forward. It moved slowly at first, as if merely stepping to correct its balance. But other small corrections followed. Soon they expanded into steps. The zombie then shuffled past us and followed the dirt trail into the forest.

"What do we do now?" Baedecker asked. "It's getting away."

"Well . . . very slowly, I suppose," I rejoined. "Let's follow it. Maybe it will show us something."

And so, Baedecker—still in the semblance of a small moving coppice—began to follow the zombie into the forest paths leading off from Bell's Hill. I went with him. It was strange work, like following a sleepwalking person. The zombie seemed largely unaware of our presence, and we strove not to "break the spell" that now made it ambulatory.

We walked deep into the forest. At every turn, the zombie displayed that it knew just where it wanted to go. It never hesitated when called to choose this or that trail. With supreme confidence, it directed us off the main trails and conducted us along smaller and smaller paths running deeper into the jungle. Soon we found that we traversed a path that might have been too small for a horse. Being a wide man in a costume, Baedecker began having some difficulty fitting past the underbrush.

After perhaps an hour of walking—with no discernable discoveries—we stopped behind the zombie and considered how to proceed.

"We have seen nothing," Baedecker pointed out. "I've changed my mind. Let us simply grab the zombie by force and take it back to our headquarters, as you originally suggested. It looks light enough."

"Wait a moment," I said. "Do you hear that?"

I cupped my ear. So did Baedecker. It seemed that on the edge of hearing, a deep and regular pounding echoed through the night. Who knew how long it had been there? Our own footsteps had drowned it out as we walked.

"It is a distant motor," Baedecker declaimed. "It is that, or the operation of machines in a factory."

"In the jungle . . . in the middle of the night?" I asked.

"Perhaps thunder, then, reverberating through the hills," Baedecker offered.

"But look," I said, pointing down at the zombie's feet.

The shambling cadaver, now a few yards ahead of us, was moving in time to the distant beat. For each resounding note, the zombie took another careful step.

"No . . . ," said Baedecker, doubting what we saw. "It is surely a coincidence of some kind."

"It is not," I countered. "He is no Kreutzberg or Wigman, but surely, this zombie dances to a beat!"

We regarded the zombie very closely. Its limbs moved in perfect time to the rhythm that resounded softly through the foliage around us. I soon saw from his face that Baedecker no longer doubted their connection.

"So what, then?" Baedecker said, after the zombie had danced forward a few more paces.

"Is he moving in the direction of the drums, drawn to them?" I wondered aloud. "Or do they command him to some other place, to some other task? I tell you, Baedecker, we will learn something valuable if we continue to follow him! If zombies are made into weapons for the purposes of the Reich, we will surely need to learn to control them. A drumbeat may be the very thing! Imagine giant radio speakers—perhaps mounted on airships or planes—beaming a beat to battalions of these creatures as they march across Belgium and France! What we learn tonight may be more valuable than what could be learned through the mere vivisection of a zombie."

"You are resolved, then, that we follow it farther?" Baedecker said, sounding disappointed.

I indicated in the affirmative.

Then the remarkable thing!

The zombie, who had lumbered no more than twenty yards down the jungle path—and was moving at the speed of an arthritic pensioner—was suddenly gone. When we looked up from our conference, the thing had disappeared completely.

"What?" I cried. "Where did it go? The zombie was there not a moment before!"

"It must have veered into the underbrush," declared Baedecker. My fellow inspector charged forward down the narrow trail to the point where we had last noticed our guide. There was nothing to see, but Baedecker continued to hunt madly for the zombie. I joined him, and we searched the woods as well as we could with our flashlights, yet our electric beams could never penetrate far into the dense Haitian undergrowth.

"There's no sign of him," my companion concluded.

"There is some mystery here, Baedecker," I said.

"Unless the thing broke into a sprint when our heads were turned," my companion rejoined.

"That seems unlikely," I said. "It looked as if it would shake apart if it attempted more than a jog."

"Should we continue down the path?" Baedecker asked.

I must here confess that despite the brave traditions from which I am wrought, I felt some trepidation at the thought of continuing farther into the dark jungle. I had only a general idea of where we were in relation to Bell's Hill and did not want to become lost. It would be difficult to gauge our position exactly until dawn.

Even as I paused to consider our next move, the beat in the distance continued to reverberate across the jungle.

"We shall continue down the path," I said to Baedecker. My confidence returned, and I reminded myself that a man of the Third Reich—the most advanced society in the world—could hardly have something to fear from a land of superstition.

"It is interesting to think," I observed to Baedecker as we strolled onward, "how it is that a society as primitive as the Haitian has stumbled upon so profound a secret as that of bodily possession and reanimation."

"Perhaps they are not as primitive as they look," Baedecker replied, having little use, apparently, for our Führer's wise opinions of the races.

"Nonsense," I countered. "Even a stopped clock is right twice a day, and even a fool sometimes hits upon an answer through sheer luck. Perhaps it is their proximity to the jungle itself that has given the Voodooists the luck of creating zombies first. This notion has always supported my hypothesis that it is a natural extract of some sort—derived from indigenous Haitian flora or fauna—that allows the Voodoo priests to create his zombies. Anyway, look at what the Haitians have done with it. By God! They have hit on the means of resurrecting the dead, and yet, have they used this power to assert their dominance in the region, or to extract a tribute from the Dominican Republic? No! They lack the intelligence and drive to use this power for any ambitious purpose."

"I do not know . . . ," replied Baedecker, his eyes downcast. "These Haitians may be wiser than you think. If we knew the secrets of zombies, perhaps we would not use them so freely either."

And with this absurdity, I raised my hand. (Initially, I did so to silence my companion's heretical speech, but in the space that ensued, we both discovered something.)

The noise was louder now. And there could be no doubt about what it was: the slow beating of many drums.

"What can this mean?" I asked. "Drums in the middle of the jungle . . . in the middle of the night?"

"These are like none I ever heard," Baedecker said. "No timpani or field drum has ever sounded thusly."

Suddenly, I spied movement in the jungle ahead of us and turned on my electric torch.

"Look!" I cried. Baedecker looked, and we both had time to see our slow-moving zombie friend pass just out of view, perhaps forty yards down the path.

"That's him," Baedecker said. "And he is clearly drawn to the drums."

I nervously extinguished my torch, and we continued after the zombie. It seemed now that the drumming grew louder—and more frequent?—with each step we took.

We fell silent. (Baedecker's insubordinately high opinion of the Haitian people needed further correction, certainly, but we both sensed that it was no longer appropriate to chat.)

The zombie came back into view. He was—for a zombie—moving quickly now (at close to the gait of a normal living person).

We began to see the flicker of large fires through the trees ahead of us. There was motion too. It seemed almost that the trees themselves bent and danced in the firelight.

"Bonfires?" whispered Baedecker.

The drums were very loud now. Multiple hands (or drummer's wands) clapped down with every beat, and the rhythms intensified. I estimated there were ten or fifteen drummers at least, all playing in perfect unison.

"And people," I added. "There are people just ahead of us."

I quickly understood that our project had once again changed. As the zombie danced ponderously toward the unseen drummers and conflagrations, I took Baedecker by the shoulder.

"It may not be safe to venture any farther," I told him. "But surely, we have found a site of importance to our research. I think the most prudent course of action would be to return to headquarters—carefully noting our route, of course—and to then return during daylight to inspect the site further for evidence and information."

Baedecker quickly indicated that my plan met with his approval.

"And yet," I added after a moment's reconsideration, "it might also be sensible to essay a glimpse of the proceedings, if we can do so safely."

Here, Baedecker dissented.

"No," I told him. "Having come this far, we must at least attempt an unobstructed view. Likely, some exciting ritual is taking place. Here, follow me into the underbrush."

We stepped off of the narrow trail and into the wet, sultry underbrush. I fell to my hands and knees—Baedecker did the same—and we began a careful crawl in the direction of the lights and percussive noises. The sound of the pounding increased with each step. (I mentally revised my previous estimates. There were thirty drummers at least—if not forty or fifty.) Our view was obstructed because of our semi-prone positions, but it seemed to me that I saw figures dancing in the shadows of the flames before us. These shadows, I decided, were men in masks, for their heads seemed unnaturally large and resembled those of animals more than men. As we drew even closer to the gathering, I smelled smoke, incense, and the scent of many people.

Edging closer still, I realized that the way forward was now directly obstructed by a boulder.

"Come, Baedecker," I said. "Secrets are ready to reveal themselves on the other side of this rock. Let us crawl around to the other side."

There was no answer.

"Baedecker?" I tried.

I looked behind myself and saw that my companion had suddenly disappeared.

I scanned the woods for him but detected no trace of my colleague. (I did not wish to risk using my electric torch so close to the gathering.)

Obviously, Baedecker's disappearance disconcerted me greatly, but I resolved that this journey should not be for naught. By hook or by crook, I would see what strangeness cavorted and drummed on the other side of the great boulder in my path! Edging my way around it, I began to detect bright flickering torchlight, the figures of dancing men, and the uniform motions of an array of drummers playing in unison like horrible, mindless automatons.

It was then that I heard footsteps behind me. I managed to make a half turn before the blow to my head rendered me unconscious.

I awoke at dawn, in surroundings that were momentarily unfamiliar. Next to me on the ground was Inspector Baedecker, heaped like a giant mound but, to my relief, still noticeably breathing. He had been stripped of his camouflage costume and wore only his trousers and nightshirt.

I stood and surveyed our arboreal surroundings. With great relief, I realized that we were back at the foot of Bell's Hill. Had we stumbled back under our own power? No. Several sets of muddy footprints leading away told the story of our having been carried back from the site of the ritual. (There were, I probably do not need to observe, a good many more sets of prints leading away from Baedecker than from myself.)

I walked over to Baedecker, intending to rouse him. Then I looked down into his face and beheld it. Ghastly mutilation!

Or . . . mutilation of a sort. For clearly, a lock of the inspector's hair had been crudely chopped away from the right side of his face, leaving his bluish white scalp exposed to the morning sun.

I roused him—at which he gave an awful start—and asked if he had any memories of the events of the previous evening. Like mine, his recollections grew fuzzy after we began crawling toward the drums and fires, and ended with complete unconsciousness. To my considerable disappointment, his memories proved no more useful than mine.

We returned to our headquarters and inspected ourselves for any other signs of injury, but found none. Other than painful bumps to the head (and Baedecker's unusual barbering), we have not been noticeably harmed.

We spent today recovering from this event. Tomorrow, we will attempt a daylight return to the site of the ritual. For whatever reason, the close encounter seems to have raised Inspector Baedecker's spirits. (He is normally given to not-inconsiderable bellyaching and complaining about our mission, living situation, and progress. However, an uncharacteristic calm has settled over him, and he remains nearly silent.)

We strongly believe that this encounter means that we are on the cusp of important steps forward in our research here. None of us doubt that we are close to something big!

Yours respectfully,
Oswaldt Gehrin

Communication 16

April 25, 1940
From: Oswaldt Gehrin
To: Reinhard Heydrich

My Obergruppenführer,

I have exciting—and troubling—findings to report in this update. Our investigation continues to take remarkable turns. First, I must relate that I have been successful in my quest to kill (or, perhaps, to "kill") the zombie grandfather of the university student Mayonette.

As you will recall, Mayonette had indicated the locations where his grandfather had recently been seen and had provided a description of the man. (It can be difficult to distinguish one zombie from another when they are in stages of advanced age or deterioration. Luckily for me, the zombie in question possessed a defining feature. He had no nose. It had been lost in childhood during an altercation with a wild dog. And while noselessness can arise from an older zombie's advanced decomposition, Mayonette assured me that I would know his grandfather when I saw him. And indeed I did.)

After just three nights' surveillance of a spot indicated by Mayonette (an abandoned outpost near a shuttered copper mine), I chanced to encounter the zombie I sought. He was just as had been described—the marks where canine teeth had taken his nose were unmistakable!—and he was alone.

I did not hesitate; I emerged from the underbrush with my Luger drawn. The zombie noticed me and lumbered forward aggressively. Ever the scientist, I did not kill it right away. Instead, I tested Mayonette's assertions about a zombie's points of vulnerability by leveling several shots at the creature's lower body. Great puffs of dust exploded as my bullets connected, and the zombie stumbled as the slugs disturbed its balance—but *it did not go down!* After a moment, it righted itself and walked as normally as it had before. It was only when I leveled my weapon at its head and fired that it seemed to be incapacitated (collapsing in a heap, exactly like a human who has been killed).

Under the conditions of our agreement, Mayonette would allow me to perform a full scientific postmortem on his grand-father's body. However, he first required me to bring the dead zombie to his grandmother's home so that—he said—they could verify that I had killed the correct one.

I placed the zombie in a thick burlap sack to insulate myself from its horrible fetor and ghastly appearance, and then hefted the sack over my shoulder. (Perhaps due to years of rot, it was surprisingly light.) Following my map, I returned to the hovel of Mayonette's grandmother. It was in the early morning hours when I arrived, but there was light from several lanterns flickering inside. Assuming Mayonette and his grandmother were still up and about, I knocked forcefully on the door.

"Hello," I called. "It is the professor! I have succeeded in my little task. Come and look."

Here, I hefted the burlap sack off of my shoulder, and it thudded to the ground before me.

No sooner had I done so than I heard the hasty unfastening of a crude metal latch. The door opened cautiously, and I was confronted by a hulking figure who was neither Mayonette nor his grandmother. The tall, wide man (who was perhaps thirty years old), appeared to be a native Haitian. He had deep crevassed scars across his face and wore a headdress bedecked with feathers from a cock. A strong smell of incense escaped through the doorway past him and assailed me. It was not unpleasant.

The man's expression, however, was. (I counted it a fifty-fifty balance of confusion and anger.)

"Hello," I said to him. "Is young Jean Mayonette—or perhaps his grandmother—at home? I have something of importance to deliver."

No sooner had the words escaped my mouth than two other gentlemen—of nearly identical age, scarring, and plumage—joined their compatriot at the door. They exchanged expressions of alarm and spoke to one another in a dialect with which I was wholly unfamiliar. (Note to RSHA Western Hemisphere Team: There may be more dialects, or even *languages*, among the Haitian Voodooists than our intelligence currently indicates.)

I attempted to explain myself, but the men became aggressive before I could finish my tale. One produced a pistol and pointed it in my direction. (Though I possessed a weapon of my own, I saw no reason to escalate the situation. I believed their anger was the result of some misunderstanding.) I raised my hands, palms outward, and began slowly backing away.

One of the large men leaned forward to investigate the burlap sack. When he had opened it enough to ascertain what was contained inside, he shouted in alarm. Then even more figures—I lost count, perhaps six or seven—emerged from the small house. All regarded the dead zombie in alarm. Their faces curled from confusion into rage, and several gestured in my direction. Sensing my options dwindling, I turned and ran into the nearest outcropping of underbrush, sprinting as fast as my legs would carry me. Some of the men followed, and at least one fired shots my way. Yet none of the bullets connected, and I evaded my pursuers by hiding in a tree until dawn.

This morning, I went directly to the university seeking to confront Mayonette. Not finding him on campus, I visited the registrar's office to inquire about his academic schedule in hopes of intercepting the lad on his way to class. Imagine my shock, Obergruppenführer, when it was revealed to me that *no student named Mayonette is enrolled at the university*. I also visited with the faculty members of the biology department. Individually and to a man, they claimed ignorance of a student named Mayonette (or any well-spoken student with a striking harelip).

As you can imagine, aspects of this encounter have been profoundly upsetting to me. We have, however, learned more about zombies (specifically, their temperament and vulnerability) than we knew before. Whilst we did not end the day with a specimen fit for dissection, we have been able to observe important behaviors in the field. Thus, I cannot say it has been an entirely bootless endeavor.

When I made my report of these events to Inspector Knecht, he suggested that we should return to Mayonette's house as a group and perform further reconnaissance. However, I pointed out that even with our entire squad present, we might still be outnumbered by hostile persons. Knecht eventually agreed with me, and I believe he is now considering alternative courses of action.

Yours respectfully,
Oswaldt Gehrin

Communication 20

May 18, 1940
From: Gunter Knecht
To: <u>Reinhard Heydrich</u>

<u>Obergruppenführer,</u>

I am pleased to report that I have witnessed a remarkable ritual that I believe sheds further light on our understanding of the Voodoo zombie. The unfortunate loss of Inspector Baedecker notwithstanding, we continue to make substantive progress here in the country. (I received your instructions not to bother myself with further searches for Baedecker's whereabouts. You are right, of course. He is probably dead.)

My witnessing of the important ritual occurred thusly: Voicing my continued interest in his "cause" (e.g., preventing another anti-Voodoo uprising), I gradually inveigled my way into the further confidences of Father Gill. Insisting that additional knowledge of the subject would allow me to better assist him, I argued that I must be allowed to meet with a Bocor personally and, if possible, see the creation of a zombie firsthand. After much argument and hand wringing (on Gill's part, obviously), he admitted that such a thing could be arranged, and an agreement between us was eventually struck. Yet even at high noon on the day appointed—as we walked from his residence to the secret location where this meeting would take place—Gill still seemed to harbor reservations.

"My dear Jesuit," he asked with some hesitation, "as it may pertain to today's proceedings, may I inquire into your degree of . . . worldly experience upon joining the order?"

Somewhat puzzled, I repeated the dossier of the fictional life of the Jesuit I am supposed to be.

"I see . . . ," Gill said after I had concluded my lengthy auto-biography. "I think I can say, then, that it is safe to assume that marriage to a woman was never in your past?"

Pretending to be shocked and astounded by his impertinence, I said, "Father Gill, I am shocked and astounded by your imperti-nence! Such a question! I have always lived my life in accordance to the wishes of the Lord and messages I received from the Holy Spirit."

"Understood . . . understood . . . ," said Gill, waving away my well-acted protestations. "And yet I hope you will not be offended if I divulge the fact that I cannot claim the same honor. For you see, I was married briefly to a girl in County Cork many years ago. She was tragically lost in an accident, and it was then that I took up the cloth."

"My condolences," I offered cautiously.

"The point being," Gill said slowly, "I have found in my own life that certain things that I surrounded mentally with mystery, awe, fascination—including, in my case, the physical act of love with a woman—proved, upon consummation, to be less sensa-tional than I had made them out to be."

"Are you saying that you are concerned that zombies will somehow fail to live up to my expectations?" I asked.

Gill tapped his forehead with his fingers and considered.

"I am concerned," Gill said, "because once the mystery is dispelled—and you have seen a zombie for the first time—you must then decide what to do with this information. Will it chal-lenge your faith? Will you stay true to your commitments? Only time will tell. But if your presence in this country is maintained only by a fascination with the unworldly mystery of the zombie, I advise you to rethink this meeting. What you know of zombies will be forever changed a few minutes from now . . . unless you change your mind and walk away."

Before I could answer Gill, and promptly dismiss the asinine "concerns" he had raised, we were distracted by a pair of men walking toward us. Or rather, I was distracted.

The men, who were elderly and of wizened demeanor (one leaned awkwardly with each step on an ancient crutch), wore thin shawls over their shoulders to shade themselves from the heat of the sun. Yet I noted instantly that one of the shawls seemed to be made of *the original forest costume that once belonged to Inspector Baedecker*. Gill noticed my distraction.

"These men approaching us are connected to the practice of Voodoo," I said quietly to my companion. "Do not ask how it is that I know."

"Yes," Gill all but stammered. "My dear Jesuit, you continue to surprise me. Yes. Those men are not intimately known to me, but I have seen them in the company of the Bocor we are going to visit."

I merely nodded.

"Your knowledge is so formidable," Gill continued. "It is a wonder that you need me to teach you about zombies, and not the other way around."

Onward we stalked through the warm Haitian day, the humidity soaking the both of us. The sun was fierce, and I was much relieved when Gill diverted us from the main road onto a path that took us under cover of foliage.

As I stopped in the shade to mop my brow, Gill said, "Do you see that house hidden down in the vale?"

He pointed to a place where the terrain sloped and a grove of trees sprouted in thick succession from the forest floor. Built into the edge of this grove was an old stone house with an empty doorway and no door.

"I see it," I told him, noting the thick green smoke drifting up from its small chimney despite the heat of the summer day.

"When we enter," Gill said, "I think it is best that you let me handle the conversation. I know that you speak the language as well as I, but you will be perceived as an outsider here. I have taken some risks in bringing you along. Our hosts will be wary of strangers, and I would hate for a miscommunication or misstep to undo any of the trusts that I have worked so hard to build with this community."

Though I found his words patronizing, I agreed to be silent throughout the encounter.

I followed Gill as he stalked into the shallow valley and approached the doorless house. While from a distance, the only indicator that it might be inhabited was the rising plume of verdant smoke. As we walked closer to the house, additional signs of life revealed themselves. A powerful odor—not entirely unpleasant—of incense, fire, and cooked meat pervaded the place. One could also glimpse moving shapes within the dark shadows inside.

Five yards from the gaping doorway, a man stepped out to greet us. He was an imposing figure—tall, without a shirt on, and his waist wrapped in strange, colorful swaddles. The man regarded Gill only for a moment, seeming to recognize him; but he let his suspicious, iron stare linger upon me as I edged toward the tiny house.

"Grandmarnier, it is good to see you," said Gill.

I raised my eyebrows as if to say, *This man is named after the libation?*

Gill glanced back at me to say, "Indeed, he is." (Though this surprised me at the time, in retrospect, I should have known that a drunkard like Gill would naturally associate with people bearing a relationship to alcohol in one way or another.)

Without a word, Grandmarnier turned. We followed him inside the tiny house, which turned out to be quite crowded.

Six men—not counting Grandmarnier—were waiting for us. Five of them appeared to be native Haitians and bore none of the exotic Voodoo trappings I was expecting. Instead, they wore simple work clothes and muddy boots. Aside from hemp necklaces and the odd tattoo, there was nothing about them to indicate anything out of the ordinary. (I went as far as to wonder if they were participants in what was about to occur, or only hired workmen.) The final member of the sextet was attired like Grandmarnier—bare-chested and with many colorful fabrics wrapped around his waist. He also wore paint on his face, in a strange variety of red and white and green hues.

"This," Gill said to me as he indicated the painted man, "is a Bocor."

Gill did not give the man any other name.

In the fireplace, a fire was raging. Its smoke was green, and its flames licked up in a variety of strange colors. The odor it gave off was one part burning wood, while the other part was some unearthly smell I had never before known. Clearly, something more than logs had been added to the unusual blaze.

Chained next to the fireplace was a live goat. A large metal basin had been set next to it, and in the basin was a long, sharp knife. (Clearly, the poor beast was not long for the world. It seemed to know it too, and sat in grim resolve with its head hanging low.)

On the stone floor, a thin layer of cornmeal had been arranged in a series of intricate patterns like the walls of a labyrinth. On top of this labyrinth—reclining, with his hands over his heart—was a deceased man, still in his graveclothes.

"So that you are not alarmed, let me explain what will happen when the ceremony begins," whispered Gill. "The Bocor's first task is to summon a spirit—some would call it a force—into the room. This spirit will help us create the zombie. However, it is understood to be a bloodthirsty specter, and can turn murderous if its hunger is not sated. Thus, the goat will then be sacrificed, and its blood will be offered up to the spirit, which will keep us safe. It is traditional to eat the goat after the ritual, although you may find you have a less-than-hearty appetite by the time that we are done here."

I regarded the condemned animal doubtfully, already feeling my appetite drain.

"Once the dangerous spirit is sated, the Bocor will direct it to reanimate the body of the dead man," Gill continued. "This will be accomplished through mystical words, the playing of associated drums and chimes, and the application of powerful balms and potions."

Gill indicated a leather pouch worn by the Bocor at his waist, which I assumed contained the magical mixtures.

"I see," I said quickly. "And can you tell me the exact ingredients involved in these mixtures? Are they of native origin? Must they be imported to Haiti? I would be very curious to know the extracts involved and their exact apportionment. And of course, the nature of their application to the corpse."

"Yes . . . perhaps later," Gill said, dismissing me. "If we are lucky, after the ceremony, the Bocor may be willing to share that information with you. As for their application, once the ceremony begins, there should be no question as to how the mixtures are applied."

Instantly, I regretted not having had the presence of mind to bring a camera, or at least some form of recording device. I resolved to take the most precise mental notes possible.

"Finally," Gill continued, "the zombie will rise from the dead. As this happens, the Bocor will take steps to ensure the zombie is contained. As the dangerous spirit vanishes, the dangerous zombie will emerge."

"And these containments?" I asked. "How are they effected?"

Gill again indicated that all would be revealed during the ceremony.

Moments later, Grandmarnier ushered the five workmen out of the small house. They departed obediently and seemed to disperse once they were outside.

"Be attentive," Gill said to me quietly. "It begins."

I followed Gill's example and sat down on the dirt floor. Grandmarnier—who seemed to be acting as an assistant to the Bocor—fetched a staff leaning against the wall and handed it to the old man. Grandmarnier then took up a drum and began to play a thunderous, unnecessarily loud (it seemed to me) cadence. The Bocor closed his eyes and began to speak in low tones in time to the cadence. As he spoke, he thrummed his staff against the ground, also in time to the beat.

As they went about their magical work, I let my eyes drift down to the motionless corpse before us. I must admit, there was an almost-electric excitement in the air. I looked hard for any movement or reaction in the cadaver, but there was none. I decided it must, of course, be too early in the proceedings.

Then a very singular thing happened.

A loud commotion could be heard taking place just outside the little house. From out of nowhere, I heard scuffling, raised voices, and muffled cries. Though alarmed, I hesitated to rise from my seated position at the ritual. (Not only was I about to learn invaluable information, but I feared that if I interrupted, or "broke the spell" of the magic, I might be censured from, or even forbidden to be present in, future ceremonies.) I remained silent despite the strange noises outside. (I did hazard a glance over at Gill, but his placid ruddy face betrayed no indication that he heard the fracas above the Bocor's rhythmic words.)

Moments later, I glimpsed distracting movement through the small house's doorway. I turned, and at that moment a group of men—perhaps ten of them—descended on us. They were all native Haitians whom I had never seen before. They were agitated and sweaty. They carried sharp-edged weapons, which appeared—alarmingly—to be stained with blood. Shouting aggressively, they pointed in our direction and let us know that we were to be the subjects of impending violence.

Gill saw them too and cried out. The Bocor stopped reciting his words, and Grandmarnier ceased to drum.

I leaped to my feet and attempted to draw my Luger, but was overtaken by the mob before I could do so. From out of the angry throng, a younger Haitian man emerged. He was better dressed than his compatriots, and horribly disfigured through a grievously uncorrected cleft palate. (Could this, I wondered, be the same cleft-palated man who had posed as a university student and interacted with Inspector Gehrin? I hardly had time to consider it!)

"This one!" he barked as two of the men held me down and wrestled my weapon from me (before, alas, I could fire a single shot). As I struggled in their collective grasp, the young man produced what appeared to be a velvet pouch from his pocket. Then he approached me and opened it, and I understood with sudden terror that it was a hood.

"Gill!" I cried out. "What do they mean to do to us?"

But I could say no more, as a ball of fabric was rudely shoved into my mouth. Moments later, the young man placed the hood over my head, and the world went dark.

I know not what befell Father Gill and the others, for I was next rudely conducted out of the small house, my arms forced behind my back and my hands tied. I was beaten about the lower body until I fell to my knees, and then struck hard on the side of the head by what I now believe was a repurposed cricket bat. The cessation of consciousness was instant.

Based on subsequent events, I can estimate with some accuracy that I was unconscious for approximately ten hours.

I awoke slowly. Even before I opened my eyes, I was aware that the velvet hood had been removed. I was, however, now tied around the waist in a standing position. Tied to what, I could not yet discern, though the ropes that bound me were clearly not tight, and I imagined I should easily be able to struggle free. I lifted my head. I could smell the salt of the sea and hear waves lapping in the distance. Upon opening my eyes, I found only more darkness at first. Yet as I raised my head and adjusted my eyes, my circumstances became clearer.

I was in a subterranean place. The air was thick with moisture. The floor was stone or rock. I gazed about, and wished that I had not. It seemed that several silhouetted figures hovered ominously in the cave around me. They were the size of large men; some of them stood close enough for me to touch them with an outstretched hand. Yet as I watched them in terror, it . . . seemed they moved not at all, not even to breathe.

Am I, I wondered, in a place with dead men? Am I to become one myself?

But no, these were not dead men at all, or even men. For when I summoned the resolve to brush my hand against the nearest one I encountered only rock.

I instantly guessed where I was and confirmed it by reaching behind me to explore the thing to which I was attached by a rope at my waist. When I felt not only hard rock but also a buckskin jacket, a top hat, and a set of carved features (accurate down to each single tooth inside a laughing mouth), I knew that I was inside the cave known as Papa Legba's Mouth. More specifically, I stood tied to the statue of Legba himself (in a position that, upon closer inspection, may well have indicated an intentional insult). The shadowy "figures" around me were nothing more than carved stalagmites.

My situation thus revealed, I took little time in extricating myself from the ropes that bound me. It was very, very dark, but because of my previous visit there with Father Gill, I believed it would not be difficult to find my way out.

As I prepared to feel my way along the rocky walls, my hand lit on the carving of Papa Legba to which I had been bound, and there I found my Luger, tied to his hand. (The bullets had not been removed, and I pocketed the firearm quickly.) After perhaps a quarter of an hour's work, I successfully navigated my way through the forest of rock to a point where I could see the open mouth of the cave. The moonlight shone off the calm waters of the inlet beyond, and I used their glare to navigate the rest of the way.

I emerged cautiously into the humid Haitian night, my weapon drawn and at the ready. Yet the scene was quite placid, and no aggressors attacked me. Though wary of another attack, I navigated my way up the cliffs and out of the cove, and returned to our residence without further incident. I did not sleep for the rest of the night, astounded and perplexed by the events that had befallen me.

Early the next morning, I lit out straightaway for the offices of Father Gill and his fellow priests. However, Gill was not at home, and his Papist colleagues could not account for his absence.

Now with a full understanding that further violence upon our person may be impending, Inspector Gehrin and I have armed ourselves against future attacks. We have opened the crate of MP 40 submachine guns and Model 24 ("stick") hand grenades that you so thoughtfully sent with us. Given the roominess of my cassock, it should prove easy for me to carry one of each with me at all times in a concealed fashion—in addition, of course, to my trusty Luger.

I have also taken the precaution of relocating our headquarters. I believe the house arranged for us by the university is known to those in the Voodoo community. (In a previous missive, I mentioned the totems that have appeared upon our doorstep.) Thus, I have secured a house of similar size—if of more modest appointment—in a more secluded area east of the city. This new house is, to the best of my knowledge, far removed from the site of any Voodoo-related encounters. It is insulated on one side by a nearly impenetrable forest, and its front door looks out on a large empty field where nothing ever happens.

Our work here will continue, but, my dear <u>Obergruppenführer</u>, it is clear that our approach must change. With the apparent abduction or murder of my most helpful contact (Father Gill), I believe it is now time to curtail my "diplomatic" approach to our operations in favor of a more direct line of inquiry.

Whilst we have already learned a great many things about the process of zombie creation—and the zombie itself—the task still remains for us to collect samples, attempt the vivisection of a "living" zombie subject, recreate a successful corpse-tozombie transformation, and send the required ingredients back to Berlin for replication by the Reich.

In my opinion, we have learned all that we can from observing the practitioners of this religion from afar. We must now aggressively collect samples—using force whenever necessary—and compel those who hold Voodoo secrets to divulge them to us, whether or not they are inclined to do so. Have my assurances, Obergruppenführer, that we will show these godless heathens what happens when dedicated men of the Reich put their minds to something.

How do the Americans put it? "No more Mr. Nice Guy."

Respectfully,
Gunter Knecht

Postscript: News has reached us that the Reich is now pushing into France and Belgium. Huzzah! We shall, despite our strained conditions, endeavor to celebrate this accomplishment tonight with what passes for beer in this miserable country.

Communication 21

May 30, 1940
From: Oswaldt Gehrin
To: <u>Reinhard Heydrich</u>

My <u>Obergruppenführer</u>,

As Inspector Knecht will have informed you, our research has taken a decidedly direct turn. After his unfortunate abduction—and, I understand, humiliation at the hands of a sodometically inclined statue—the inspector has directed that our activities moving forward shall consist only of two activities: 1) the collection of samples and 2) the interrogation of subjects regarding Voodoo techniques used to create zombies.

Under the newly enthusiastic direction of Inspector Knecht, we resumed a nocturnal surveillance of Bell's Hill. Per Knecht's new directive, we sought either a Voodoo practitioner (for interrogation) or a zombie (for vivisection). It did not take long for a suitable specimen to emerge.

After only a few days, I chanced to encounter a female Voodoo priest leading a single shambling zombie along the forest paths near the hill. It was the hour after midnight, and they were the only moving beings in sight. (I say "I chanced to encounter them" instead of "we" because Inspector Knecht had suddenly contracted a tropical fever and was convalescing in our new abode.

Determined that a flu bug should not impair our work, I undertook that evening's surveillance alone.)

That this strange young woman was steeped in the Voodoo arts, there could be little doubt. She wore the heavy rope necklaces with dangling idols that I have come to realize are associated with the arts of the Bocor. On her brow was a headdress embroidered with colorful patterns of eldritch origin. In one hand she held a rope loosely tied around the neck of the zombie. In the other, she gripped a rattan cane with a cluster of cock feathers attached to one end. (It may be worth noting that our only previous sighting of a female Voodoo priest involved a giant ovoid woman who was mostly abhorrent to the eye. Whilst I thought this might be indicative of the typical physical manifestation of all female priests, the woman I now beheld was a striking example to the contrary. Her bosom was ample, but complemented by a modest waist and shapely hips. Her legs were long, and her long strides down the jungle path were a beautiful thing to behold. Though African of origin (and thus, as our Führer reminds us, inherently inferior to an Aryan woman), her beautiful features had a stunning effect on me, exhibiting a pleasing symmetry and appearance. I must confess that I felt a great engorgement of pleasure upon beholding this woman's visage and figure, having fraternized, you will recall, almost exclusively with men since the beginning of my time in this country.)

With my courage thus tumescent, I emerged from my hiding place and addressed the young woman and her zombie.

At first, she smiled pleasantly, and it seemed as though she would happily engage me in polite conversation. Then she espied the submachine gun swaying on its cord over my shoulder, and her face coiled into a horrible mask of anger. She emitted an audible hiss like that of a snake. (This caused my infatuation to dim somewhat, though not completely.)

Remembering my mission, I lifted the offending weapon and fired half of the clip into the brain of her zombie (a crusty old fellow who appeared to have been in the earth for many years). Its brittle head all but exploded, ripped apart by the gun's powerful blasts. The torso fell to the ground in front of us, still and unmoving. For all her serpentine bluster, the Voodoo priestess was quite disarmed, and she put her hand to her mouth.

I shoved my gun's hot barrel into the space between her breasts.

"You will now be coming with me, young lady," I said to her. "We have much to discuss. If you are forthcoming and honest, then you have nothing to fear."

She regarded me icily but did not protest. I moved behind her and nudged her forward with my gun. Taking back roads and discreet jungle paths to avoid being seen by any third party, I conducted her back toward the abode I share with Inspector Knecht. (Though I knew my compatriot was feeling under the weather, I hoped that he would feel well enough to help me interrogate this remarkable specimen.)

My guest remained silent as we trekked through the jungle. For a moment, I became concerned that she might be dumb. (An interrogation with a subject who could not communicate would obviously reveal nothing useful.) To test her tongue, I attempted a conversation.

"I mean you no harm," I said to her. "I am . . . a visiting scientist and student of Voodoo, only seeking to learn more about your great and historic culture."

Here, of course, I was forced to suppress a laugh.

"Am I correct," I continued, "in assuming that you are a practitioner of the Voodoo arts? A Bocor?"

At this juncture, the woman responded with a strange word I had never heard before (though it seemed she might be referring to a tropical fruit.)

"Come again?" I said.

"Mambo," she repeated. "When it is a man, it is a Bocor. When it is a woman, it is a Mambo."

"Ah, I see," I responded, thankful to see that she was capable of coherent speech.

"It's strange that the most basic distinctions of our religion are unknown to a 'visiting scientist,'" she declared icily. "Perhaps you are not a very good one."

"I—," I began.

"Am German," she finished my sentence in her own way. "I can hear it in your accent. Are you perhaps one of the visiting butterfly researchers who have been so clumsily bumbling about the area? We do wish you would all go away."

I did not reply.

"By your silence, I see that you are indeed one of them," she continued. "I also see by your conduct this evening that you are more than simply a student of tropical insects."

"It is enough for you to know that I am a faithful servant of my country!" I exclaimed, becoming annoyed by the precocious tone of my captive.

"As were the French before you," she said. "And the British. And all the others . . . back to the Spanish in the time of my great-great-great-grandmother. All of them were only faithful servants of their countries. All of them, eventually, decided to try to take things with the tip of a gun or a sword. Does it not concern you, my German friend, that all others have abandoned their projects here? Only a few outposts remain, and they are mostly staffed by harmless religious zealots whom we have learned to humor. What makes you think you are any different?"

I disliked the presumptive nature of the Mambo's question and the tone in which she delivered it. I remained silent for the rest of our journey.

Eventually, as the hands on my watch moved close to two in the morning, our circuitous route wound back to my headquarters. As far as I could tell, we had made the trip unobserved. No zombie footfalls pursued our own, and no ominous drums beat in the distance. Even so, to make our approach less conspicuous, I took us along the forest that abutted the house on one side—as opposed to across the wide field on the other—until we arrived at the back door.

We entered the dark, quiet house without event.

"Hallo!" I called to Inspector Knecht. "It is Gehrin! I have returned with a female Bocor—who is called a Mambo—so that we may interrogate her, per your instructions."

My calls were answered with only a low moan. The fever that had overtaken my colleague had been as sudden as it was severe. All afternoon he had been very sick. When he finally did emerge from the upstairs bedroom, I saw that Knecht was covered with sweat and could only support himself by leaning against the guardrail of the staircase.

As my sickly colleague slowly made his way down to the house's first floor, I busied myself tying the Mambo's body to a chair. She did not resist. As I secured her, she regarded my colleague with what can only be called an evil eye.

Knecht descended the old wooden staircase slowly and seemed to run out of energy upon reaching the final step. Instead of approaching us, he sat down on the staircase and rested his chin in his hands.

When the Mambo was tied quite tightly, Knecht motioned that I should approach him. I did so. He leaned in close and spoke to me in whispers.

"Gehrin, I am still very weak from this horrible fever," he rasped.

"I can see that," I said. "I am sorry to have roused you. I assure you that I am fully capable of conducting an effective interrogation on my own. Please, return to your bed if you are not well."

Knecht waved this idea away: "No, I insist on being present. I'm sure that you are capable . . . but even so, I wish to be here. "

"Very well," I said, turning my attention once more toward our comely captive.

No sooner did I swivel around to face her than the Mambo began to laugh. (It was not a pleasant laugh—no light expression of joy or delight—but the low, evil chuckle of a person contemplating revenge.)

She was not looking at Inspector Knecht or myself but, rather, out the window into the open field at the front of the house. Concerned that she had seen something, I rushed to the pane and peered outside. There was nothing beyond, however—only the empty sky, the short grass, and the low-hanging moon.

Frustrated, I slammed the window shut and closed the shutters. Then I stalked back to the laughing Mambo and turned my attentions to her directly.

"This is no time for levity, young lady," I said to her. "Let me be direct: My colleague and I are in the business of extracting information. We have been carefully trained in this art and are capable of making uncooperative subjects feel pain beyond their wildest imaginings. That said, if you are cooperative and forthcoming—which I hope you will be—there shall be no need for physical persuasion at all."

The young woman nodded seriously, yet a smile was still upon her lips. Although she clenched her teeth, an amused titter still escaped every few seconds.

"I see that you are not convinced," I said to her. "Have no fear. You soon will be."

I then took a chair from the kitchen and moved it in front of the Mambo. I sat facing her and took out my notebook and pen. I looked over at Knecht, who nodded in approval from his position at the foot of the stairs.

"We wish for you to tell us the means by which a lifeless corpse is transmuted into a zombie," I said to her. "As a female Bocor—a Mambo, that is—you are in possession of this information. You see, there is much that we already know about you."

Here she stopped her tittering and raised an inquisitive eyebrow.

"I see that I have your attention," I told her. "Yes, we are aware of much of the ceremony. The goat that must be sacrificed . . . the drumming . . . the designs drawn upon the floor and over the corpse in cornmeal."

As I finished this litany, the Mambo cast her eyes around the room as if waiting for the punch line of a joke. When it became clear that I had finished speaking, she once again broke loose with peals of dark laughter that seemed to spew forth from an evil subterranean cave within her.

"Yes!" she cackled. "It is clear to me—someone has made you aware of something, indeed. Haha!"

I did not have to look over to Knecht to know that he wished me to correct the situation. I stood and gave the jocular witch several hard blows across the face with the back of my hand. The Mambo presently fell silent. Though I had bloodied her nose and lips, she still managed to smile. I sat back down across from her.

"I can assure you that that was nothing, young lady," I said sternly. "If you will not become immediately cooperative, we shall begin the interrogation in earnest. My colleague seated on the stairs is not as kind as I. His predilections usually call for me to begin by removing a subject's fingernails and teeth, and then to move on to more serious methods. It would be a pity if you forced me to disfigure a face as comely as yours, but you must understand that I would not hesitate to do it."

For a moment, the young lady only stared at me—still smiling, always smiling.

"Yes," she said with a confidence that seemed out of place. "I think that teaching you to raise the dead—here and now—is *exactly* what needs to happen."

"Good," I said cautiously. (Probably my tone reflected my surprise. I had not expected her capitulation to come so freely. Given the woman's fiery spirit, I was betting that the extrication of at least a few fingernails would come before any useful progress.)

"But you must untie my hands," the Mambo said. "There are certain . . . motions involved . . . that I cannot describe with only words."

"Very well," I told her, "but have no confusion. Any attempt on your part to escape will be met with brutal—or fatal—consequences. My colleague may be under the weather, but he can still shoot a gun. And the surrounding hills are rife with Bocors and Mambos. It would be a very small matter for us to kill you and obtain another."

The Mambo smiled icily as I loosened the ropes that bound her upper body, and she worked her arms free.

"Now," I said, taking up my pen and notebook, "how does one create a zombie?"

"There are many totems and trappings in our ceremonies," said the Mambo. "But these are merely decorations. Formality. The *real* power of the Bocor and the Mambo is in one thing alone."

"Yes?" I said, my fountain pen dripping on the page in anticipation. "And what is it?"

"A chant," said the Mambo. "The power is found in an ancient chant that has been passed down to a select few since the oldest days. It is older than Muhammad or Jesus or Moses. It is older than the first men who sailed in barks from sea to sea. It is as old as the Old Ones themselves, who are older than men."

"And how does it go, this chant?" I asked, hoping that my years in the conservatory would allow me to accurately record any musical subtleties to the incantation.

"I shall sing it . . . but then you must sing it with me," the Mambo said. "Two voices are required. It is one chant upon another chant. Therein may be found the power. Listen to what I sing now, until you know it well enough that you can reproduce it perfectly."

She then began an almost indescribably guttural and blunt-tongued cant. The words she spoke—if, indeed, words are what they were—seemed almost entirely devoid of verbs. There were animalistic clickings, spittle-filled stops, and trills of the tongue that were closer to the language of insects than men. As her mouth emitted these remarkable noises, the Mambo lifted her hands over her head and snapped her fingers to punctuate certain words (again, if words they even were). Her eyes rolled back in their sockets, and she seemed to enter a trancelike state.

At first I attempted to record the sounds with my pen, but it was quickly clear to me that I lacked the holographic lexicon for such an undertaking. (Looking back at my notes now, I see that I got as far as "XXthoxx Nthuxxx. XXthoxx Xthulu Xthulu Fghthxxxn. Xthulu Xthulu Fghthxxxn" before giving up.)

Resolved that the sound of the magical words should not be lost, I rose from my chair with the intention of retrieving our audio recording device.

"No!" cried the Mambo, suddenly shaken from her trance. "But I must record this," I insisted.

"You must *learn* it," the young woman countered forcefully. "Then I must sing the second chant while *you* sing the first. Record *that* if you want to."

Her reticence frustrated me. I desired to record all parts of the chant—the separate parts and then both of them sung together. However, I glanced over at the sickly Knecht, and he waved his hand to indicate that I should indulge the Mambo.

"Very well," I told her. "Begin again, and I shall attempt to learn the song."

The Mambo's eyes rolled back once more, and the horrible, guttural song recommenced. For several minutes, it remained an unintelligible cacophony. However, as time passed, I began to recognize phrases that recurred. I began to memorize them and sang along with the Mambo each time they came around. Before half of an hour had passed, I was singing along more often than not. After a full hour, I was copying the Mambo precisely. I even snapped my hands in perfect time to her own.

As our voices and hands fell into perfect synchronization, the Mambo stopped. She came out of her trance, and her eyes focused on mine once again.

"Good," she said softly. "Very good. You have learned it well. Now you shall sing it alone, and I shall sing the second chant on top of it."

"Very well," I said and began the series of guttural noises and clicks I had just memorized. As I did so, Knecht slowly rose and made his way back upstairs to fetch the recording device. Moments later, the Mambo began to sing the second part of the incantation—

and my god!—though I would have deemed it impossible, it was even more guttural and gravelly sounding than the first! Had I not known better, I would have guessed the Mambo was imitating a large animal in the final stages of childbirth (or at least copulation).

As we sang our strange noises together, I began to notice an eerie organization to it. The Mambo was clearly timing her incantations to my own. There were moments where our two voices seemed to answer one another, like a conversation. At other moments, we spoke a phrase or made a sound identically—our voices melding as one—before once again diverging into horrible dissonance. We sang together in this manner for several minutes.

Moving very slowly under the weight of his fever, Inspector Knecht eventually returned with the recording device and set it next to us. With a ponderous hand, he adjusted the spools of tape and depressed the pertinent button to begin recording. At that very moment, the Mambo stopped her song.

She looked up at me and smiled an evil smile.

When it was clear she would sing no more, I stopped my chant as well.

"We are recording now," I pointed out to her, indicating the spools with my finger. "Please continue the song so we may preserve it . . . or have you forgotten what I said about your teeth and fingernails?"

She only smiled at me. It was a confident smile. The smile of one with secret knowledge.

"Continue the song!" I demanded. "I command you, in the name of the Third Reich, to continue the song!"

"Unnecessary," retorted the Mambo. "It has already been effective."

At this insolence, I rose from my chair and struck her across the face as hard as I could. (Though her hands were now free, she did not flinch or block my blow. I hit her powerfully in the cheek.)

"Continue the song, now!" I shouted.

She only smiled icily. I drew the Luger from my waistband. I fully extended my arm and pressed the barrel hard against her forehead.

"Continue!" I cried. "Continue the—"

And here I stopped, for the sound of an unexpected blow echoed across the room. It was as though something had been thrown hard against the shuttered window facing the field.

The Mambo's smile brightened.

Then—*kramm!*—the sound of another blow echoed off the window. Then a scraping sound. Then silence. Then a powerful blow again.

The Mambo threw back her head and laughed, exposing a row of glistening white teeth.

"I believe your guests have arrived," she said.

"What nonsense is this?" I asked. I stalked over to the window and threw open the shutter.

The sight that greeted me is difficult to describe.

I found myself staring into the face of a zombie. He was ancient, covered in mud, and missing his nose and teeth. He emitted a roar from lungs that had not drawn breath in many years. I involuntarily flinched away and discharged my weapon into the wall.

But that was not all that I saw.

Beyond the zombie, in the field, were many others like him. *A least a hundred.* All of them looked positively ancient—decades dead, at least. Some were so decayed and desiccated that it was hard to recognize their forms as human. Some crawled or scuttled on the ground like insects or crabs. Others slunk forward slowly, on legs stiff as stilts. They were deformed. They were horrible to behold. Each of them that could moan, moaned. Every single one of them had turned to face (or, in some horrible cases, "face") the house.

The ground on which they stood—formerly a placid field, empty and pristine—was now a mess of upturned earth. In a horrible shocking instant, it became clear to me that not only had our song awakened the dead, but that they had heard our siren call *whilst underneath the very earth itself*!

"Europeans are idiots, each in their own way . . . but you Nazis take the cake!" cried the Mambo gleefully, as if our dire predicament were only a joke to her.

I trained my Luger on the zombie in the window and fired several times into his head. He moaned and fell to the ground, unmoving. Another stepped up and took his place almost simultaneously.

"Only the world's biggest fools would choose the house next to the old Grangou burying ground in which to interrogate Mambos on the art of raising zombies!" the young woman cackled from behind me.

"That isn't helpful!" I shouted, and then emptied the Luger into the field of zombies. At least two others fell; but, again, more zombies quickly took their place. It was clear the house should soon be swarmed if I did not improve my firepower.

"Knecht!" I cried to my colleague. "Thank God you opened that crate! We must fetch those machine guns and grenades immediately."

Suddenly, behind me, I heard a door slam.

"Knecht?" I cried and swiveled around.

The inspector was still sitting at the foot of the stairs, looking more overcome by his fever than ever. With an effort that clearly required great exertion, he lifted his arm and pointed to the chair. It was now empty. The Mambo had apparently untied her legs whilst my back was turned, and had just run out of the house and into the forest. The door was still ajar.

I wondered for a moment if Knecht and I ought to follow her. I approached the half-open door, intending to stick my head out and look beyond. No sooner had I grasped the handle than a moldy, teetering zombie stuck his head around the corner. It had no eyes, but it clearly sensed my presence and snapped at me with a jaw full of crooked teeth.

I recoiled in horror, kicked the door shut, and locked the zombie outside.

"Knecht," I shouted, "we are under siege! Where have you put the crate of armaments?"

My fellow inspector, who seemed on the verge of passing out from weakness, managed to point to the room at the back of the house where he had made his office.

I bounded over to the little room and found the crate underneath a blanket. I grabbed one of the MP 40s and began shoving grenades and ammunition clips into each and every pocket (and even down my trousers).

"Gehrin," my colleague moaned from the other room. "I think they are breaking through the window."

I raced back to the front of the house to find that Knecht was not exaggerating. A whole platoon of zombies seemed to be gathered around the window overlooking the field. They had smashed the glass, broken through the storm shutters, and now several sets of flailing arms reached inside. The smashing glass and gnashing teeth were not the only noise they made. The zombies emitted low moans. Now and then, they almost seemed to form coherent words. It was profoundly unnerving.

I pulled out my submachine gun and began firing into the mass of arms and teeth. I uttered a war cry that I hoped was worthy of a man of the Reich and watched as my bullets riddled the wriggling zombies. I tried my best to aim for their heads, but the mass of body parts and limbs writhed and thrashed violently, making precise aiming a near-impossibility.

As you may be aware, my Obergruppenführer, the clip on an MP 40 exhausts itself after only a few seconds of constant fire. I was forced to expend several clips before I had pushed the crowd of zombies back enough that it felt safe to lob a grenade through the window.

"Take cover!" I cried to Inspector Knecht and flattened myself against the floor.

"You fool!" he coughed. "The walls of this house are far too thin for that."

No sooner had he issued his warning than the ensuing blast conspired to prove him right. The grenade detonated—handily dispatching the remaining platoon of zombies lurking just outside the window—and tore a man-sized hole in the side of the house.

Dirt and dust rained down for a moment, and then all was silent. I stood and inspected the hole. It did not seem possible to repair with any haste. Looking beyond it, I saw the pile of dead zombies I had just created, but also dozens more still lumbering toward the house from across the field.

"Damn and blast," I cried. "Now they will overrun us if they reach the house. We must not allow that to happen. I'm going up to the roof through the hatch in the second floor. My only hope is to pick them off before they reach the opening. Knecht, you must go to your office and bring me the rest of the ammunition and grenades!"

"I can hardly stand," Knecht protested.

"All the same, you must do it!" I called, racing past him up the stairs. "Think of the Führer and be inspired."

As quickly as I could, I raced to the attic of the two-story house and popped open the hatch that allowed for access to the roof.

Luckily, the slope of the roof was quite gradual, allowing me to stand and balance myself easily. The moonlight revealed a field filled with lumbering zombies. I would have to eliminate them one by one.

Seeking to conserve ammunition, I began by throwing grenades at places on the field where the zombies were clustered. This produced good results. Whether the zombies were unaware of my grenades or simply did not care about them, they proved almost entirely incapable of evasive action. This made my work as easy as a soldier's training exercise. Again and again I threw the grenades at the stumbling worm-eaten corpses that groaned and gnashed their teeth. Again and again, they failed to take cover, and were blown apart. Limbs, heads, and (on occasion) entire zombies were lifted into the air by the force of the blasts, and they rained down upon the field.

This grenade lobbing was highly effective, but it was still a challenge to explode the zombies before they reached the house. The field was very large, and I could only throw the grenades thirty or forty yards without losing my footing under the force of the throw. (And I could not throw the grenades too close to the house, or, as we had just seen, the structure itself would be damaged in the blast). Sooner than I liked, I had thrown my last one. Where was Knecht?

"Knecht!" I called into the roof hatch as I prepared my submachine gun. "Come quickly with more grenades!"

I fell onto my stomach, extended the collapsible stock of the MP 40, and braced the weapon against the edge of the roof. I then fired several rounds at the zombies nearest the house. Hitting the slow-moving fellows was no problem, but it proved maddeningly difficult to achieve the head shots required to bring them down. My natural inclination was to aim for the torso. By correcting this, and seeking to aim only for the head, I often overshot the shambling corpses. In most cases, I expended *an entire clip of ammunition* in the course of bringing down a single zombie. This was no way to work.

I was quickly down to my final clip, and still no sign of Knecht.

I stared hard into the field, where many zombies remained upright. Should I begin shooting with my final clip, or should I wait before expending it? These walking dead showed no signs of stopping. If I did not do anything, they would soon start entering the first floor of our house.

Suddenly, I detected a slow, lumbering movement right below me. Assuming—in that startled instant—that a zombie had risen from the dirt at the foot of the house, I hastily turned my gun on it and loosed a single round. No sooner had I done so than I realized the figure was not a zombie but Inspector Knecht.

He dropped the ammunition in his hands and slowly crumpled to the earth.

"Knecht!" I cried.

He did not respond.

Abandoning my plan of a rooftop defense, I scuttled back through the hatch and raced down to the first floor of the house and leaped out of the grenade hole through which my colleague had stumbled. There I found Knecht, facedown in the soil. The ground beside him was littered with the grenades and clips he had been carrying. I took a knee beside him and flipped him over. He moaned.

It appeared that my shot had only nicked his leg.

"Knecht, can you walk?" I asked urgently. Zombies were approaching from several directions, some less than ten yards away.

"For you . . .," Knecht moaned and squirmed, attempting to gesture to the grenades and SMG clips he had carried. Obviously, I should never have sent him to fetch ammunition. How I regretted this horrible mistake!

I gathered as many of the grenades and clips as I could, and then I lifted Knecht over my shoulder (thank goodness he is a relatively light and wiry man). No sooner had I done so than a dusty zombie lumbered to within an arm's reach of us. I leveled the SMG at him and fired until his head disintegrated.

It was difficult to replace the clip while holding Knecht, so I set him back down. (He was close to babbling from the fever—and, doubtless too, from the stress of the attack—and seemed only marginally aware of what was happening to him.) No sooner had I replaced the clip (and was ready to once again hoist Inspector Knecht over my shoulder) than another zombie drew within ten feet of us. This time I was more careful with my ammunition and brought him down with a single blast to the forehead. Then another directly behind the first lumbered forward, and I laid him back to the earth in similar fashion. Then yet another.

It soon became clear that carrying Knecht back up to my rooftop perch would be a dangerous (and probably impossible) undertaking. In a trice, I decided to make my stand then and there, in front of the house.

The fighting that followed was long and exhausting. To the bats that occasionally passed overheard and looked down on the scene below, it must have appeared that the remaining zombies circled around me the way water circles around a drain. The walking dead men seldom moved in a straight line, but always they found a way to careen or corkscrew in my general direction. As they stumbled within my range, I dispatched each one as quickly and efficiently as I could. As the night wore on, spent clips littered the ground around me, and the bodies of the zombies encircled me from all directions.

Finally—in the culmination of an effort I do not overstate as nearly superhuman (for, as the Führer reminds us, we Aryans are supermen)—I dispatched the final zombie. It was a frail Haitian girl, teeth gnashing and eye sockets gaping obscenely. I shot her through the forehead with what was nearly my final bullet. The sun had just begun to rise.

Utterly exhausted, I fell cross-legged on the ground next to Knecht (who was nearly buried underneath dead zombies). I tried to work up the strength to enter the house and get a glass of water. I surveyed the empty field as I sat. Before, it had been as smooth and green as the pitch on a golf course.

Now it was a no-man's-land of muddy craters where the dead had risen from their slumbers and clawed up through the broken earth. Nothing moved on this strange, blasted moonscape. I was thankful—at least—for that.

Then, unexpectedly, something did.

At the far edge of the field—over a hundred yards away—I saw two humanoid shapes. I had not noticed them before because they were unmoving, but now they turned to face one another. I could not discern if they were zombies or humans. One was a smaller, lithe-looking black woman. She looked not entirely unlike the Mambo we had just met. The other was Caucasian and had a hulking, almost-planetary carriage that closely reminded me of Inspector Baedecker's.

I took up my SMG and readied myself for the eventuality of dispatching two more zombies. And yet the figures made no move to approach me. After seeming to converse for a few moments, they simply turned and walked away. In a moment, they passed over the horizon and were gone.

Thus concludes my account of our first successful participation in the creation of zombies.

While we were not able to record the dual-voiced song that seems to be the secret, we now understand that this auditory phenomenon is a salient part of the ceremony, and that the rest is, as they say, window dressing. The potential for weaponizing this in the cause of the Reich is grand indeed. I envision zeppelins—equipped with great loudspeakers—broadcasting the chants across enemy territory. (When our enemy's armies are exhausted from fighting their own dead, then we shall strike them with the full might of the Reich! In their weakened and spent conditions, we shall annihilate them utterly!)

I have been able—I believe—to perfectly recall my half of the guttural chant, which I have reproduced on the enclosed spool of tape. Given that we now know exactly what we are looking for, I am optimistic about our chances of quickly capturing a second Bocor/Mambo and inducing them to divulge the second voice for our recording device.

I am also happy to report that Inspector Knecht is making a slow but steady recovery from his tropical fever. He was well enough on the day after the events described to assist me as I dragged the dead zombies into a great pile and set them aflame.

Please find enclosed the spool of tape featuring my singing, as well as a request for a new shipment of munitions to the address provided.

Yours respectfully,
Oswaldt Gehrin

Communication 27

June 29, 1940
From: Oswaldt Gehrin
To: <u>Reinhard Heydrich</u>

My <u>Obergruppenführer</u>,

Since taking up residence with Inspector Baedecker in the Voodooist settlement, I have witnessed many strange and exotic rituals—the majority of which I have not the time or space to limn here. However, I have twice witnessed the Song of the Jeje used to raise zombies. It has proven itself to be the same song that I sang in the presence of the Mambo.

The village is a small one, though its character varies greatly depending on the time of day. Any traveler discovering it during daylight hours will see a modest collection of fifteen or so homes and a population apparently engaged in subsistence farming. By night, however, the encampment comes alive with bonfires, singing, drumming, and dancing. The population seems to triple or quadruple; and men, women, and children engage in all manners of rituals, cavorting, and worship—often until the dawn's first light. In this dark nocturnal carnival, I have seen things that I never would have credited as possible.

I have seen a wild pig emerge from the forest walking on two legs and seemingly converse with humans who knew it as a friend. I have seen ghostly apparitions with human forms appear at the edges of the Voodoo gatherings and then melt back into nothing. (They leave behind a strange, ethereal mucus on the trees.) I have seen a circle of Voodooists seem to levitate six feet off the ground as they chanted and sang—seemingly unaware that this was an unusual consequence of chanting.

If anything, dear <u>Obergruppenführer</u>, the wonders and powers of the Voodooists have been underreported in the Western world.

There is a hierarchy to the structure of the Voodoo practitioners here, and it is more complicated (and involves more subtlety) than a casual observer might give it credit. Yet there can be no question that it is an ancient, wizened Bocor who occupies the central position in the group's power structure. The man—his name is Grandmarnier—is reputed to be 102 years old (though he looks perhaps sixty). He is also said to be able to change his appearance through sheer force of will and sometimes appears older or younger. I have not yet seen this feat accomplished, though I *have* seen the man raise zombies.

(In connection to this presumed agelessness of Grandmarnier, Inspector Baedecker remains convinced that the ultimate value of our discoveries may be a means of preserving life indefinitely. It is his hope that through scientific refinement, the Reich will be able to reanimate its members as fully sentient zombies, with little or no taste for flesh. I do not disagree that this is an admirable goal, however lofty, yet I continue to see a more immediate value in the creation of murderous zombies for use in the European conflict.)

Grandmarnier appears to have taken a particular shine to Inspector Baedecker. I do not know what actions—taken prior to my arrival—fostered such a wealth of good feeling between the two men, but it cannot be denied. And upon Baedecker's vouching for me, I have also been accepted, though somewhat more hesitantly, into a circle of trust. The Voodooists seem completely unaware that we intend to use their rituals for military purposes. Neither Baedecker nor I have given them any impression that this is the case. (Following Baedecker's lead, I have presented myself as a

European with a wanderlust, keen to find a more "authentic" and "natural" way of living. I give no hint that I am aware of the practical applications for their technologies.)

Grandmarnier, like the rest of the Voodooists in this cloistered village, does not seem to regard his powers as supernatural and exotic—or even as unusual. Great secrets for controlling the natural world are tossed about as though they were mere trifles or magician's tricks. (Further, he is keen to share them with willing acolytes.)

Thus, the most exciting news: Grandmarnier has agreed to teach us the second voice in the Song of the Jeje. (I am relearning the part I sang that ominous evening with the Mambo, and Baedecker is learning the Mambo's part.) Obviously, this is momentous, because it will allow us to create zombies on our own. Though the song is onerous and complicated, I believe we will have it mastered within hours of Grandmarnier delivering the lesson. At such time, the correct course of action will probably be to connect with one of our U-boat teams and return to Germany (where the song can be recorded, analyzed, and utilized as our glorious leaders see fit).

I feel we are close to success, my <u>Obergruppenführer,</u> and your helpful guidance has been the force behind our accomplishments here. Upon our return to Germany, we shall make clear to everyone that you are the one who deserves credit for this valuable discovery that shall so greatly strengthen the Reich.

Yours respectfully,
Oswaldt Gehrin

Communication 30

July 1, 1940
From: Oswaldt Gehrin
To: <u>Reinhard Heydrich</u>

My <u>Obergruppenführer</u>,

Our successes compound!

Under the tutelage of Grandmarnier, the Song of the Jeje is now perfected! Inspector Baedecker and I have mastered the ritual. How it works is still largely unknown to me, but I can attest that it does work. And with the permission of Grandmarnier, Baedecker and I have raised a zombie! (Baedecker has jocularly christened him Hans, after a primary school classmate he apparently resembles.)

Using a corpse procured from a burial ground several miles away, we performed the song on a starless night in a clearing lit only with torches. At my own suggestion, we sought to use this ritual to distill the Voodoo down to its most essential (and functional) elements. Thus, we commenced the song with none of the decoration or affectation of the tradi-tional Voodooist. Only the song was used. The corpse was placed on the bare ground before us. Drums, feathers, and ceremonial garb were not employed.

Yet much to our delight, it was still effective! When the song was through, the fingers of the corpse began to twitch. Moments later, the thing sat up and looked at us. There was comprehension in its eyes as its gaze met our own. Baedecker and I were jubilant.

"We have done it!" Baedecker cried and began to dance a happy jig, right there on the jungle floor.

The result was near disaster.

For in the midst of his dance of joy, Baedecker—you will remember that he is an awkward and overweight man—slipped on a root and hit his head on the side of a tree, falling unconscious.

Zombies, as I hope I have made clear at this point, are slavering and innately violent creatures. They want nothing more than to eat human brains. They can, however, be controlled and rendered relatively docile through the use of certain powerful (dare I say magical?) words. (Other things, too, seem to have this ability. Certain drums can attract zombies like a homing beacon. Certain signals and markings do not divest a zombie of its aggressive aspect, but they nonetheless protect the wearer from the zombie. We are learning much. It is fascinating!)

It was these very magical words (already taught to Baedecker by Grandmarnier) that he intended to share with me after our animation of the zombie.

As Baedecker lay prostrate on the ground beside me, Hans rose to his feet with a murderous look in his rolling yellow eyes. His teeth began to grind, and he extended his arms like a blind man feeling his way forward.

"Baedecker!" I cried, but my colleague was surely unconscious.

The murderous zombie began to stumble forward.

"Stop!" I cried, a great fear coursing through me. "I am the one who has created you. You must respect me!"

Yet alas, Hans did no such thing. Onward he came, his hands—they seemed more like claws—snatching violently at the air.

As our ritual was to be a scientific exercise conducted in relative safety, I had not brought my Luger. As Hans drew nearer—his grave breath cold and stinking—I prepared to flee. But of course that would mean disaster! While I might easily elude the stumbling zombie, it should surely then turn its attention to Baedecker. Both my colleague and the valuable knowledge he carried would be lost.

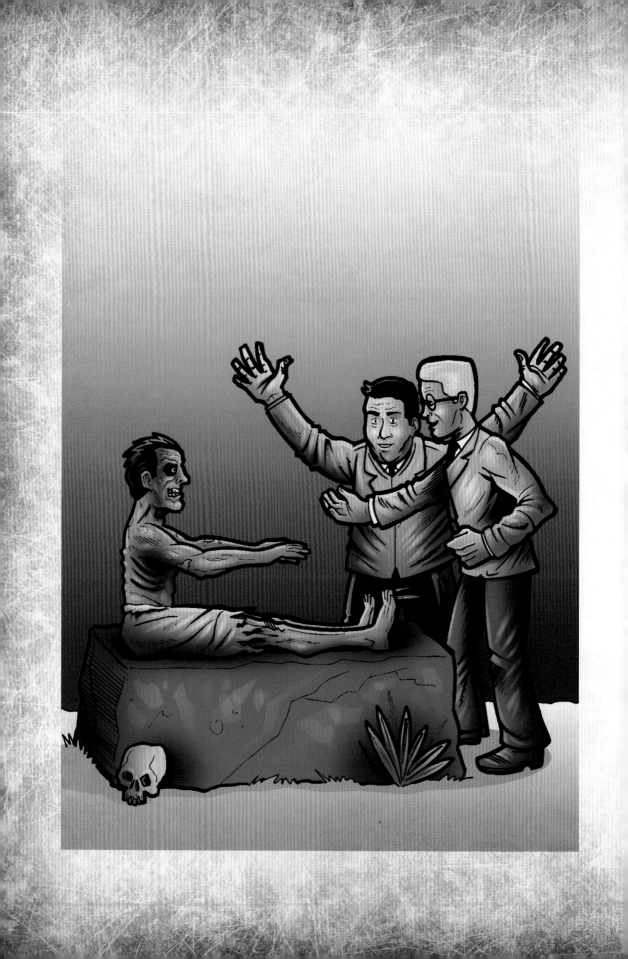

Suddenly, as the zombie's yawning mouth drew near, I heard a strange voice deliver a familiar-sounding utterance of the Voodooists. The zombie collapsed unmoving at my feet.

I looked over at Baedecker. But no! He was still unconscious—his breathing visible, but only just. Someone else had spoken!

Looking around wildly, I detected a shadowy figure half concealed by the darkness. He stood at the clearing's edge opposite me. I could not make out his features in the flickering torchlight, but he wore the black clothes and collar of a man of the cloth.

It is Knecht, come to kill us! I thought to myself, and my blood ran cold anew.

But then the figure edged forward into the torchlight, and I beheld a visage entirely unknown to me. He was an older man with silver hair. He bore the ruddy signs of drink upon his cheeks. In addition to his clerical collar, he wore the clanking ebon necklaces of a Voodooist (nearly concealed—black on black—against his dark clothes).

"Who are you?" I asked anxiously.

"A loyal servant of the Voudun," the man answered in a thick Irish brogue. "You, my friend, cannot say the same."

"What?" I responded, but the man put up his hand to stay me.

"Let me save you some time," he continued. "My name is Father Gill. Your colleague—who I sincerely hope is now dead or back in Germany—would likely have spoken to you about me."

"Oh . . . ," I said, genuinely baffled. "He did speak of you. But . . . but . . ."

"Let me save you some more time," said Gill, again raising his hand. "You are German operatives, sent here to learn the secrets of Voodoo—like the French before you, and the many, many others before them."

"And you are a supporter of that gangster Churchill, I suppose," I answered defensively. "I fail to see why you people insist on meddling in Continental affairs! My nation has only ever acted defensively!"

"Save your patriotic speeches, for I care not a whit for Churchill or Chamberlain," seethed my guest. (His tone was aggressive and curt.) "It matters not from what nation you people come. The fact that you are here to steal as your spoils the secrets of the Voodoo religion is the only matter of consequence. I offer you one choice, and one alone: Leave here this instant, return to your homeland, and speak nothing of what you have learned."

"You cannot be serious," I answered. "You are a man of the cloth. Knecht, before his insanity, told me of your mission to convert those *away* from the Voodoo faith toward the religions of Europe!"

"A necessary ruse," replied Gill. "It is true that I came here as a servant of the Catholic Church to convert the heathens, but it was I who was converted. Now I use my position under the Pope only to protect the country's native religion from missionaries and other interests. I am a member of a sizable—though necessarily secret—confederacy, and we are committed to preventing the exploitation of Voodoo secrets by sniveling outsiders."

"So then . . . ," I began.

"I could tell right away that your colleague was not all that he seemed," Gill continued. "Yes, he had researched his cover story well, but I have seen so many interlopers over the years that they have become easy to spot. At first, I tried to convince him that there was nothing to see. When he would not believe me (perhaps because of things he—or, come to think of it, *you*—observed), I tried to make it clear to him that investigating the Voodooists any further would be dangerous to his person. Perhaps he told you of the ritual I took him to—completely staged, of course—at which I fed him incorrect information about how zombies are created, and then gave him the impression that his own life was in danger."

"He did," I said, thinking on it.

"In retrospect, it would have been easier to have killed him," Gill explained. "Of course, that would only have prompted your government to send others to take his place. The only satisfactory resolution is always to convince interlopers that there is nothing to find, or to send them in the wrong direction entirely. Of course, I did not know how much Knecht knew. Had he heard of Grandmarnier? Had he seen actual zombies? Based on my educated guesses, I think I did a very good job designing my charade."

"Did you know about us?" I stammered, pointing to myself and Baedecker.

"Yes, I was made aware of Knecht's colleagues, who I assume are the two of you," Gill answered coolly. "I gave instructions that I thought would culminate in either your leaving the country or your outright deaths. And yet, I see that you are here, and still alive."

"Who are you to speak for the Voodooists?" I asked forcefully, my shock changing to rage. "Grandmarnier has personally invited us to become his acolytes and has freely shown us how to use his arts to raise zombies. Who are you to keep us from his secrets?"

"Grandmarnier is as ignorant as he is powerful," Gill declared. "He does not understand that Voodoo's powers are in danger of exploitation by evil men. He has no experience of the world outside of this tiny country. Types such as yourselves would use his secrets for your own gain—perverting and distorting the magic he freely teaches. You are here because you dream of creating an army of invincible zombie soldiers to serve your leader with the ridiculous toothbrush mustache. Do you deny it, sir? I know it is the truth!"

I opened my mouth, but nothing came out.

"This is about more than who rules Europe for the next thirty years," said Gill. "This is about the most ancient secrets men ever stole from gods. Yes, *gods*! And if you will not swear, this instant, to abandon your plundering and leave here forever, then we have nothing more to say to one another."

Here my anger became uncontainable. Not only did this man— whoever he truly was—stand in the way of our valuable mission, he had *insulted the Führer's mustache.*

It could not stand.

"You are a damned fool if you think the secrets of zombie creation are for you alone!" I spat. "The Third Reich is the greatest entity ever known to man! It is for the Reich—and the Reich alone—to determine the best use for zombies."

"Then I see you have made your choice," Gill responded coldly, and in the same instant drew a Colt revolver from his pocket and leveled it at me. "Like all men who have sought to steal the secrets of Voodoo, you shall meet the end that you deserve!"

Before I could think, there was a deafening report . . . yet it was Gill who dropped to the ground dead!

I looked over and saw the reclining Inspector Baedecker holding his Luger, the smoke from its barrel mixing with the omnipresent smoke from the torches.

"Baedecker, you came to!" I stammered.

"And just in time," he replied, slowly rising to his feet. "That man was a fool, but a dangerous one. He shows how determined our enemies are to stop us."

In a few moments, Baedecker had recovered completely from his fall. Without further word about the interloping priest, Baedecker began his tutorial for me on the verbal control of a zombie.

As I write this letter, Hans the zombie is sitting at my feet, as tame as a kitten. Yet were I to utter the right set of syllables, he would become as murderous as a homicidal maniac. It is a strange feeling to have such complete and utter power over so potentially deadly a thing. Imagine the feeling of a lion tamer . . . but no, that is inadequate. (Though lions can be tamed, the tamer must never let his guard down, lest he be surprised. Further, the lion must be carefully coached for months or years to respond correctly to a tamer's whip.) Imagine the feeling of an inventor who has constructed the perfectly obedient and deadly automaton—yes, that is it precisely—and you have perhaps some notion of the sentiment that runs through my veins. I can loose the zombie on my enemies, and it will bite and claw until my foes' brains are eaten and the zombie sated. I can rest it by the door to my hovel, where it will stand as a trusted sentry. Or I can command it to stand in the corner and stare at the wall for hours on end if doing so should somehow benefit me. (And for all of these tasks, no training on the zombie's part is required.) It is truly awe-inspiring to wield a power so complete, and I am firm in my belief that the Aryan is the only race capable and truly qualified.

Baedecker and I have now mastered the commands enabling one to have control over a single zombie; however, as my colleague pointed out, we must learn how to control *groups* of them if we are to have any hope of marching a zombie army across Europe. Several other Bocors and Mambos in the encampment seem to have this ability, including Grandmarnier, who orders groups of zombies around with great ease and facility.

After some discussion, Baedecker and I are agreed that it is worth it to remain here a little longer to learn these somewhat more complicated "group commands." We shall then return to the Reich, carrying with us the momentous knowledge of how to create and command an army of zombies.

A final thought before I end this transmission: Our encounter with the late Father Gill was, of course, deeply troubling. The fact that an outsider could penetrate our cover is unnerving. (Perhaps Inspector Knecht's skills in deception are not as accomplished as he believes them to be.) After he was shot, we left Gill's body where it was, on the forest floor. A few hours later, it was not there, yet I have no doubt that the man was completely dead. He claimed to speak for Grandmarnier, but neither Grandmarnier nor anyone else in the village has remarked upon him (and we, certainly, have not brought it up in conversation). Could there have been truth to Gill's ravings that other European nations have previously attempted to learn and export zombie Voodoo technology? My own knowledge of Caribbean history suggests that it is possible. (Yet I am not surprised that representatives of the Third Reich are succeeding where those from lesser nations failed.) We must—in these final days in this country—insulate and protect ourselves from any others in Gill's cadre. It seems impossible that he operated alone, and we know not with whom he may have been aligned in his mission.

The incident with Gill illustrates that Baedecker and I are in mortal danger. However, we are also in the good graces of the most powerful Bocor in the country, armed with Lugers, and now in command of our own personal zombie named Hans.

I, for one, like our chances.

Yours respectfully,
Oswaldt Gehrin

Communication 32

July 5, 1940
From: Gunter Knecht
To: <u>Reinhard Heydrich</u>

<u>Obergruppenführer</u>,

Zombies are real.

Zombies are real. Zombies are real. Zombies are real.

I stare up at the Haitian moon that illuminates the page as I write these words . . . and can scarcely credit their truth. And yet I know it to be so. I have seen the evidence myself.

My suspicions have been wrong all this time. For, my dear, dear *Obergruppenführer*, zombies are real!

What happened was this: I was deep in the jungle. I had been traveling for hours and was exhausted. For days I had been searching for any clue as to the whereabouts of Baedecker and Gehrin. I had found nothing. I questioned every farmer and villager I encountered. I bribed those who seemed receptive to it and threatened those who were not. Yet every lead took me nowhere. I found myself directed to white men who were not my colleagues, or else to empty places where I found nothing.

I was distraught and tired. My canteen had been empty for hours, and my feet ached terribly. I longed to return to my temporary headquarters.

Cutting through a swath of forest as dusk began to descend, I passed through a small village. I had previously surveyed it and found nothing of value—just a few straggling mud farmers and ramshackle homes. However, I discovered that by night the place changed remarkably. The settlement was a carnival of Voodooists cavorting here, there, and everywhere! Some danced in strange circles. Some sat together and spoke to one another quietly. Several were preparing an evening's meal.

Then, in a lonely corner of the clearing, I saw them.

Gehrin and Baedecker. The former still wore the uniform of a butterfly catcher, and the latter sported a strange suit of feathers, drawings, and animal bones. They stood beside a group of five or so Haitians, who milled absently in front of them. Gehrin and Baedecker were acting like drill sergeants, spitting out commands in a strange guttural language. Some of the group appeared to be reacting to these barked orders, while others were less receptive.

Then a villager carrying a torch walked past the parading troops, and I saw that they were not Haitians at all . . . but *the reanimated bodies of the dead*!

There was no question about it. The ghastly figures had horrible, rotted skin that was falling from their bodies. Many lacked eyes, left with only empty soil-filled sockets. Worms crawled amidst what was left of their hair. They moved in a horrible shamble and often gnashed their teeth murderously. Indeed, their facial expressions seemed to indicate a ravenous madness that was barely being kept at bay.

I did not react rationally. I realize that now.

As an officer in the service of the Fatherland, I understand that I am expected to maintain my wits at all times. I must be unshakable. I know that. It is my responsibility. And yet the sight shook me utterly, to my core.

It was not only that these fools had been right all along about the existence of the walking dead. It was their arrogance. Their damned arrogance! The grins of confidence upon their idiot faces! These fools had stolen secrets that were rightfully the Reich's, and they clearly reveled in it. They looked so pleased with themselves. So full of hubris.

The fools . . .

No, my instincts told me, they were something worse than fools. Traitors.

It could not stand.

Before I knew what was I was doing, my hand had flown to the MP 40 that hung from the strap over my shoulder. I loosed my bullets upon the impostors and their zombie parade.

In a matter of moments, my clip was expended. Baedecker, Gehrin, and their undead horde still stood. Everyone in the village looked around in alarm. Several villagers gestured in my direction. I instantly understood that I had acted rashly. (Soon these people would be after me.) Suddenly, as I was considering this, Baedecker and Gehrin produced their Lugers and fired back. I turned and fled into the jungle.

I ran until I thought my lungs would give out. The Voodooists pursued me relentlessly, yet I was always the quicker and the stealthier. I secreted myself within a mossy bog and waited motionless until the last of them gave up the chase.

Now, secure inside my new headquarters, I am plotting the destruction of Gehrin and Baedecker. They are untrustworthy outlaws. This is known for certain. They must be eliminated, and our mission completed. I know where they are, and I know how to do it!

Prior experience—namely, Gehrin's evening spent singing with the Mambo—has already shown that a properly motivated Voodoo priest can divulge all the secrets necessary for the creation of zombies. Thus, I shall execute the traitors Gehrin and Baedecker and capture my own Voodoo priest. (If a fool like Gehrin can accomplish this task, then it should give me little trouble.) I shall then surrender myself (and my captive) to a U-boat crew. The inter- rogation can take place in Berlin. I know what to ask the Voodooist, and the secrets should come quickly once the interrogation gets underway. (Again, if Gehrin can do it . . .)

But first things first.

I acted rashly in the earlier encounter, allowing myself to be overcome by anger. Later this evening, I shall instead employ the cool precision for which we Germans are known. Armed to the very teeth, I shall return to the village of Voodooists, kill my traitorous cohorts, and then find a suitable hostage.

Thank you for being patient with me these many months, Obergruppenführer. I intend that—in just a few hours—your patience should be rewarded.

Respectfully,
Gunter Knecht

Communication 33

July 6, 1940
From: Gunter Knecht
To: <u>Reinhard Heydrich</u>

Gehrin and Baedecker are dead. I have killed them.

I am sitting next to their bodies. Gehrin's face has been smashed beyond recognition, and his brains dashed out across the dirt floor. Baedecker has had an entire MP 40 clip emptied into his considerable chest.

For all their SD and RSHA training, it was surprisingly easy.

Just before dawn, I retraced my steps and found the Voodoo village. It was wrapped in a strange, thick fog that gave the place a ghostly aspect. Many torches and cooking fires still burned, but it appeared that the residents had retired for the night (or departed from the village entirely). Neither man nor zombie moved. All was stillness. All was silence.

Concealing myself in the shadows, I crept to the place where I had seen Gehrin and Baedecker directing their zombie parade. Directly adjacent was a modest hut with a thatched roof. I moved in close and looked through the open doorway of the hovel. Inside, Gehrin and Baedecker slept peacefully on straw mattresses. I crept inside stealthily, intending to do the both of them in with my knife.

Suddenly, Gehrin's eyes opened. He saw me, sat bolt upright, and exclaimed, "You!"

Instinct took over. I dropped my knife and readied my gun. Gehrin was quick, though, and pounced on me like a jungle cat. With an acrobatic move remembered from my combat training, I caught his blow and used his own momentum to send him careening to the ground. Then, before Baedecker could rise, I turned my MP 40 upon him and pulled the trigger. (I intended to shoot him only twice, but in the fury of the moment, I emptied the entire clip into his massive body!) I then turned back to Gehrin, who was only just righting himself. Gripping his head, I brought his face down on a wooden stool. It seemed to knock him unconscious. Taking no chances, I gripped the stool like a club and beat it against his head—again and again—until his brains were literally dashed out.

I then reloaded my submachine gun and prepared for the onrush of Voodooists certain to come. (My weapon's blasting had been loud. Even a single shot should have been enough to awaken the village's lighter sleepers.) I paused at the doorway to the hut, looking out into the dark village and flickering torches beyond.

But nothing stirred.

Was an attack building? Were the Voodooists coordinating a movement against me?

I waited, my MP 40 at the ready. Then I waited some more. Then more still.

Nothing.

Still hesitant, I knelt down in the hut next to the corpses of the traitors and considered my next move. Dawn broke slowly, but the fog stayed where it was. Though the sun was now upon the horizon, this ethereal mist—which was quite thick and dense— still made the village a strange and dream-like place.

Confident that if attacked I could simply disappear into the clouds all around me, I summoned the resolve to leave the hut. I still intended to kidnap a Bocor or Mambo as quickly as possible and then to make my way to a U-boat.

Yet something very strange had occurred.

The village—which I had seen populated by twenty or thirty people by day, and which was a veritable social gathering at night—was totally deserted. I moved from hovel to hovel and found every home empty. Stalking through the thick fog, I encountered neither man nor beast. Within thirty minutes' time, I had made a thorough search of the entire place and found not one person. Signs of recent habitation were all around, but there were no people. It gave me the uneasy feeling of having accidentally wandered onto an empty theater stage just before a performance.

Though impossible, I began to feel as though I had dreamed the village as it had been—populated and lively.

I crept back through the smothering fog to the hut of Baedecker and Gehrin. I half-expected them to have disappeared too, but they were just as I had left them.

I am sitting now in the hut, preparing this message for you. The fog has abated slightly as the sun has moved higher in the sky, but the village remains deserted. I have resolved to take a quick nap here on the hut's floor—I am very exhausted from the night's work—and then to press on.

This was not a totally optimal outcome, and I admit that freely. However, the elimination of Gehrin and Baedecker is an important accomplishment (for which, I can only trust, I will find myself congratulated at a later date). I shall make it my mission in the coming hours and days to capture a Bocor or a Mambo capable of singing the zombie-creating song, and then return swiftly to Berlin.

I now know exactly what I must do. The power of the zombie will soon be within the grasp of the Reich!

I am, my dear <u>Obergruppenführer</u>, so very, very close.

Respectfully,
Gunter Knecht